UNFORGIVABLE

An inCapable World Novel

SARA HUBBARD

UNFORGIVABLE

Copyright © 2016 Sara Hubbard
Published by Sara Hubbard
Edited by The Red Pen Coach
Cover design by Perfect Pear Creative Covers
Cover image by Lindee Robinson with models Tyler Koronich and
Ashley Hanson.

The following novel contains strong language and sexual situations. It is recommended for adult readers.

Discover other titles by Sara Hubbard at http://www.sara-hubbard.com

Sign up for Sara's newsletter at http://eepurl.com/NDwi5 to be notified about new releases and to receive bonus content.

First edition June 2016.
ISBN eBook: 978-1-988212-03-6
ISBN Print: 978-1-988212-04-3

CHAPTER ONE

How many times have I been told to get my shit together? I keep making the same mistakes over and over again. All because of my obsession with men—or bad men.

I trudge into my Aunt Mona's pub, blowing through the entrance to the back room to change into some sensible shoes for work—one inch versus three-inch heels. As I pass Aunt Mona's office, her gaze lifts and our eyes meet, but I keep walking so I don't have to hear another one of her lectures. I soon hear her heels marking time with mine.

When it comes to other people's business, Mona usually sticks to her own. When it comes to mine? She's like a dog with a bone.

I fall onto the couch and kick my feet out of my shoes, sighing. I hug my designer purse against my chest like it's a lifeline. Once upon a time, I used a teddy bear for comfort. But as a grown woman, my Michael Kors bag will do just fine.

Mona appears in the doorway, her flaming red hair a few shades darker than it was yesterday. At her age she should be gray, but this fiery lady isn't about to grow old gracefully. Not a chance. She leans against the frame, studying me.

"Problem, Beth?" she asks, crossing her arms over her chest.

"Have you seen Evie yet?" I ask, frowning.

Mona's face tightens as her brows pucker.

"Please don't look at me like that." I avert my eyes.

"Maybe you should have gone to see her at the hospital," she says dryly.

"Yeah, maybe." Evie is a new friend and a coworker. I had a hand in her starting work here, but I also had a hand in getting her almost killed. One thing about me I always felt good about until recently? I'm a good friend. Well, usually I am, but the other night I got drunk and when Evie wanted to leave the club where we were partying, I let her leave—alone. And I didn't even visit her when she lay in the hospital, bruised and beaten afterward. Nope, my guilt wouldn't let me. Seeing her in pain would have just given me a permanent visual reminder of my huge mistake. And I don't like to look my mistakes in the face.

"You fucked up, Beth. Don't do it again."

"I need to change," I say. Letting Evie leave alone was selfish and stupid. She's a grown woman, I told myself at the time, ignoring the fact that she only recently moved to the city and she's perhaps the most innocent person I've ever known. If I hadn't been drinking...if I hadn't been so focused on Mason Cross... *Mason Cross*. Ugh, just thinking his name makes me feel violent.

He's a prime example of the kind of guys I seem to gravitate toward. The kind of guy who distracts me with promises, affection, and easy smiles but who always disappoints.

"I don't know...I'm just thinking if I could go back to that night at The Pipeline..." I chew on my nails, wishing I could go back. Could I have saved her from the attack? Or would someone else have taken her place? Could I have saved them too?

Mona picks up an apron sitting on the table to her left and chucks it at my face. "Don't dwell. It'll give you wrinkles. Just don't do it again. But yeah, you need to change. I'm sick to death of having to bail you out of the stupid situations you constantly get yourself into. You know...you could've easily been the one attacked. Then what?"

"I know," I exclaim in frustration. But that's not what I'm frustrated about. Truth be told, I wish I'd been the one attacked—if only to lessen the guilt that weighs so heavy on my shoulders right now. Drinking and partying without a care in the world has always worked for me, but now? Evie's attack is making me reevaluate a lot of things in my life.

"You're twenty-four years old. When are you gonna smarten up?"

"I feel awful, okay? You don't even know how much."

"What were you doing that was so fucking important, anyway? Drinking? Partying? Flirting?"

I glare at her.

"Come on. Tell me. Why couldn't you make sure your friend got home safe?" She purses her lips and gives me the smuggest expression. She can see right through me, I swear.

I refuse to reply.

"It was a boy, wasn't it? And I bet he's a winner."

You know what they say about glass houses... I bite my tongue to stop myself from reminding her that she married a sociopath that went "missing" a few years ago. Not sure if she had anything to do with it—but that's beside the point and I wouldn't blame her if she had.

"I don't date boys, Mona. I date men. Unfortunately, they're all pricks and liars."

"Don't swear. I'll wash your fucking mouth out with soap."

I chuckle at her poor attempt at humor. But then, she's probably not joking. It's okay for her to swear like a sailor, but it isn't for her niece—though I know I mean much more to her than that or she wouldn't be berating me right now. She practically raised me since my mother brought me over from Poland when I was almost thirteen. She was the one who convinced my mother to let me stay when Mom went back home. Though I'm sure it didn't take much convincing. Some women are born to be mothers and some aren't. My mother falls in the latter category. I almost think she was relieved to get rid of me.

"He's married, Mona," I say, and immediately regret offering this piece of information.

"Who's married?"

"Never mind. It's just this guy I've been seeing."

"The guy you ditched your friend for?"

Ouch. I frown up at her.

"What's his name?"

I shake my head. My aunt is one of scariest women you'll ever meet. Seriously. Think Annie Oakley meets Bonnie of Bonnie and Clyde. People that piss her off go missing. That goes for her brother, too—my cranky Uncle Mickey. So giving her the name of a man who managed to hurt me isn't something I'm about to do, no matter how much I might like to see him suffer.

"Tell me," she demands.

"Forget about it."

She sighs and shakes her head. "I know first-hand how bad boys can seem appealing. Or, at least, the thought of them. I fell for a guy who was completely wrong for me and I'm lucky I got out alive. You don't even know how bad it got before...he left." When she speaks, she refuses to look my way. Her relationship with Ralph is not something she normally talks about, which only serves to capture my attention.

I hated that man. From his voice to his constant sneer, he

unnerved me. I debated going back to Poland just before he left, because I found it hard to live with him, especially when I saw how much he hurt my aunt. Funnily enough, he disappeared soon after I spoke to my aunt about booking a flight. It's rather ironic now that I find myself gravitating toward men from the same crop.

"You need a nice guy. One you can settle down with."

"God help me."

Declan Lewis appears behind her, his gaze moving from her to me. Declan is beyond hot. Once upon a time, I would have done anything to get his attention, but when Mona took him in, he became more of a brother than a potential bedmate. He's also quite annoying and tends to get overprotective about me at times. Even if he comes in a muscled, tattooed, and beautiful package.

"What's going on?" Declan asks, though he seems distracted and simply trying to make conversation. I doubt he actually cares.

"Boy trouble," Mona says, a hint of acidity in her voice.

He groans and walks away. "Need to borrow something from the basement," he says, his voice trailing off.

"Put it back when you're done." Mona pauses for a moment. "On second thought, throw it in the harbor." She turns her attention back to me.

This is my family: Criminals. And I'm just close enough to their shit that I can hear it, taste it, smell it...they just make sure I never see it. That *no one* sees it. They like to keep their illegal activities hidden from me, but then, I'm not an idiot. Mona has a small arsenal in her basement, and though she never goes down there anymore, it doesn't mean she doesn't have it on standby. Mickey and Declan tend to peruse her selection from time to time. Here, they talk about picking out a gun as casually as they would talk about Sunday dinner.

"I guess he's not mad at me anymore," I say.

Declan has fallen hard for Evie and he didn't exactly keep quiet about how shitty I was to let her leave alone that tragic night at The Pipeline. But he's talking to me now, so he must forgive me.

I think.

"He does care about you, you know," Mona says, referring to Declan.

"Maybe. But his feelings for Evie far outweigh any he has for me."

"She's good for him."

I shrug. "Yeah, I know." I stand, kick aside my leopard print shoes, and snatch my black ones to the left of the couch. *Wish I could find someone good for me.* I slide my feet into my work shoes, already appreciative of the extra room I find in the rounded toe.

"Beth, if you want to change...then change. Stop dating assholes who don't give a shit about you. And stop obsessing about them. Don't become *me.*"

"Mona..." I say softly, but she cuts me off before I have the chance to say anything that might comfort her.

"You need someone who won't put up with your bullshit. Someone who will *take care* of you."

Here we go, Mona to the rescue. Playing matchmaker again, just like she did for Declan and Evie. "I don't know why I started this conversation," I say under my breath.

"I told you before, Mickey and I won't always be around to save you," she says.

"Why do you keep saying stuff like that? You'll be ninety years old and still on my case."

She stares at me blankly and takes a breath. "I know the perfect guy. He just moved back here and—"

"Not interested."

"He's a Marine, or an ex one. Whatever the fuck you call them."

This stops me. I'll admit a man in uniform has a certain appeal, but a Marine? Don't they stick their dick into any hole they can find? Yeah, that's just what I need. "I'm good, Mona. I can find my own man."

"Just go out and meet him."

I laugh out loud. Of course, he's in the bar. "What's so great about this guy, anyway? You don't like anyone."

"You're right. I barely like you."

I blow her a kiss.

"There's something about him, Beth. I can't quite put my finger on it, but he's the guy for you...He's a bit like Declan in a way... quiet...a little sad...maybe a little lost. And he could put up with your bullshit and take care of you."

Again, with the taking caring of me. "This is your sales pitch? Sad and lost? He's like Declan? Declan annoys the hell out of me on his best days. And I can take care of myself."

"Uh huh."

"I'm serious." Okay, so maybe I haven't up until this point. Even my rent and clothing are partially paid for by gifts from men. But all of that's going to change now. Once I found out about Evie, I took a long, hard look at myself in the mirror and I didn't like what I saw. In fact, I couldn't stand to see my reflection at all.

"He's sitting at the bar," she says. "Longish brown hair, big brown eyes, and a five o'clock shadow. He's got too many tattoos for my taste, but you probably like that sort of thing."

Sigh.

"Oh, and his name is Damien."

I roll my eyes at her words as I walk past her on the way to the bar. "Stop playing matchmaker, Mona. It doesn't suit you." The last thing I need in my life is someone like Declan. He's got more baggage than a freight ship. But when I push through the double swinging doors leading to the front, I can't help but nonchalantly search for this guy who Mona thinks might be my perfect match. Perfect match? Hah. Relationships don't last. The only lasting relationship in life is the one you have with yourself. But Mona is right about something, though...I need to stop relying on my family so much, and stupid assholes who promise the world and deliver next to nothing. Maybe I'll get a cheaper apartment. That would be a start.

It's lunchtime and the pub is more crowded than usual. The noise level peaks, the muffled sound of at least fifty different conversations happening all at once. Add the sound of Irish music playing in the background and I can barely hear myself think. I head to the bar, not intending to look for Damien, but my curiosity won't let me forget about him.

He's easy to spot, even though every seat at the bar is occupied. He has the body of a military man: tall, lean, and muscular with tattoos. His hair is short on the bottom and long on top, a haircut perfect for a guy who hid his hair under a hat or beret or ball cap or whatever it is that they wear in the Marines. He wears a short-sleeved black shirt, his tats stretching down the backs of his hands. He's thick, but not beefed up like a guy who spends long hours at the gym pumping iron while staring at himself in the mirror. Just fit...lean. And I'm a little in lust.

Damn, Mona.

He leans over the bar, his hand firmly around a glass of something or other. I don't approach him initially. I pour some drinks, get rid of some dishes from the customers who leave, and then wipe down tables. When the place has quieted and is filled with only the regulars, I finally make my way over to him. First I make sure Mona's not around, because I don't want to fuel her meddling fire or have her shout 'I told you so' at me when it's clear that I find him attractive.

I hate that she knows me so well. If only she could match make herself so I wouldn't have to see her alone all the time. Not that her brothers-in-law would allow her to remarry or anything. Her missing husband was a Dante and in this small city that means something—actually, it means everything. The Dante and the Hill families are like the mob in Sterling.

"Another drink?" I ask him.

He doesn't look up at me; he keeps his eyes on his glass as he offers a single nod. It kind of hurts my ego a little. I'm not used to guys ignoring me. Blonde hair, blue eyes, small body and ample breasts, I'm used to guys coming on to me, and submitting to my every whim until they've managed to get me naked and underneath them, like Mason did. *Asshole*. Guys I take an interest in end up married or emotionally unavailable. Story of my life.

"What are you having?" I lean over the counter, knowing full well the curve between my breasts is visible in my low V-neck shirt. He doesn't even raise an eyebrow. Maybe he's gay. Or maybe he is as advertised—another Declan. Before Evie, I could have sworn Declan was batting for the other team.

"Whiskey and water."

"Water? That's a serious drink," I say.

"What can I say? I'm a serious guy." He tilts his head up to study me. A hint of a smile crosses his full lips.

I'll admit I like the way his face looks when he engages me. Like he's focused on me and no one else. I also like those big brown eyes; they look like they have a story to tell and I'm nothing if not nosy. And the scar that passes over his left cheek that puckers slightly when his cheeks lift has me intrigued. I imagine it's from the military, but then it could be from something much less glamorous, like falling off a bike when he was a kid.

I make his drink and set it down on the hardwood counter in front of him. "Where are you from?"

"Here. Originally."

"Never seen you before," I say without a second thought, but the longer I look at him, the more I have to admit there is something vaguely familiar about him. His hooded eyes? His full lips? That dimple? I don't know, perhaps he just has one of those faces.

His smile builds. "No, I don't suspect you would have."

Whatever that means. "But you know my aunt?"

He tips his head to the side.

"Mona Bilski?" I offer.

"Yeah, I know Mona. And you're Beth."

Not a question. He definitely knows who I am and I wonder how much information Mona has thrown at him. Or how many pictures she's shown him.

"I'm Damien." He holds out his hand and I stare at it, noting the roughness and the nicotine stains on his fingers. Hesitating, I take his hand. It's so big it practically engulfs mine. His grip is firm, confident, and makes me squirm a little.

Could I be intimidated by him? No way.

I have to give it to Mona, there is something very sexy about him, something undeniably raw, because as I stare at him, my hand still locked with his, all I can think about right now is how it'd feel for him to touch me in other nameless places.

"How do you know my aunt?" I demand, not caring if I'm prying or bordering on rude.

"Pen pals."

Slowly, I slide my hand free from his. What did he just say? I grimace and take a moment to find my voice. "Excuse me?"

He chuckles. "I'm not even kidding. We met a long time ago. She did me a favor and we've kind of kept in touch ever since."

"You must have made an impression on her. She doesn't like a lot of people, and she likes you enough to think we're soul mates."

He chokes on his drink. "Wow, she wasn't kidding when she said you were bold."

"Did she tell you that she thinks we're perfect for each other?" I roll my eyes.

He smirks at me, shaking his head.

"She must have forgotten to put that in her letters, huh?" I raise my eyebrows in challenge. He must think I'm a complete idiot. Pen pals? He has to be pulling my leg.

"Uh...I...I'm not sure what I'm supposed to say right now."

"You don't have to say anything."

"So why do I feel like you're standing there passing judgment?" he asks.

I shrug. "Maybe I am. Or maybe I'm just trying to decide if you'd be worth my time."

He laughs out loud. "That's if I'm even interested." He holds up his glass as if to toast me. He takes a small drink and sets it back down, circling the rim of his glass with the tips of his fingers.

"Oh, please," I say, refusing to lose my nerve. "One kiss. One touch...and you'd be interested."

"Don't be so sure," he says, winking at me before downing the rest of his whiskey.

I like that he's giving me as much sass as I'm giving him. Guys love confident girls and I try hard to play the role with finesse, even if inside I'm just as self-conscious as the next girl—I'm just a better actress.

"It wouldn't have worked anyway," I say matter-of-factly as I stand back to survey his handsome body.

He chuckles, "Yeah, and why is that?"

"You look like a shitty kisser. I wouldn't have been able to get over that."

His eyes widen, and though my comment seems to have shocked him, he gets over it quickly. "I've never had any complaints."

"Perhaps they were stunned into silence."

He laughs out loud. "Let me prove you wrong."

I scoff at him. "Sure, show me what you got."

He stands up, pushing his stool back and out of the way. I never imagined him to be as tall as he is, and I have to admit I like it a lot. He's got a good foot and a half on me, and when I glance down I see a bulge I'm a little impressed with—unless he stuffs his pants like some other guys I know.

My stomach is in knots and I can't explain why. Guys don't make me nervous. Not one bit. But this guy...Mona was right. Like Declan, he's a little unnerving and perhaps a bit unpredictable. He's going to follow through. I didn't expect him to, and now I can't back down, either.

My stomach aches as unfamiliar butterflies dance wildly inside me to a song that I've never heard before. He lifts a hand and with a single finger, he motions for me to come closer. I shrug at him, refusing to be scared.

He puts his hands on the counter, leaning in and I stretch up on my tiptoes, forcing myself to meet him the rest of the way. He reaches up to stroke the side of my face and my eyelids flutter until they fall closed.

What the hell am I doing?

He whispers in my ear, something low and husky. "Is this what you want?"

I nod, unable to stop myself, and my cheek tingles against the rough feel of his fingers. Then, as I wait for him to touch his delicious lips to mine, he presses a kiss to my other cheek. And then... nothing. His fingers leave my face and his breath is no longer a weak wind in my hair. When I open my eyes he's smirking at me. He leaves me hanging. *Me!* And I want to slap him hard and go masturbate in the bathroom all at the same time.

"Asshole," I say as I turn from him, ignoring the sound of him chuckling at my back. This is Mona's idea of a perfect guy? A guy who wants to play games? And who loves every minute of it? Fuck him. Fuck him sideways with a bent spoon.

I storm out back, straight to Mona's office and when I reach her doorway, I put my middle finger up sky high as I give her a death stare. She laughs riotously at me. "Met your match, Little Bird?"

"Not even close," I say as I stomp away. "And don't call me Little Bird."

Thanks for the not so subtle reminder about why I need to stay the hell away from men. Perfect match, my ass. No doubt he's just like all the other guys I've known and let myself fall for. And I'm not about to make that mistake again. Not now. And certainly not for him.

CHAPTER TWO

With a coffee in hand, I lock the heavy wooden door to Mona's Place and turn the sign to *Closed*. I walk back to the bar through the dying fog of smoke to retrieve a cloth for the remaining dirty tables. One of these nights, we're going to get shut down for letting people smoke in here. Then again, it's not like the cops are foolish enough to come into Ralph's widow's place and start giving Mona shit for inconsequential things.

Tonight, we closed later than normal because one of our regulars passed out at his table. Even when he regained consciousness, we couldn't get him to walk to the door. We had to call Mickey to come and take him home.

After Claire, Hannah and I finish cleaning up, we put the chairs upside down on the tables and then it's time to mop. Claire and Hannah look as exhausted as I feel, so I offer to finish up so they can leave.

"Are you sure?" Hannah asks.

"For sure. It won't take me long." No point in us all suffering.

"I'll owe you one," Claire says, and I know she means it.

Everyone here at Mona's looks out for one another. We all do our part, take our turns, and I know they'd cover for me if I asked.

When I'm done mopping, I kick off my shoes and pad out back with my lukewarm coffee to check in with Mona. She's in the kitchen—alone. The cooks usually leave shortly after we stop serving food and that's hours before close. Mona is always back here late at night, baking rolls and bread. If there is one thing I like about this pub, it's the after-hours scent of yeast and baking bread in the kitchen.

Mona's eyes flash up at me as she smashes the dough about on the floured countertop. I hop up on the counter opposite her, dangling my legs like I used to as a kid.

Mona likes to be by herself while she bakes, but sometimes she'll let me keep her company. Sometimes we sit in silence and other times we chat about nothing and everything. Some of my best talks with her happened right here. In fact, my first sex talk was here when I was fourteen.

"So, this Damien guy?" I begin, a bit of an edge to my voice.

She smirks and continues to work the dough, pounding it like a boxer would an opponent.

"He's not even *interested* in me."

"He doesn't know what he wants. He's still shell shocked after a bad deployment and an even worse ex-girlfriend."

"Oh, well. He's the perfect guy for me then, isn't he? Fucked up."

"Watch your fucking mouth."

I tap my fingers on the counter and pinch my lips together.

"I told you. He's perfect for you. Neither of you know it yet, though."

"Stop playing matchmaker, Mona. You're not very good at it. If anything, I need to stop focusing on guys for a while and not have one pushed on me."

"So you're not interested in him, then?"

Groaning, I hop off the counter and set my coffee down, resolving to stop drinking it. It's cold now and there's nothing worse than cold, black coffee. "Nice guys don't exist, and if they do, they certainly don't go for girls like me, Mona."

I believed in fairy tales once upon a time. I even thought I could have one of my own, but...seeing my mother abused by her endless stream of greasy boyfriends and then my aunt by her husband, I wondered if they truly existed. When I'd thought I finally found one, he turned out to be an asshole, too. 'You're the kind of girl guys fuck, not the girl guys marry,' he told me after I gave my virginity to him at prom. I've never forgotten the way his voice sounded when he delivered those sharp, poison-filled words or how they made me feel the second they hit my ears. Or how he rolled off of me and pulled up his pants and stood to look down on me like I was a piece of trash. It was like he'd hauled off and hit me in the face and kicked me in the stomach all at once. Sex, making love, fucking—whatever you want to call it—became less magical after that. It became a tool to satisfy a need. That's it.

"You only need one guy to prove you wrong."

Mona's voice pulls me from my memories. One guy, huh? If only it were that simple. I shake my head at her, refusing to let her hopes build up mine. Disappointment is a bitch I'm all too familiar with. And since it seems we're going to have to agree to disagree, I decide not to continue this conversation any further. I head to the break room and put on my heels and jacket.

After hours of being on my feet, they throb from the pointed toe. I almost want to take them off and borrow a pair of sneakers from Mona—well, almost. I put on a scarf and some mittens and return to the kitchen. Mona is smoking a cigarette now, leaned over the countertop lost in thought. With her back to me, I wrap my arms around her middle and she stills. As I lean my head on her shoulder, I take a breath and her scent fills me. Cigarettes, vanilla hand cream and bread.

She's smiling. I know it, even if I can't see it.

I love you. "Don't think I don't appreciate you, even if you piss me off." My voice is as quiet as a mouse, but she has ears like a hawk.

"Ditto, Little Bird."

I take a step back and leave through the back door. It's late and dark, and after Evie's recent attack, I decide to take a cab. Whoever grabbed her is still out there and she's not the only girl who's been attacked these last few months. The cab ride is quick and I can barely understand the driver when he tells me the fare, so I look over the seat and glance at the display on the meter. I pay him the fare plus tip. I make a living on tips so I'm not stingy when it comes to giving them out to others.

When I walk into my apartment, I'm struck by the silence. Sometimes being alone gets to me, while other times I enjoy it. Tonight it's the former. My small living space suddenly seems too big and leaves me feeling empty. A cat would help, maybe... Or a dog. Man, would I love to have a dog. But I know it's not practical. I'm never home. I work a lot of hours at the pub, and on my free days, I'm usually out with my best friend, Carrie. Partying like we're still teenagers without a care in the world.

Until recently, this suited me just fine. Now? I don't know. Evie's attack got me thinking. Here today and gone tomorrow. Do I want to be remembered as the thoughtless girl who partied hard and went through more than her fair share of men? How sad is that? No, not sad, it's fucking depressing.

Ugh. I shake off my thoughts because they're just making me feel worse. And I don't know if I believe people can change. What am I going to do? Go to school? Get a trade? Screw that. I sucked in school. I never could pay attention. Mind you, my dyslexia didn't help. It was easier to tune out than try to train my brain to work differently.

So I'm twenty-four now and I'm stuck. One day I'll take over Mona's pub, but that's the best I can hope for. And a good guy? In my social circles? Hah! I run with the mob.

But I have to do something. If only I could figure out what that something is...

I take a shower and get in bed, leave my blinds open so I can look out the big window and see the gray moon shining in the midnight blue sky. I toss and turn, unable to fall asleep. My apartment is too hot; it's too cold; my sheets aren't tucked in and then they're wrapped around me too tightly. Just as I'm about to throw off my covers and grab a sleeping pill and a strong drink, I hear a knock at my door. At first, I decide to ignore it, but then, after several knocks it becomes increasingly clear that whoever is here is not going away.

I mutter a curse when I look at the clock and read 3:05 a.m. Who the hell would come knocking at this hour? After kicking off my sheets, I pad to the door wearing nothing more than a tank top and some boxers I stole from an ex. I press my hands against the wood and stretch up on my tiptoes to look through the small peep hole.

It's Mason—the married guy. I lean my head forward to rest on the door and lightly bang my head a few times.

I shouldn't open the door...

I should tell him to piss off or just ignore him...

But that's not what I do.

Maybe it's because I felt so alone when I came home tonight... or maybe it's because I want someone to touch me. No matter how hard I try I just can't seem to get close to people and I guess that when I'm having sex, it feels like I am—if only briefly. I don't know. But for whatever reason, I open the door, ignoring my decision to stay away from men—and this one in particular. And it's not that I like him that much either.

"I should have told you," he begins. Not, "I shouldn't have lied," or "I'm sorry I hurt you." He just wishes he could have kept on lying so he could continue using me. But as I think about all the reasons he needs to leave, I decide that, right now, this relationship suits me as much as it suits him. He can't hurt me if I'm using him too, right?

So I swallow my convictions and act on instinct, not caring about the consequences or how much it will hurt in the morning when he leaves to go home to his wife. In this moment, he wants me and only me and I desperately need to be wanted. For five minutes? For ten? It doesn't matter how long; as long as his need consumes him and overwhelms me in the here and now, I could care less. His cock strains against the zipper of his jeans and he licks his lips. There's something a little desperate about desire, and I suppose I can understand it—in a way.

"You're the only one I want," he says.

It's bullshit. I know it. But I let myself believe him because tonight I can only think about now and how everything will feel better if I let him come inside my apartment and then inside of me.

WHEN I WAKE I am full of self-loathing. I mean, I knew I would be, but the sharp point of the guilt stick is more bothersome this morning than I'd imagined.

He's married, I tell myself. *What if he was your husband?* Maybe this is why I can't find nice guys. Because I do stupid shit like this, and karma's a bitch.

I get out of bed and head for the shower, still berating myself. "This is why you'll never get married," I say out loud. Men cheat. In my experience, they all do. How many guys have I dated that I can say this about? Tony? Adam? Ricky? Greg? Wow. Every single one. Though, to be fair, they didn't cheat on me in most instances. They cheated on someone else *with* me—not that I knew I was the other woman when I started dating each of them. That always came later. Was I ever the girlfriend? The real girlfriend? Or just the girl on the side?

Always the bread and never the main course.

And Mona thinks this Damien guy is different? Fat chance of that. How many women has he cheated on in his lifetime? Ugh. I don't want to think about this anymore. And I don't need to continue this negative cycle. No more married guys, I tell myself. Never again. I mean it. I really do. And while I'm at it, no guys at all. I need to just focus on me for a while. Maybe figure out who I am without the distraction of men and the drama that comes with relationships. I all but chant this on my walk to work. *Fuck men.*

The sun is out—mostly. The sky alternates between sunny and overcast as gray clouds pass by overhead. It might rain, but it won't rain long. I pick up my step and reach Mona's in record time. She's in her office, her head tilted back in her chair, her mouth open, quiet snores coming from her red, lipstick-rimmed mouth. I shake my head at her, feeling warmth in my belly, like I often do when I catch her off-guard like this, acting like a normal person. Because let's face it, my aunt is anything but normal. And I wouldn't have it any other way.

The cooks—Carey and Henry—arrive and fire up the stoves, warming the cool space. Another waitress, Carla, comes shortly after. She's pretty new to Mona's but not new to waitressing. I think I had her follow me for one shift a few weeks ago, but it wasn't a whole one. She can put me to shame now. She's fast on her feet and I swear she gets the best tips in the joint. Secretly, I kind of hate her. She makes me look bad. I do a good job—most of the time—

but I also get sidetracked, chatting with customers. I can argue that this is important, though. That my customer service ensures customers keep coming back.

I tell myself this, but it's only a half-truth, because most of the clients that come here, do so because my aunt was married to a Dante. Or, is married to one still, I guess. Until they find his body. Right now, he's just a face on a milk carton. Sometimes I have to wonder if she had anything to do with it. To the world, she looks like a grieving widow when his name comes up, but privately, she mumbles "fucking bastard."

Carla has the place set up and the doors open in record time. I get the till ready while she does her thing. Then I make coffee and brew it strong—the way I like it. When she's done, she comes behind the counter and pours herself a cup. She makes a face after one sip. "Man, Beth, this is rancid."

"Just the way I like it."

"You know you're the only one who'll drink this shit, right?"

"My Uncle Mickey drinks three or four cups every time he comes in."

"Then I guess liking awful coffee is genetic," she says, her face sour.

I fake smile at her and she fake smiles back.

The place picks up and I'm practically run off my feet. We aren't usually this busy, but we're short staffed after Hannah called in sick. Thankfully, Evie has agreed to come in and help. This will be her first shift back since the attack and I'm kind of nervous to see her. My stomach turns as I imagine her outside The Pipeline late at night, waiting for a cab, only to have a man spring from the bushes and pull her in.

When she walks through the front door, I heave a sigh and note the bruising on her face and arms and her blackened eye. I want to talk to her the moment I see her, but I'm ringing someone in at the cash. I'm thankful for the time to collect myself. It allows me to build up some courage to face her and apologize for my mistake— which I don't usually do. But this one can't be avoided. I'll never forgive myself if I don't.

She grabs a cloth to clean the recently vacated tables but I take it from her. "Oh, just relax," I say. "We can do that later." I stare at her injuries.

"What's up?" she says.

"Up?" I shift my weight onto my other foot. "Nothing's up... I just feel like we haven't talked much lately. Maybe we could hang out again sometime...go someplace a little *safer*?" *I'm sorry. So sorry.* Why can't I say these words when my mind is screaming them inside my head?

"Because that worked out so well the last time," she says, grimacing.

I don't think she's trying to be mean, but her words sting me, and I frown at her and lower my gaze to the floor.

"Hey, Beth," she says, gripping my shoulder. "Don't blame your-self. Going home alone was my stupid decision. I own it. You have nothing to feel bad about. If anything, I should feel bad about wrecking your dress and shoes—which, by the way, I'll replace."

Is she serious? She was attacked and she's concerned about wrecking the clothing she borrowed? Just when I thought I couldn't feel like a bigger jerk. "Oh my God. Don't you dare. I never wore them anyway."

"Maybe not, but I ruined them and I'll replace them," she says. "I—" She stops mid-sentence and her eyes go wide. Her bottom lip trembles and she starts to shake. When I turn to see what or who has got her so rattled, I'm at a loss. "Evie, you're as white as a ghost."

Sam Tanner glides into the pub and takes a seat near the bar. He's wearing a wicked grin. His eyes are focused on Evie and she can't seem to take her gaze off of him. Now, I'm confused. The two of them are from completely opposite social circles. Besides that, Mona married a Dante and this guy belongs to Danny Hill's crew. His men aren't welcome here and they know it.

I take her hand to comfort her, but also because I'm not entirely sure she has the strength to continue standing. "Evie, you're freaking me out."

"It's him," she whispers.

"What do you mean?"

Sam licks his lips and purses his lips as if to blow a kiss. It's only then I connect the dots, because only the man who attacked her could inspire her to respond like this. It was Sam; he's the sick bastard who tried to kill her. Heat swallows me whole and I see red. I try to keep calm, keep the anger from my voice but can't manage it.

"Evie, go out back and I'll take care of this."

She shakes her head.

I charge past her and head out back to grab Mona. She's tapping away on her computer, one finger at a time. "We got a problem," I say quickly. "We need you out front, right now."

"What is it?"

"The guy who attacked Evie is out there. It's Sam fucking Tanner."

"Who?"

"One of Danny Hill's boys."

"Oh, no, he fucking doesn't. Come into my fucking bar, will he?"

Mona reaches into her desk and pulls out a handgun. She raises it chest-high and cocks it with a sneer on her face. She powers by me, the gun at her hip, and I follow, close on her heels. Out front, she lifts the counter arm and marches over to Sam who continues to smile widely, not even fazed by the red-haired woman heading for him with a gun hanging at her side.

Some of the customers spy the weapon and quietly push away from their tables and leave the pub. They don't look surprised by the scene or remotely concerned by it. Just a normal day in Sterling, I guess. And they know enough to get out of the way.

Mona raises the gun and points it at Sam's temple. His smile finally fades. "Hello, Mona."

Evie rounds the counter and slowly moves toward Mona. I stand between them, high on adrenaline. I'm not much of a fighter, but I have a temper, and if my aunt needs backup, I'm ready to kick ass.

"You're not welcome here," Mona snaps at him. "Stand up and walk out or I'll put a round in your head right now."

"I sincerely doubt that you're going to kill me in front of all of your customers."

"Anyone see anything?" Mona yells to the people still left in the room. I watch as a dozen heads shake and a few of them mumble quiet 'nopes'.

"Mona?" Evie says, putting her hand on Mona's arm. "You don't have to do this."

"Ain't about you, kid. No one comes in here and upsets my staff. Period."

"Mona, you pull that trigger and there'll be a lot of trouble for you," Sam says.

He stands tall, with his shoulders back and his chin up. It's like he's an animal trying to puff up his size and show dominance. Yeah, like that'll work with my aunt. He obviously hasn't met her before.

"I'll take my chances." Mona closes in and lines up her shot after lowering the barrel to his crotch.

"Mona? Please," Evie says, her face strained and her eyes teary.

"Please?" Mona parrots. "Are you serious? He attacked you. Beat you. He deserves this and a hell of a lot more."

"Mona!" she yells. "Please. You don't understand. There's more going on than you know."

Mona studies Evie's face, then flicks on the safety and lowers the gun. To Sam, she screams, "Get the fuck out of here!"

He walks backward, toward the door, his hands protectively cupping his cock and balls. "I'll see you again," he says, tipping his head to Evie. "Soon. Real soon."

Mona raises the gun again and he disappears through the doors. Evie and I heave sighs of relief, but before my racing heart has a chance to slow, Mona grips Evie's arm and drags her out back. I'm left stunned, not sure what to do next. That's not true. I want to follow Mona and Evie, but when I go out back Mona's office door is already closed, and I have a feeling they don't want company so I putter around, cleaning and wiping down tables and chairs, hoping Sam doesn't come back and Mona doesn't go Annie Oakley again.

A few hours later Declan strolls in looking for Evie. I'm sitting by the bar, devoid of energy from the adrenaline rush I experienced earlier. I have my phone at my ear, talking to Carrie. I give him a friendly nod, but he responds with his usually sour face so I give him the finger and he gives it back, making me chuckle. I can't believe I used to think he was hot.

He sits down at the counter opposite me and waits for me to hang up my cell phone. I could try to prolong the conversation, just to be a stubborn bitch, but chances are he'd just take my phone and hang it up for me so I cut my call short.

"Hey, crank. What's up?"

"Evie around?"

I roll my eyes at him. "Of course. Anxious to see her?"

He stares blankly at me.

"You're so not friendly, you know that?"

He rubs his temples and sighs at me. "Go get her."

"Get her yourself, ass."

"Always a pleasure, Beth." He pushes out from his bar stool and the scraping sound it makes along the hardwood floor makes me wince. After ducking under the arm of the bar he disappears out back.

"Be nice to her," I yell, loud enough for him to hear. "She had a rough night."

I don't see Declan or Evie again tonight. I don't see Mona either. This surprises me because she's always checking up on us out front. At close, I lock the doors and turn the sign around. The waitresses leave and when I head out back to get my stuff, I'm surprised to see the cooks are still there. They should have left hours ago and it gives me pause. Eyeing them as they're rooted in their spots, I wait for one of them to speak. When they can't find their tongues, I help them.

"What's going on?" I snatch my jacket from one of the hooks by the back door.

"Look, I wasn't going to say anything...it's not my business," Henry says. He removes his ball cap with one hand and runs his other hand through his hair.

"Say anything about what?"

"It's Mona. When...uh...she left earlier...she and Evie were packing," Carey adds.

"Packing?" I still. "Were they going after Sam?"

Henry shrugs. "Don't know. Not my business. But...you might want to give Mickey a call—just in case." He starts to leave and then turns back quickly. "Don't tell Mona I said nothing. She's fucking scary when she's pissed."

I nod. "No, I won't. Thanks, Henry."

As the cooks leave, I stand by the open door. The wind blows in, chilling me, and the fine hair on the back of my neck stands on end. I rub my arms and worry my bottom lip between my teeth. Carey and Henry seemed genuinely concerned and not much rattles them. Plus, like Mona, they're usually pretty consistent about minding their own business.

Am I worrying about nothing? Mona carries a weapon all the time, so it's not like this is strange and unusual. But after today...her threatening Sam...I have to wonder if she's about to do something really stupid—or if maybe she has already. *Fuck, Mona.* Because if Sam turns up dead, Mona is likely to be the first person the cops question.

Motive? Yep. Deadly? Um, absolutely. And she flat out threatened Sam.

Oh, Jesus. Carey and Henry are right to be worried. Why couldn't they have told me this earlier? I punch Mickey's number into my cell phone as I pull the heavy door closed with a thud that seems to rock the walls. Every ring on my phone makes my heart beat faster.

CHAPTER THREE

When I called Mickey earlier, he didn't answer. Neither did Mona. After a half dozen voice mail messages, it becomes clear to me that they're not going to answer until they're good and ready. But I can't shake the feeling that something is seriously wrong. It's a gut feeling that leaves me practically sick.

I curse them both as I sit in front of the television in my apartment, biting at my nails and continuously checking my phone to make sure the ringer isn't off. After a few hours, I can't help but fall asleep. It's been a long day and working on my feet takes its toll on me. There are times when I feel like I have the body of a seventy-year-old. Without meaning to, I sleep well into the middle of the night, dreaming about poor Evie and the man who beat her up, except I feel every punch, every kick. I taste blood in mouth. Though I try to scream, nothing comes out.

Bang, bang, bang.

My eyes pop open. I take a breath and wipe the sweat from my brow. The dream felt so real.

Bang, bang, bang.

Dazed from sleep, I reach for my phone but after another rap at my door, I quickly realize the noise isn't coming from my phone. I turn the clock around and frown at the digital reading: 5:00 a.m. That better not be Mason. I swear to God I don't have the patience for him tonight and sex is the last thing on my mind.

Bang, bang, bang.

I scurry to my apartment door and stretch up on my tiptoes, hoping to God it's Mona or Mickey. My heart plummets into my stomach when I see two men I don't recognize: two men wearing blazers and collared shirts—with jeans. It doesn't take a genius to recognize them for who they are: cops.

Please be okay. Please, please be okay.

I open the door, but leave it latched. I'm wearing a tank and panties—not that it matters, but I don't exactly want to give them a free show. Plus, I've been trained not to trust cops any more than I trust criminals. They try to make you feel as if they're your friends when they're really looking for information or attempting to nail your ass to the wall. Cops might just be the fakest people I know.

"What do you want?" I ask, my voice still hoarse from sleep.

"Beth Bilski?"

"Who's asking?"

One of the men reaches to his waist and removes a badge from his belt. I catch the butt of a handgun poking out from under his arm when his blazer hitches.

"I'm Detective Keith Russell, and this is my partner, Detective Mitch Connor."

I stare at them blankly, waiting for them to tell me why they're here at this ungodly hour.

"May we come in?" Russell asks. Although his smile looks forced, his chocolate brown eyes look sincere. Still, I'm skeptical, and talking to cops in my world is a mortal sin—one people don't recover from.

"You can talk to me from there," I say.

Russell opens his mouth to speak but Connor taps Russell's chest with an open hand and shuts him up. "Look, we've got some news. The kind of news you don't want while staring at us through a half-open door. You understand?"

"Give me a minute." I shut the door and grab my old white robe from the back of the bathroom door. After wrapping it around me and tying it shut, I open the door while taking a deep breath to prepare myself for the worst. But nothing can prepare me, because I know in my gut what's coming and I'm not ready for it. I want them to tell me Mona fucked up and she's in jail...or on the run. It's funny how the thought of losing her makes me wish for her criminality. I just want her to be okay. I'm not ready to be alone any time soon.

I wave for them to come inside and they file in, Russell first. I don't have much space in my apartment and my endless supply of clothes is littered around my bachelor. I pad forward, grabbing armloads of clothes from the couch and tossing them behind it.

"Wow," Russell says, scanning the mess.

"Maid's day off," I say.

"I'm not going to beat around the bush, here," Connor says. "This kind of news is hard to deliver and even harder—I'm sure—to hear. So I'm going to go right ahead and say it. Last night your Aunt Mona was shot. She was taken to Sterling General Hospital but... I'm afraid she died en route."

The room goes silent and I reach for the chair behind me to sit down. I don't feel anything at first; it's like my whole body has shut down. It hurts to breathe, hurts to think...it just plain hurts. And I feel like I might be sick.

"Oh, God." I lean forward and rest my elbows on my knees. For all intents and purposes, Mona has been my mother all these years. After hyperventilating for a minute, I whisper, "Are you sure?"

"'Fraid so, kid," Russell says.

Connor walks around the room, eyeing my bookshelf, and fingers through some books and papers. I don't have the strength to chastise him or kick him out. All I can focus on is this building tension in my gut and my chest, like I can't get enough air because I'm so constricted. *Mona. Dead.* This can't be happening. It just can't.

"We won't always be around to take care of you," she said. Like she knew her days were numbered. How could she possibly know?

Russell clears his throat and approaches me, tentatively laying his hand on my shoulder. "Is there someone we can call for you?"

"Does my Uncle Mickey know?"

When I look up at Russell, he shakes his head and his face softens. He bends down so we're eye level. His voice is soft, comforting. "We've been trying to locate him but so far have been unsuccessful." Russell pauses a beat before adding, "Do you have any idea where he might be?"

"No." And I wouldn't tell you if I knew. "He's not answering his phone."

"I see," Russell says.

"Who did this to her?" I ask. I bat away tears and try to control my breathing but I'm not sure that's possible right now. I assume it was Sam Tanner who's done this to Mona, but I'm not about to throw out his name. That's not smart when you're talking to cops. The fewer details you give them, the better.

"We can't go into the details right now, ma'am," Connor says.

"You can't go into details?" My voice grows stronger, louder. "Are you kidding me? My aunt is dead and you can't tell me who's responsible?"

"The man who shot her was also killed," he says, as if that makes this situation any better.

I narrow my eyes, confused. What aren't they telling me?

"*Declan*," I say quietly. "Mona practically raised him. Oh my God, I need to call Declan."

I attempt to rise and Russell puts out his hands to gently push me back down. I don't like the look on his face and am afraid he has more bad news. Just what the hell happened last night?

"Declan was injured, but he's stable. I'm afraid you can't see him right now. He's in protective custody."

"What?" I stand now, getting angrier and angrier. None of this makes any sense at all. Declan is the most hardcore person I know, but if he's in protective custody then that means he's a rat. Declan would rather die than work with the cops. "That's bullshit!" I snap.

"I'm afraid it's true," Connor says, picking a sticky note up off the countertop, next to my cordless phone. "He and his girlfriend."

"Evie?"

Connor offers a slow nod.

"You need to leave. *Now*."

"Connor, give us a minute, will ya?" Russell says.

Detective Connor shrugs, tips his head at me as he passes. I hold my middle finger up sky high.

"You, too," I tell Russell.

"I know you're upset and I'm very sorry for your loss—"

"Really? Is that why your asshole partner was leafing through my shit?"

"No, I'll be honest: we're trying hard to find your uncle. I have a feeling he's not going to let Mona's death go unpunished and I don't think I need to tell you what will happen if he does—not just to him, but to everyone he cares for as well."

"I hope he kills everyone who had a hand in her death."

He sighs and puts his hands firmly on his hips. "I know this is a terrible blow. I just hope when the dust clears that you'll realize that following in your aunt's and uncle's footsteps will only lead you to more chaos and pain."

He closes the distance between us, holding out a tentative hand to touch my shoulder. I flinch and pull back as he touches me, away from his reach, and flash him a disgusted look.

"I'm going to give you my card. I really hope you use it."

I tear it up into small pieces and throw it on the ground, staring up at him with a heart full of hatred.

He takes another and sets it on the countertop. "You seem like a smart girl. I hope you're smart enough to realize that your uncle is going to end up like your aunt if we don't find him quickly."

"Get out!"

"Of course." He backs away.

"Now!" I snap since he isn't moving fast enough.

"Be careful," he says.

"I don't need any advice, thanks. I just want to be left alone."

Detective Russell ambles to the door and I follow behind him, waiting for him to step out into the hall so I can slam the door and find my phone. But that's not what I do. When they're both gone and the door is tightly sealed I fall to the ground and shed a thousand tears for the woman who loved me like I was her own—even if she had trouble showing it. *Oh, God. This pain.* I can barely handle it. I wrap my arms around my legs, put my head down, and rock back and forth. The world fades into silence and black emptiness. I don't know how long I stay like this. But when I've had my fill, I decide to never shed another tear and pick myself up and take a deep breath.

I'll never be the same. I know it, but I can't crumble to pieces right now. Not when Mickey is in danger of leaving me, too.

I need to find him.

Before it's too late.

I check the obvious places first: the pool hall, his favorite burger joint, the Laundromat. Mickey seems to spend an awful lot of time doing laundry, although to be honest, I'm pretty sure he does more business in that old white paint-chipped building than underwear.

When he doesn't turn up at any of those places, I decide to visit his whores. I'm no saint. I've been with my share of men and I can hardly cast stones at women who sleep around, but the girls Mickey likes to hang with are ones who typically exchange sex for money. Maybe not when it comes to him, because older girls seem to love his whole bad boy with gray hair thing, but they're still working girls, even if they give it away for free from time to time.

Sandra's Place is an old white Victorian house down on Fairview. On the outside, it looks like a family home, with shutters, rose bushes, and lawn gnomes. On the inside, it's all business. And it's owned by the Dantes—the girls all foreign and illegal either by age or by nationality. Sandra is the woman who manages it, and she's tough as nails. Like a weathered and heavier version of Mona. Mickey's regular date, Fancy, works there five evenings a week out of seven.

"Haven't seen her," Sandra says as she tosses a boa over her shoulder.

Sighing, I shift my weight to my other foot as I stand in the entryway of the house. "Can I leave you my number?" I ask.

She eyes me, not suspicious-like, but in a way that makes me believe I need to offer her some incentive. I reach into my bag and pull out a twenty after jotting my number down on the back.

Sandra stuffs the twenty in her ample cleavage, down deep, past the heart tattoo on her left breast and the cross on the right. "I'll pass on the message."

"And if you see...if you see my Uncle Mickey, could you ask him to call me too?"

"Mickey?" she says with a sneer. "Mickey Bilski?"

I nod slowly, wondering why the hell she looks so pissed off. He might be one of her best customers.

She glances around and then walks to the door with me practically tripping on her stilettos. When I'm on the other side of the door, under the cover of the porch, she lowers her voice and all but whispers, "They're watching." Her eyes roll up and to the left and I spy the camera up high in the corner of the porch. "I can't help you. They're looking for him."

"The Dantes?"

"Don't come back here."

She attempts to slam the door in my face but I push back on the door, refusing to let her dismiss me. "Please!"

She shoves hard and the door slams shut, the glass vibrating within the dark-stained frame. I slap my open hands against the glass, kick the door. "My aunt is dead!" I scream. "Please. Tell me what the hell is going on!"

The lights in the entryway to Sandra's turn off, casting the house into shadows and I'm left to stand on the porch in the dark, confused, and breathing heavy from fighting to get back in the house. "What the hell is going on?" I whisper. *They're looking for him*, she said. She can only mean the Dantes or she would have helped me. None of this makes any sense, but it certainly adds credence to what the cops were trying to sell me in my apartment. Mickey is in danger and I could very well be, too.

As I hurry back to the car I borrowed from Mona's garage, I fish my phone out of my purse and scroll through my phone numbers, looking for someone I can pump for information, someone who works around the Dantes but not necessary for them. Someone I can trust. Someone who's not loyal to them. But as I look through all the numbers there isn't a single name I find that I can bet my life on. That doesn't mean I give up, though. I keep looking, driving around all night, hoping to glimpse Mickey's old fixed-up sedan. Only when I'm yawning and fearful of going off the road do I finally head home, defeated. I promised I wouldn't cry, wouldn't cry ever again, but my eyelids feel like dams, no longer able to bear the weight of my tears.

So they fall, no matter how hard I try to fight them; they fall hard and fast, blurring my vision. I pull over on the side of the road, unable to see, and pound the shit out of my aunt's steering wheel. Shout every obscenity I've ever heard and make up some of my own.

I need you, Mickey. God, I need you so much right now. "Where the hell are you?"

CHAPTER FOUR

The elevator dings and opens to the hallway of my apartment floor. With my head bowed, I trudge forward, dipping my hand into my large purse to search for my keys. I feel the metal and hear the clank of the keychain as I pull them out, snatching the key to my apartment door. If the Dantes are looking for Mickey, it's only a matter of time before they come looking for me. I try to fit the key in the keyhole but my hand is shaky and I have to use two hands to slide it in.

Declan...Mona...Mickey...they've always had my back. I never needed to worry about trouble because I never found myself in any amount of trouble that they couldn't help me out of. Now, I have no one. I told Mona I can take care of myself and now when I have no choice I'm not sure that I can. I don't even know how.

The Dantes will come for me. I know it. They'll assume Mickey will reach out to me. Hell, I assume it too, but what if he doesn't? What if that's it? What if I never see him again? What if he's dead, too? Then they'll torture me as I tell them 'I don't know' and they'll call me a liar.

Fuck.

After the lock clicks open, I take a breath and open the door, only to find myself at the end of a double-barreled shotgun. Holy fuck! I yelp and jump backward, my side colliding with the door-frame. I curl my hands into a fist, my keys jutting out between two of my fingers to use as a weapon. I'm about to scream for help when the light flicks on and I see his face.

I push the barrel away and wrap my arms around his neck. My whole body instantly relaxes as I melt against him. "Oh, Mickey! I've been looking everywhere for you!"

"I know, kid. I saw you checking out the Laundromat, but Jimmy's bitches were watching and I couldn't approach you. Couldn't approach you at Sandra's, either."

"What is going on? The police told me Mona was murdered."

"I know. We don't have much time." He removes my arms from around my waist. "Get your shit. We need to leave."

He pushes past me and storms over to my dresser. I peek my head out the open door and glance in the hallway, looking both ways to ensure there's no immediate danger. Satisfied when there's no one there, I shut the door and lock it. Mickey is in my closet now, pulling things out and tossing them on the floor.

"What's going on? Declan and Evie are in protective custody. Nothing is making sense right now."

"You have a bag packed? For emergencies?"

I nod.

"Get it. We need to leave right now." His voice carries an edge and my heart skips a beat. Emergency bag? Being associated with the Dantes, I know that any minute I might need to run—for my life, from the law—in a hurry. So I always keep a bag packed. I've spent years here and I never thought I'd need it, but here I am, with Mickey in front of me, sweating like a whore in church.

"Mona killed her husband years ago and she felt the need to share that piece of information with the Dantes last night."

"What? Why?"

"It's a long fucking story, kid. And we don't have time to waste. The short of it is: the Dantes want me to come in and I ain't about to do that. They know I ain't going to let this shit lie."

"And Declan?"

"We don't have time for this!"

"You've worked for them for years. Maybe they'll trust you enough to let this go if you walk away. The cops said whoever killed her is dead."

"Your aunt fucked us. She was wearing a wire when she was shot."

I pause, and let that thought sink in. "Mona wouldn't do that."

"Well, she fucking did, so get your stuff. The Dantes want blood and so do I. They won't listen to a word I say right now."

Most of my stuff is ready; my passport, some tip money—at least a grand—and some clothes. I kick off my heels and slide into some running shoes. I don't work out and I don't ever wear sneakers, but I bought this pair especially for something like this.

Mickey goes to the window as I grab some pictures off my dresser, one of Mona and I at the beach when I was much younger, and one of my mother holding me before she left for the last time on a plane. Mickey cracks the window and opens it wide. He puts one foot out on the fire escape landing while keeping the other inside. The breeze whirs inside, making my long curtains whip about, hiding Mickey behind them. They settle when the wind does and Mickey rolls his hand through the air, motioning for me to hurry up.

My door rattles on its hinges and I stop dead in my tracks. "They're here."

Mickey barrels toward me, grabs me by my shirt and then drags me to the window. I hop over the windowsill to get outside. He follows my lead. Every step we take on the ladders to the alleyway below sounds like echoes in a canyon. I glance up to find Gerry Mills and Markus Simon sticking their heads out the window.

"There they are!" one of them screams.

Gerry climbs outside and I look away, trying desperately to pick up the pace. Every step we take my heart beats faster and faster and I swear I can feel it pulsing in my neck and chest. We get to the second floor and I climb around to the other side of the ladder and hang on tight as it lowers to the ground below. When I jump off, the ladder goes back up and Mickey is quick to hop on. But then he's jumping off in mid-air before I can count to three.

We run fast, faster than I've ever run before, and faster than I thought I could. Adrenaline is on my side, and yet I can't keep up with Mickey and he's pushing sixty. He grabs my arm and drags me forward. My breathing is labored and I can't stop looking over my shoulder. I trip, falling over my feet, and Mickey helps to right me.

His car is a few feet ahead of us and when I recognize it, I find the strength to push for another moment. Tires squeal in the distance and then get frighteningly close. As we climb in Mickey's old car, Markus shows up in the end of the alley, revving his engine in a big, old truck. Oh, God. We're trapped. But we're not. Mickey floors the car in reverse, colliding with a garbage container with such force it rolls away to smash into the building adjacent to mine. Then we're on the street and I don't remember how we got here; it's as if I've lost time. Cars swerve to avoid us, honking, while drivers scream at us through their open windows.

Mickey pulls away, gunning it to race through a red light, almost getting us into an accident. When I turn to check if Markus is following us, two cars smash into one another, t-boned, one with a stop sign wrapped around its hood.

I try to calm myself and control my breathing. Mickey is

straight-faced, calm as usual. How the hell can he act as if this is just another day in the life for him? How is he not freaking out right now when one of the biggest crime families in the city has men out looking for him? And now me, too?

A loud smash sounds and my ears throb with pain as a bullet whips by my head and connects with the windshield. A web of cracks spiral out from the hole. The back window is blown out and there are pieces of glass all over the backseat. Holy shit! I stifle my screams and hold my breath as the houses and trees and bushes whizz by us. Mickey pushes the accelerator to the floor and the engine roars. I grip my seat with my heart in my throat.

"They're gaining!" I cry, but Mickey isn't concerned.

Or is he? Mickey's car flies down the dark road, swerving around turns and flying over bumps that have me reaching the roof when we land.

"Take the wheel!" Mickey screams as he slides out of the window to sit on the edge of the door.

"Mickey, no!" I lean over, try my best to put my foot on the accelerator while I work hard to steer from where I sit. My seatbelt is still on and I can't slide over any farther, but I don't want to take my belt off for fear that I can't control the car.

Bang!

I hear a smash and an explosion as the sky is lit up behind us in the rear view mirror. I slow down, figuring they've lost the chase, and I remove my belt. But somewhere between my letting go and Mickey trying to climb back inside, we lose control and we fishtail before hitting the shoulder. Mickey takes the wheel. I curse loudly while he tries to yank the car back over to the road, but it's too late. We bounce hard and the car tips sideways. Down, down, down we roll over the edge of an embankment and land in a brook.

The water pours in.

And the world fades to black.

~

THE CAR IS right side up, water flowing in through the crevices and broken glass. It's so cold; I'm shivering. I lose my breath and my teeth start to chatter. My eyes flutter open and my hands spring to my throbbing head. Wet sticky liquid covers my hands and my palms are stained crimson. It takes me a moment to orient myself and realize what's happening. I need to act. Now.

Mickey? Where is Mickey? I pull on the door handle and try to force it open, but it won't budge. There's a hole in the window and Mickey's body lies outside of the car on the water's edge, his work boots sticking out through the tall weeds.

"Mickey!" I cry, hoping he'll at least respond and I'll know he's safe. "Mickey?"

But I hear nothing. I push and shove and when it's clear the door won't open I remove the seatbelt biting into my chest and waist and crawl over the seats to get out of Mickey's door. After poking my head out of the window, I crawl out. It takes seconds for my clothes to swell and grow heavy with water. My body tenses, but the cold helps numb the pain from my wounds and so does fear for my uncle. I stumble through the muck and weeds in the water and I fall forward, gasping with the chill. Crawling, the water to my chin, I close the distance.

"Mickey? Mickey? Answer me?" I reach his body and his whole abdomen is covered in blood. Too much blood. I know how bad this situation is, but I also know it's about to get a hell of a lot worse.

"Don't leave me," I cry.

Mickey stirs, mumbling incoherently.

"Tell me what to do. Please, I can't do this on my own."

"No hospital," he says, sputtering.

"What? You can't be serious."

"I'm as good as dead," he says. "Docs on payroll..." His eyes roll back in his head and he lays limp. My heart pounds in my chest and the world slows, the wind whipping my hair around my face. I'm sure I've lost him until I press my fingers to his neck and find a weak pulse. I know Mickey. If I call the hospital he'll lose his mind. He'll never forgive me. Never. Plus, even if he survives, the Dantes will find us. There are few people in this city who can't be bought. It wouldn't take long for someone to talk and for his men to come into the hospital, ready to fire another bullet, this one aimed at his head.

I reach into my back pocket and find my phone. I thought the waterproof case wasn't necessary when my aunt suggested it and here I am, being proven wrong again. My finger hovers over the 9.

Life or death.

Now or later.

I know I should call 911. I know this is the right decision but I can't push the buttons. Mickey always knows what's best and I can't ignore that fact right now, even if it seems completely foolish. So I call the only other person I can trust.

"Hello?" Carrie's soft voice echoes through my cell phone. The service out here sucks and the line crackles for a minute before I find my own voice.

"Carrie, I need help."

"What time is it?"

I ignore her. "Please tell me you know a doctor or a nurse or something. We were in an accident." I sniff away tears and wipe my forearm across my nose, noting the streak of blood it leaves on my flesh. I wipe again and there's less this time. "Oh, God. I don't think Mickey's going to make it. There's so much blood."

"Call 911," she says, her voice firm.

"It's not safe. He'll find us. He said no hospital."

"Who'll find you?"

"I have so much to tell you, but not now. I need help. Just please, come and help me," I say, my voice pleading.

"Where are you?"

"Um...," I look around and focus on the sign I can still see a few yards ahead. "Just before the turn off to Seabright."

"Hang tight, Beth. I'll be there as soon as I can."

Hang tight? I'm not going anywhere, but Mickey might very well be. I take his hand in mine and caress the back of it. I caress the top of his head, too, moving his wiry gray and black hairs out of the drying blood sticking to his scalp. I've never felt so alone in my life. Or so vulnerable. Growing up, Mickey was always the protector. No one touched me or messed with me because of the threat of Mickey—a hired gunman to one of the biggest crime families on the upper east coast. And if the threat of him wasn't enough, if someone hurt me—emotionally or physically—he took action and they lived just long enough to regret it. I never agreed with his methods or how he's lived his life, but I have to admit, growing up I felt safe. He gave that to me—him and Mona...and Declan.

Minutes feel like hours and Mickey is fading fast. I fear Carrie will never get here. I pick up my phone again, knowing I can't wait any longer for help when Carrie's old sedan finally comes barreling down the road, dust kicking up around her. I leave Mickey and run up to the road to flag her down. She drives so fast that when she stops, the wheels spin out and she fishtails into the opposite lane. She doesn't bother to correct it; she's out of her car and by my side. I breathe a sigh of relief. I have no idea what's next, but I'm confident Carrie's got a plan. If not, we'll be at the hospital within thirty minutes, twenty the way she drives.

After she helps me carry my uncle to the backseat of her car, she races down the highway, taking turns so quickly I clutch at my seatbelt for fear we might tip over again. I glance over my shoulder every few seconds, each time breathing a sigh of relief to see Mickey's chest still rising and falling.

"He's lost so much blood," I say. "I just don't know if he'll make it."

Carrie chews at her lip as she swerves to avoid a cat darting across the road. She narrowly misses him and I let out a curse. "Jesus, Carrie. That's if we even get there in one piece." *Wherever we're going.* I assume at this point it has to be the hospital, but then she zooms right by it. "I hope you have a plan, or some secret doctor boyfriend I don't know about."

"Don't worry. I got it under control."

"I hope so, because if the Dantes find us we're as good as dead."

"Dantes?" she says, her eyes wide. "What the hell happened?"

"I'll tell you everything. Just not right now, okay?" And what's to tell? Mickey never got to fill me in, either. I'm in the dark as much as Carrie is.

"Where are we going?" I ask.

She chuckles nervously and shrugs her shoulders. I know that look and I don't like it.

"Carrie?"

She hesitates before glancing at me from the corner of her eye.

"Carrie!"

"Relax, I have it covered, okay?" When I groan at her, she follows up with, "Have I ever let you down?"

Has she? Probably. Though at this moment, I can't think of a single instance and she is my best friend. Whatever she has cooking, she has to believe it's for my own good. I don't trust many people, but her? Yeah, I would follow her off the edge of a cliff if she promised me there was something soft to land on.

Mickey moans in the back. He's conscious again—barely. He coughs and sputters and blood bubbles from his mouth. "Fuck." I slam my head back against the head rest. And then again. It doesn't take a genius to know blood coming from his mouth is bad—really bad. Internal bleeding, for sure.

We continue into the East End. Not good. That is exactly where the Dantes rule and I can't be seen here. For a moment, I panic and wonder if my trust is misplaced. I can't help it. Look who my family is. Mickey and Mona always told me trust no one but yourself and maybe they were right.

Just before we get to The Pipeline, and I'm about to pee in my pants, we make a left down a street I wouldn't walk on in the day, let alone the night. "Carrie, you better start talking—fast."

Carrie refuses to answer.

"We're a block from The Pipeline! Jimmy Dante's goons already shot Mickey. Are you trying to give them a shot at me, too?"

"Jesus Christ, Beth. Calm the fuck down." She turns down an alley and slams on the brakes to stop short of a large metal garbage container. My head is knocked forward but the seatbelt holds me tight and I flinch at a sharp pain. I didn't even know I'd injured my chest and stomach but I can sure feel it now. Mickey has rolled off the seat and onto the floor. *Shit*!

Carrie and I get out of the car and try to get him comfortable.

"Stay here," she says, running off to leave me in the middle of the alleyway in the dark.

"Where the fuck are you going?" I cry out. My hands are wrapped around Mickey, under his arms. There's no way I can move him myself.

I hear the bang of metal and a slow creak. When I look up and to the right, I see Carrie facing an open door and the silhouette of a man inside, though I can't see his face. *Please be someone safe,* I pray.

Carrie's heels click on the pavement as she jogs back to us. A hand pushes me aside and though I don't protest, I want to. Who is this guy? I glare at him, immediately distrusting him, but then I see his longish, brown hair, trimmed neatly along the bottom, his barely-there beard and his tattoos peeking out from the collar of his T-shirt and the hems of his sleeves.

Damien.

"Why are we here, Carrie?"

She holds up her hands. "He's trained."

"Trained? What do you mean he's trained? What does *that* mean?" Mona said he was in the military, but she never said what he did for them.

Damien approaches Mickey with a bag in his hand. He takes a look at Mickey, shoves a shit load of bandages over his wound, and then tapes it in place. He seems to know what he's doing and he's confident about it. The tension in my shoulders relaxes momentarily until he wraps his arms around Mickey's waist and tosses him over his shoulder like he's made of feathers.

That can't be good for his wound.

"We can help you carry him," I say, with more sass to my voice than I intend.

"Nope. I got him." He passes me and then tosses out a, "You're welcome," over his shoulder.

Carrie starts to follow him, but I grab her shoulder to stop her. "Carrie?"

"Now's not the time. I promise he knows what he's doing."

I refuse to let go of her.

"Your aunt trusted him. That should be enough for you, too."

I narrow my eyes. How the hell does she know that? I'm missing something and I don't like the way it feels. "Is he a doctor?" I ask.

She frowns.

"A nurse?"

She shakes her head. "A corpsman...and a paramedic."

She reaches out her hand and waits for me to take it. Though I hesitate, I reach out and grip hers. A paramedic. Okay, that's not so bad. This could work. But can he be trusted? She certainly seems to think so or we wouldn't be here, but she must see my continued apprehension because she says, "He's saved a lot of lives. You can trust him, I promise."

My body relaxes, if only a little, and the tension in my neck and shoulders dissolves into slight discomfort.

We follow the narrow staircase inside the building up to the second floor apartment. Through another unlocked and open door, I find Damien in the kitchen and Mickey lying unconscious on the table. Damien takes a pair of scissors and quickly cuts down the center of Mickey's shirt, exposing his chest and the hole in his abdomen. I gasp as the blood pools in the broken skin by his belly button.

Damien takes a long swig of whiskey and then pours some of the liquor on the open wound, making Mickey flinch.

"You think that will help?" I say.

"For who?" he asks. "Me or him?"

"Either," I say sourly. Him drinking right now does not help engender my confidence in him. Though he clearly doesn't seem to care, spitting back his response to me as sourly as I delivered it. He turns and grabs a bag with a red cross on the side. With a quick unzip he's dropping things onto the table. "Hold him down."

Neither Carrie nor I move. He looks at Carrie first and then me before I come back to life, hurrying over to Mickey's side. I stroke the side of his face. "It'll be okay, Uncle Mickey. I promise."

He jabs a needle in Mickey's leg and Mickey doesn't even flinch. "Help me roll him; I need to see if it went clear through." Mickey groans in pain as we log roll him onto his side. Damien nods and says. "Okay, it went through. That's good. We'll just have to sew him up and hope to God it didn't slice through anything important."

"You think it did?" I say, gulping.

He shrugs. "I don't know. It's pretty close to some major organs.

If he lives, he'll be lucky. You should have taken him to a doctor. His chances would be better."

"I..." I can't finish the sentence because I know he's right. I know I should have, but Mickey always knows what's best. I have to trust him, because dealing with this shit is so far out of my comfort zone but probably well within his.

While Damien rolls my uncle back onto his back, I hold my hands over Mickey's ears to make sure he doesn't smack his head. Damien jabs a needle into Mickey's skin, a few inches from his gunshot wound. I wince as Mickey moans and I want to question Damien about what he's doing and why, but then he pulls out a kit for stitching him up and lays out his equipment. The way he holds his tools and the thread... And the way he attacks Mickey's wound... There's no hesitation. Only confidence. He threads so quickly that I can't follow his movements. His hands move like they're dancing—lacing and threading. Before I know it, Mickey's wound is closed tight and Damien is cleaning up the blood on Mickey's stomach.

He leaves me speechless.

"Told you we could trust him."

With my uncle, yeah, I'll give her that. But with our lives? That remains to be seen.

"Thank you," I finally say after letting go of a deep breath. Tears spring to my eyes. This is going to work. I did the right thing. He's going to live...because of Damien. I want this to be true and yet part of me still worries. I may still lose him. The thought shakes me and a sob threatens to bulldoze through my body.

Bilskis don't cry. Not ever. I'll be strong for Mickey, because he needs me to be and because I don't want to be weak. I want to be strong like my aunt, stronger than I've ever been. I'll give him a firm hand to hold just like the one he always gave me. I'll give him what he needs. No matter what.

"Hey," Damien says, holding my gaze. "It'll be okay."

"I don't think anything will ever be okay again." My voice is barely a whisper.

"Might never be the same. But that doesn't mean it won't be okay. And if you need a shoulder, lean on people who care about you."

"People who care about me?" I mutter. "I'm not sure how many of those I got left."

CHAPTER FIVE

Mickey's still breathing, or at least, I think he is. I watch his chest for movement and am relieved to see the slow but certain rise and fall. His bandages are stained, but for the most part, it looks as though the bleeding has slowed. There hasn't been any change in his condition since Damien stitched him up.

Damien.

I shake my head just thinking about my unlikely savior. Never in a million years did I expect Carrie to bring me to him and for him to know exactly what to do to help. I owe him so much. More than I can ever repay. I'm not accustomed to feeling this way and I don't exactly like it—not when I barely who he is or how much I should trust him. Or if I should trust him at all.

Mickey groans and I reach out to dab the beads of sweat on his forehead. "I'm here," I say, squeezing his hand with my free one. "Don't you dare go anywhere. You hear me? You have to pull through." I lower my voice to a whisper as I lean forward.

My hand clutches his until he settles and falls back asleep. Damien happened to have some painkillers on hand—I'm not going to judge him—and thankfully, he was able to get Mickey to swallow them. He seems to be comfortable now, aside from the occasional quiet moan, which I don't even know for sure means he's in pain. For all I know he could be dreaming or delirious.

I loosen his grip on my hand and sit back on my heels. Pain radiates down my back and I rise to my feet. Not the most comfortable night I've had, but I wouldn't have slept anywhere else. I had to be here for Mickey in case he needed me. Reaching around, I try to rub the kinks out of my lower back. I don't want to leave Mickey's side, but I know if I get back in that chair right now I won't be walking tomorrow.

It's after four in the morning. The moon shines a ray of white light onto the carpet, reaching the tips of my toes. The apartment is quiet and I wonder if Carrie is still here. Damien must be and I will feel so much better if Carrie is, too.

Because Damien unnerves me. Not because he's scary—he's actually quite the opposite. The way he took charge and mended Mickey and comforted me... I'm not used to someone being soft around me like that—and meaning it. I can't deny his sincerity. It draws me to him. But then, I'm only drawn to assholes, so that can't be a good thing. My judgment is poor at best. That alone should be enough for me to keep my guard up and firmly in place. I can't let myself be distracted or lose focus. My life is just too complicated.

The last time I lost focus, Evie paid the price and the aftermath resulted in my aunt's death. The truth is, if I hadn't let Evie leave that night at The Pipeline she wouldn't have been attacked, Sam wouldn't have threatened her, and Mona wouldn't have intervened. My life would be normal right now. Declan and Evie wouldn't be in custody, Mona would be alive, and Mickey wouldn't be fighting for his life.

All because I have some deep-seated need to be wanted, to be cherished. How fucking pathetic is that?

And here I sit thinking about Damien? What is wrong with me? Even if I could trust myself, I have to admit I know nothing about him. I still don't know how he and Carrie know each other, and this bothers me because it's as if she's been hiding things from me. And then there is Mona's supposed familiarity with him. I mean, who is this guy?

The list of conversations I need to have with the people who surround me seems never ending, and makes me want to scream in frustration. I can't just sit here and let my mind spin. Besides, I need to pee and I have an enormous headache that is growing by the minute. I venture to the bedroom door and listen for life on the other side. Still quiet. I hear a clock ticking and the steady hum of an old fridge, but otherwise there is silence. I pull on the door and cringe when it creaks, but as I try to go slowly, I swear the sound climaxes. *Fuck.* I walk through the half-open door sideways, and try to get my bearings. Last night is a blur and all I remember is that the kitchen is to the right. There's a door across from me and it's shut and so are the other three doors. Fantastic. All I need is to walk into Damien's room and find him sleeping—or not. I'm sure he'd appreciate that.

I creep to the kitchen and cover my mouth to stifle a scream when I see him sitting in the living room in the dark by the open window, the moon casting him in shadows. He's smoking a cigarette, blowing the smoke out through the crack. I feel the breeze and a chill walks through my body, so I hug myself for warmth. And yet he sits there, shirtless.

"I couldn't sleep," I say.

He reaches over and flicks on the small lamp on the end table by the chair. "Did you need something?"

"A new life? Could you manage that?"

"Hmm. If I could, I don't know that I'd be sitting here right now."

"Fair enough. I'll settle for a bathroom. Maybe a change of clothes?" I point to the clothes I've worn since yesterday. My once white high-collared sweater is now splattered with blood and so are my jeans.

"Right across from the bedroom you came out of." He stands and flicks his cigarette out the window before cranking the window closed. "If you want to go do your business I can bring you some clothes."

I nod and turn away from him, but before I disappear down the hallway, I look over my shoulder, pausing as I try to find the strength to say the words I should have said hours before. "Thank you. For the clothes, for the place to stay, but mostly for helping my uncle."

His solemn face is immobile, and I don't suspect I'm going to get much more than that from him, so I tiptoe to the bathroom. I lock the door behind me, take a deep breath, and lower the toilet seat cover. I don't pee right away. The closed space and the privacy gives me something I didn't know I needed—the ability to let myself go and just *feel*. Behind the locked door, I rock back and forth as I cry quiet tears for the aunt I lost; for Declan, the protector I might never see again; and for Mickey, the uncle I still might lose. I don't know how many minutes pass but the sound of the knocking on the door pulls me from my private moment.

I breathe through the tears and wipe my cheeks and eyes with the backs of my hands. In the mirror I see how positively wretched I look. My hair is in knots, matted with spots of dried blood and stray weeds. My eyes are red and puffy and my cheeks are cut up and so is my head. I don't feel any physical pain, just emotional. I can't let Damien see me vulnerable so I open the door just a bit, push my hand through, and allow him to put the clothes in my hand. I pull them back in and lock the door again. I never asked for a shower, but I don't figure he'll mind, so I take a quick one, noting all the bruises on my body. They're nothing compared to Mickey's. They don't even rate. I feel completely foolish for noticing them. Like they have any sort of importance in my life right now.

Damien has no shampoo or conditioner, just body wash—Axe— and I use it to clean my body and my hair. When I'm done, I smell like men's deodorant, but it's a considerable improvement from the stench of blood and sweat that surrounded me so thickly I swear it was visible.

Damien is a lot bigger than me. I'm average height for a girl, but Damien has to be pushing six three, maybe even six four. I'm drowning in his T-shirt and jogging pants. If they didn't have a draw string waist I'd have no hope of keeping them up, and I have to roll up the bottoms or risk tripping on them.

A shiver overcomes my entire body, even within the steam still lingering from my hot shower. I rub my arms before opening the door and walking to the living room. Damien sits in the exact same spot he claimed before I left him.

"Better?" he asks.

"Much. *Again*, thank you…"

He offers a small shrug.

He pushes off the windowsill and approaches me. The light coming in through the windows is enough for me to make out his expression. Solemn. Thoughtful. Intent.

"Did Carrie leave?" I ask, refusing to meet his eyes.

"A few hours ago. She has to work in the morning."

He stops a foot short of me, too deep in my personal space for me to feel comfortable. I clear my throat, and as I avert my eyes I get an eyeful of his firm, defined abs.

"Take a seat," he says, his voice but a whisper.

"Um…what?"

He reaches up to touch my forehead and I lean back, away from him. He waits for permission before trying again and though I don't know why he's about to touch me, this time I let him. He moves slowly, his fingers brushing against my temple. Right where he skims I feel a throbbing and burning ache. It was bleeding earlier and though it smarts, I don't shy away now. I close my eyes.

"Let me clean this for you. You might need a few Steri-strips."

"Huh?"

"Your wound."

"Oh...right."

There's a recliner to my left and I reach down to feel for it before lowering myself, my eyes inches from his taut body. The smell of him is divine, like the Axe in the bathroom but stamped with his own personal scent...earthy...like cedar and cigars. It's...comforting...safe... It kind of reminds me of being young again and living in Poland. Of staying out late in the woods and playing with friends. If I close my eyes, it's like I can smell the trees and the burning woodstoves in the distance.

When I'm sitting with my hands crossed on my lap, he kicks over the ottoman until it lands in front of me. He cocks his leg over mine and sits, straddling my closed legs with his, then he grips my waist and pulls me to the edge of my seat.

I swallow a hard lump in my throat and lose my breath. The way he looks at me...like nothing else in the room exists. I know he's focused on my cut, but for a moment I let myself believe that he's focused on me—on the girl inside, beneath the pretty face and hair. I wonder if he can see me—the real me—that no one else has ever wanted to take the time to find.

He reaches for the medical bag on the end table, and his chest brushes against my arms. Chills overwhelm me and a tingling sensation radiates through my body. He stops and turns to me, as if he felt me shiver, and when he's sitting up straight again, he holds my gaze before opening his kit. He pulls out some gauze and soaks it with a solution. With the gentlest touch, he dabs my cut and as he pulls the gauze away, I see spots of crimson. I thought the cut had stopped bleeding, but apparently not.

"You don't have to do this, you know."

"It's nothing." He takes another piece of gauze and does the same thing. I flinch as the solution stings my tender flesh.

"No...not this." I point to my head. "I mean...looking after Mickey and letting us basically crash here...even after Carrie left. That's more than I can ask of a friend, let alone a stranger."

"I know you, Beth," he says. "I know you better than you think."

"Because of Mona?"

He nods. "She had a lot to say about you over the years."

"I still don't buy this pen pal thing."

"I'm not asking you to."

"So are you helping me for Mona? Or for Carrie?"

He sighs, and as he removes some thin white strips from plastic packaging, a flash of sadness crosses his face. "Both." He pauses a beat. "Carrie told me Mona was murdered. I...don't even know what to say about that."

"I can't believe she's gone. I don't think it's really sunk in yet, because I feel like when I go back to her place she'll still be there, waiting in the background for when I need her. Or waiting to shout out a snarky comment just because she can."

"Yeah. I'd like to say it gets easier, but..."

"That's comforting," I deadpan.

He frowns. "I just mean you'll get used to it and it won't consume you after a while, but it'll always be there, like a hole dug out in your chest that you just can't quite fill no matter how hard you try."

"Did you lose someone?"

"I've lost a lot of someones. Brothers. Not by blood, though..."

"The men you worked with? In the Marines?"

He clears his throat and nods before pressing some of the cut strips over my cut. "You expect some people might die when you deploy, but it doesn't make it any easier when it happens...or when it happens in front of you." His hand lingers at my brow before his rough thumb strokes my skin.

"Are you real?"

"Real?"

"You just...you're easy to talk to...and you seem..." Sincere. Honest. *Different*. It is an act? Is he playing with me?

With raised eyebrows, he sits patiently, waiting for me to finish and I just can't. He makes me feel vulnerable and I can't afford that. Every word I say puts me in danger of getting too close and he needs to stay at an arm's length. I don't want to feel foolish or let my guard down. As long as I stay in control, I can maintain the upper hand and I need that. No matter how different he seems. "Never mind...you just seem different, is all. I don't know how to handle you."

"Handle me?" he says with a chuckle. "Why would you handle me at all?"

"Nothing. It was stupid. Just forget it."

"It's forgotten."

I open my mouth and snap it shut. That was easy. Too easy.

With our eyes locked he says, "How did it happen?"

"How did what happen?" I'm caught off guard and I don't even know what we're talking about anymore.

"Mona. How did she die?"

His hands are on mine now and I can't say when he put them there. He has me completely unwound, just with his warm, soft tone. I shy away, pulling from his touch, no matter how nice it feels.

"I don't want to talk about it. Besides, the cops wouldn't tell me anything, only that whoever shot her is dead."

"But there's more to it than that, isn't there?"

"Why would you say that?" I ask.

"Because your uncle is in the next room with a bullet to the gut."

"Yeah...well."

"So I think if there's more to share, you might want to let me in. I took a risk letting you in last night. You owe me that much."

"I don't owe you anything and if you want us gone, I can make that happen." I try to stand and he doesn't resist. The ottoman slides back a foot, rolling across the faux wood flooring.

He waves to the door leading to the staircase. "Then, please, by all means."

I glare at him. He knows very well I can't take off with Mickey like he is. I hate that I need him and I hate it even more that he knows it. Smug bastard. Here I am again, needing someone. Depending on someone and there's not a goddamn thing I can do about it. I wish I could take it out on him—beat him senseless with my fists and scream in his face. Anything to get rid of my building frustration.

But I know it would be misplaced. He doesn't deserve my anger. If only he weren't being so fucking nice to me. *Be a dick!* I can handle dicks. I know how to treat them, but he...he has me spinning.

Of course, I don't tell him that.

"Whatever," is the stupid response I come up with instead as I sit my ass back down. "I don't know why Carrie thought it was such a good idea to come here."

He frowns. "She didn't think it was a good idea. You told her 'no hospital', remember? Or did you conveniently forget that?"

"You're a fucking asshole," I say, folding my arms across my chest and turning away.

"An asshole who saved your uncle's life." He groans in frustration, making me turn to glare at him.

"And do you realize how much you swear?" he adds. "I mean, I'm a Marine, but you and your aunt could put my unit to shame."

I take a deep breath and try to calm myself. Getting pissed off and lashing out isn't going to do either of us any good and as much as I hate to admit it, I really need him right now and he really doesn't need me. That's the crux of this situation and it's one I have a hard time swallowing. I could just hear my aunt if she were here right now. *"Eat crow and like it, kid. If that's what you gotta do to save your ass, then that's what you gotta do."* But crow tastes like fucking shit.

I take a deep breath to calm my nerves. "The problem I have with all of this is that neither of them has mentioned you before."

"I've been away a long time. And I would wager that you don't know as much about your friend as you think you do."

"Does a person ever really know anybody?" This fact has only been made clearer with my aunt's death. I feel like I didn't know her at all.

"I thought Carrie was exaggerating when she said you have trust issues."

I point to the bedroom Mickey lays in. "I think I have good reason."

"Fair enough," he agrees.

"Just tell me who you are. I want to understand, because you appear out of nowhere...and you're pen pals with my aunt?" I laugh, "I mean, what the fuck? Mona has a pen pal?" I quiet for a minute. "Then all of a sudden you're the guy my best friend turns to when I have an emergency. Why haven't I ever heard of you?"

"You're welcome," he says, grinning.

"Bastard," I mumble as I move to my feet. I wait for him to move his leg out of the way so I can walk away.

I glare at him and he takes the hint, rising to tower over me. I spin on my heel and stomp away. As I reach the hallway, he starts talking and I slow to listen, touching the wall as if I need to be held up.

"I met your aunt just before my eighteenth birthday, right before my mother married husband number four. Daddy-to-be and I didn't get along so well and one night your aunt broke up a fight between us. I was much smaller then…maybe half the size I am now. Not short, but thin. He all but knocked me unconscious and she stopped it."

"So…that's it? You became friends?" I sigh, looking over my shoulder. "I didn't even know Mona had friends." I turn and start walking back to him, but I maintain my distance.

He smirks. "I came to her pub one night to thank her for saving my ass and she handed me a wad of cash, told me to get out of town, and get away from this place. She said Sterling has a way of destroying everything good in your life. And the way she said it…I could see real sadness in her eyes. I couldn't stop myself from really listening to what she had to say. I didn't want to leave on her dime, but then…your aunt was persistent."

"You don't say?"

"So I took the money and I left."

"And then what?"

"Wow, you're very much like your aunt, you know that? You like to control conversations."

"Only when people avoid my questions," I say.

"Back to your issues with trust, are we?"

"So you're not going to answer?"

He scratches at his neck and then settles back down on the ottoman like he might be there for a while. "All right. I'll let you have your way this one time." He flashes me a wink and I glare at him. "I joined the military. It was my way to stay away from my stepfather and his influence."

"He's a bad guy?"

Damien nods, his face grim.

"Then what?"

He grins, shaking his head at me. "Soon after I signed up, I did a tour in Afghanistan and when I had the money, I sent Mona a letter, along with the money she'd given me. She...uh..." His smile touches his whole face, even leaves small lines along the corners of his eyes. It's as endearing as fuck and a little distracting. "She sent it back with a picture of her giving me the finger. Then she said I could keep writing her if I wanted to, but not to expect her to write back because she had better things to do with her time." He gives me a small smile but it doesn't touch his eyes and I get he can't fully enjoy the memory, not when he knows he'll never have any more with her.

"That sounds like my aunt," I say quietly.

"One of the best laughs I had on that tour. So I kept writing. And for a while she didn't send anything back. Not until I stopped writing on my second tour. I...uh...got myself injured and was kind of out of commission for a while. She wrote that first time to makes sure I was okay."

"She actually asked?"

"Not in so many words. But, yeah. After that, she always wrote back. For the last six years."

"How could I not know that?"

He shrugs. "I think she's the type of person that only tells people what she wants to tell them."

"I feel like I didn't even know her, like I only got a piece of her. I mean, how is it that I'm discovering a whole different side of the woman I thought I knew the best?"

"I feel like that too. I'm sure everyone who knew her did. That was her way, I guess. She gave pieces of her to the people who needed it. Always holding back...for what, I never could figure out.

Maybe, like you, she was afraid of showing her hand. Giving away too much and leaving herself vulnerable."

I chew on that for a moment, running a finger across my bottom lip. I worry he sees through the same façade I put up, and for the exact same reasons she did. Both of us hurt by people we cared for and unwilling to trust others completely. But, more importantly, his insight hurts me. Makes me feel a pang of jealousy. How could I have lived with her for years and not known about Damien? About someone who obviously meant a great deal to her? Did I rank on her list of people she couldn't trust? How foolish I'd been to think I might have been the only one she could have been completely open with. She was that person for me.

"What about Carrie?" I say, before swallowing hard. "Another pen pal?" Part of me wants confirmation that he's not into her, though I don't know why. The furthest thing from my mind right now should be a man. There's no way I can see myself through everything going on if I get hung up on someone.

"Our fathers are brothers."

"She's your cousin?" I shake my head and count to ten. "Is everyone keeping shit from me?"

"You're angry she didn't tell you she has a cousin? Did you expect her to offer up her family tree when you decided to become besties?"

Besties? He says it like we're two kids on a playground.

I jump as his warm hand reaches for mine. He's back in my personal space, making me uncomfortable all over again. "I lied to you," he says.

"Of course you did," I say, angrily. "But about what in particular?"

"I asked your aunt to introduce us."

"What?"

"She talked about you so much when I was away I couldn't help but feel like I knew you too. When I came back to town, she helped me find this apartment and when I dropped her off at the pub last week, you were just getting there. It was raining...your hair was wet against your face and neck. She told me to stop staring and I didn't even know that I was." He pauses, takes a step even closer so I can feel his breath on my face. "I asked her to introduce me to you and she laughed. She told me I couldn't handle you."

He wanted me? Wants me? So he was playing a game with me in the pub. Is he playing with me now? This is just further confirmation that he can't be trusted, and it stings. I expected it, and yet I hoped he might actually be the person to prove me wrong. *"One man,"* Mona said. *"One man to prove me wrong."* But not this guy. His soft voice and his intense stare and kindness...it's an act. Of course it is.

He inches closer, his head tilting down so his lips are close enough to brush against mine.

"Is this what you want?" I ask, moving my lips across his. I can play just as well as he can.

He smiles as I try to pull back, but he grabs a hold of me and spins me around so my back is against the wall. I struggle against him, grunting as I try to break free from his grasp. He's too strong, his thick muscles stretched taut as he grips my wrists. I want to hit him for restraining me and for lying and for making me consider he might be trustworthy. It seems the more fight I give him the stronger he becomes and after a strangled scream I give up. My whole body relaxes and my arms go limp. He releases me but stays in my space.

"Feel better?"

"No!" I snap.

"Not everyone is out to hurt you, Beth."

"You lied to me. Why?"

"Because I didn't think a girl like you would look twice at a guy like me."

"Why would you even care?"

He closes his eyes and sighs, pushing away from the wall. He looks like he wants to say something, but instead of speaking his head tips forward, as if in surrender.

I repeat my question. "Why? Because of the way I look?" I say, frowning.

"Maybe. Or maybe because I see something inside of you that... feels familiar to me."

"I'm not the girl for you," I tell him. "I'm not sure I'm the girl for anyone."

He lifts his head and I see pain behind his eyes that makes me swallow hard. It's like he's looking right through me. And I'm afraid of what he'll see. Of showing him too much. I try to look away but his fingers catch my chin and his lips crash into mine, taking my breath away.

When he breaks away, his breath is in my face and I can still taste him on my lips. I lick my lips and struggle to find my way through the fog I find myself in. No one has ever kissed me like he just did, like our lives depend on it. Like his soul is speaking to mine.

"Who are you?" I say softly, more to myself than to him. His familiarity hits me again. I can't shake it. I know him. He knows me. He has to. There's no other way to explain that kiss.

He takes a few steps back. His cheeks are rosy and there's ample strain in his jeans. I try not to stare, though I'm sure he's caught me, and my cheeks start to burn.

He turns from me and saunters to the closet, snatching a stray shirt off the recliner along the way. I want him to come back and answer me but I fear if he does, we'll be doing a lot more than talking.

He pulls the shirt down over his chest before grabbing a leather jacket and sliding his arms through the sleeves. The hem of his shirt inches up just enough to see the faint line of hair leading from his navel to below the belt of his perfectly fitted faded jeans. I lick my lips and clench my thighs.

Then he pulls me from my burning desire as he snatches his keys.

"Where are you going?" I say before I can stop myself.

"I need some air."

"Air?"

He nods, his expression solemn.

"How can I be sure you're not going to talk to someone about Mickey and me?" As soon as I say it, I feel like an asshole. I fidget with my fingers, looking at my feet.

"Try not to miss me," he says.

"I won't."

A confident smile curls along his full lips, showcasing a small dimple in his left cheek.

"I know you, don't I?"

He shrugs. "Do you?"

Yes. Every inch of me feels it, and yet, I can't place him Why can't I place him?

"Try to get some rest while I'm gone. You're safe—for now."

With that, he walks out the door, closing it gently behind him.

CHAPTER SIX

Two minutes after Damien leaves—when I'm sure he's gone—I start searching for my phone.

I need to talk to Carrie.

Damien wants to avoid my questions? Fine. I'll get my answers the old-fashioned way. I'll ask Carrie, then I'll Google him and... wait...what's his last name? I don't even know his last name. How have I not asked him that already? Better yet, why hasn't he volunteered it? There's a better question.

Is he trying to be mysterious? No, that's ridiculous.

The only reason that makes any sense is that he's hiding something from me. Something *unforgivable*. And if I could just remember him, I would have my answers. But I have nothing. No memories at all, just a nagging feeling in my gut.

I check under cushions, in my clothes, under Mickey's bed, in the bathroom. Where the hell did I put it?

"Not everyone is out to get you," he said. Hah! And I'm supposed to take his word for it? Trust him because he's so open and honest.

He's already admitted to lying to me and playing games with me in the bar. I should have punched him in the nuts for that.

Where the hell is my phone? I pick up cushions and toss them back down on the couch.

I should hope he has nothing to hide. That would make life easier—for both Mickey and me, but I don't hope for that. Not even a little. I want him to prove me right, to be the asshole I expect him to be because then I'll know how to deal with him. Otherwise, I'll feel lost and vulnerable and completely out of my depth.

"Ah ha!" I say when I find my phone under the radiator by the chair I slept on. Then I cringe when I glance at Mickey and worry I've gone and woken him up. He moans in his sleep but continues to snore, puffing air out through his pursed lips. I tense and hold my breath while I try to turn my phone on, like it will make the action quieter. I don't know why. It doesn't surprise me when the screen remains blank.

Fantastic. Cursing under my breath, I toss it on top of my folded, dirty clothes and bite my nails as I search the room and find no landline. There isn't one in the living room either, or the kitchen, or his bedroom.

He must have a cell phone. But he didn't look for it before he left or have it in hand. It's got to be here somewhere. I search the kitchen countertops and the coffee table and end tables. I come up empty and have to widen my search. Then it dawns on me. Why am I looking for *just* his phone? Why do I need information from Carrie? I mean, blood is thicker than water and if Damien's her blood, she might hold out on me when I drill her about him. No. I need to do some digging on my own.

I return to the kitchen, yanking on every door and moving around junk and utensils and random lighters from like fifty states, looking for... I really don't know what, but I'll know it when I see it. Another drawer searched and nothing stands out. Keys, lots and lots of keys. Some loose change, some rank insignia. A faded black case with a trio of medals inside. I hold the open case in my hand, guess what each one is for, but in truth I know nothing about that stuff so I can only imagine he was good at his job. Though I have no idea why he left the military. For all I know, he could have been dishonorably discharged.

Time ticks away on the digital clock above the stove and I begin to panic, unsure when I'll get another opportunity like this. I all but jog down the hall, desperate to go through his room before he gets back. He never said where he was going or how long he'd be gone, but something tells me my time is limited. He's left strangers in his home after all—but then I'm not exactly a stranger to him.

His room is practically bare. Some clothes in the closet, some underwear in the drawer—boxers, not briefs—and socks. All his other drawers are empty. He did say he just moved here, so I guess that makes sense, or maybe he's a liar and I can't check his story. Maybe he doesn't really live here at all. Maybe it's a cover. My nerves are firing; panic is building inside of me. What will he do if he catches me? I've already discovered how easily he can overpower me.

What if he has a temper like Uncle Ralph?

The thought takes me away, back to the last night I saw Mona's husband. He and Mona were yelling at each other, as they often did. I was in my room, trying to get through my homework, and not very successfully. Their angry voices were like an awful song stuck on repeat, one that I could tune out after a while no matter how much I didn't like it. Monotonous. I guess that's how I'd describe it. It was only when it got quiet that I stilled and worried about my aunt. She was a strong woman with one hell of a right hook, but when it got quiet, I knew Ralph was trying to assert his dominance. I debated creeping out of my room to check on her, knowing that as awful as Ralph was, he never put his hands on me. Perhaps even he had his limits and that meant at fourteen I was somehow safe from him.

When I got to the stairs, I peeked down and saw his hands tightening around Mona's neck while she tried to slap them away. I wanted to scream and run and get the phone and dial 911. But I was paralyzed. When she finally broke free from his chokehold, she fell forward, coughing and sputtering. Ralph looked up and met my eyes. The coldness inside of him shined through. He was a devil if I ever saw one. I believe it to this day. This image of him is permanently etched in my brain—the look of evil. The look of hatred, of unchecked rage.

This is the image that haunts me when I witness a man's anger.

And that image looks nothing like Damien. But I don't know him, and this is just another reason why I need to.

If I were Damien, where would I hide something? Definitely not in plain sight. I look up in the corners of the room, then the floor. A hidden floor board? I tap my foot on random boards. This place is too clean and I don't believe for a second he doesn't have something hidden here. The bed? Why am I so stupid? I get on all fours and lift up his sheets, checking underneath, but all I see are rabbit-sized dust bunnies. Hmm. But wait...his mattress lies just a little uneven. I lift it up and jackpot. A .40 caliber handgun. A Browning. I tip it to the side and notice the serial number is shaved off. Huh. You don't get a gun like this unless you intend to hurt someone and not get caught. I press the button on the side and let the magazine slide down and into my hand. One hundred percent loaded and there's one in the chamber.

I sit cross-legged on the floor, Damien's gun in my lap, staring up and out the window as the sun finally reaches the clouds. The stream of light funneling in through the blinds warms me, but it does little to soothe me. This gun could mean nothing. He might just have one for protection...but then why shave off the serial number? I considered getting one not so long ago when I got roughed up outside a club. Stupid me got so blind drunk that I couldn't take care of myself and I had to call for help—as usual. Declan came to my aid that night.

The door swings open and I hear a sweet, "Hellooooo." A woman. Shit. I stand and pad to the door, hiding behind it. The gun is heavy as I clutch it in my left hand.

"Damien? Are you up yet? Damien?"

Her high heels click on the hardwood as she approaches his room. She's going to see me.

"Damien? Where the hell are you?" I hear the musical sound of her pressing buttons on a phone. Then silence. "Damien, it's your mother."

I know her voice.

Why is it so familiar to me?

"I swear you could at least pretend to sound happy to talk to me," she says. "Where the hell are you?" Pause. "No you're not, because I'm at your apartment." She's quiet for another moment. "Hello? Damien? Are you there?" The woman mutters curse words under her breath and I let out a quiet sigh while I anxiously wait for her to leave. She doesn't give up easily. She clicks her way back to the living room and I hear her puttering around in the kitchen. I peek through the crack of the door where it meets the hinges, trying to see her as she moves about the apartment, but I only get a view of her back. Dark hair. Long legs.

I lower myself to the floor and wait. Holy shit, woman. When will you leave?

I don't know how long I wait. It seems like forever has passed when the door flings open and Damien appears. I perk up, leaning in closer to see and hear what transpires next, hoping to glean some information.

"Mother? Seriously? What are you doing?"

"I'm making coffee." Annoyed. "Would you like some?"

"No. How did you get in?"

"Does it matter?"

"Actually, it does. Because obviously, I need a bigger lock."

"I could pick any lock you throw at me, son."

He runs his hands through his hair and his eyes train down the hallway to meet mine. Or I think they do and I lean back. Though I'm probably imagining it, he seems to want to keep my presence as quiet as I do, because he hasn't ratted me out. I have to give him points for that, at least. He wants to keep me hidden.

He sighs and takes a seat at one of the bar stools at the counter. "This isn't right. You have to know that?"

"Oh, get over it. I needed to see you. I've had the worst night of my life and I needed someone to talk to that isn't...well, you know."

"No, I really don't." He folds his arms over his chest.

"Jimmy is still in jail. That bitch Mona Bilski was working with the cops. And because of the wire she wore, he won't make bail."

What the hell?

I sit up a little straighter and Damien's head turns just enough to meet my eyes. Mother fucker. Liar! He knows them! He's with them. I clutch the gun a little tighter, waiting to spring at any minute. Carrie had to know. How could she not? The wretched ache of betrayal consumes me and it takes all my self-control to not pull the trigger right here and now.

Bitch! I'll give you bitch!

"George is trying to get him out, but it seems his voice on tape is pretty compelling evidence." I hear a loud bang and it startles me, making me jump enough to knock the door. A small creak echoes through the space.

"What was that?"

Damian shrugs. "Radiator."

"Damien, I need you right now. I'm so depressed. I had to take an extra Valium last night to get some sleep, and you know how I function without sleep. I'm just a mess."

"I don't want to hear any of this. It was only a matter of time before he ended up in jail. He's a crook."

"Don't say that about your father!"

"Jesus, Mom, stepfather. And I made it clear when you married him I want nothing to do with him."

Damien Mendes. The name hits me like a punch to the gut. Oh my fuck. I was right. I did know him. Or...I knew of him, maybe met him a couple of times before he left for the military. We were in the same grade, though our high school was so big I don't remember seeing much of him. Maybe in a few classes, but that's it.

Carrie brought me to Jimmy's stepson's house.

Realization sinks in and memories flash through my mind. First of Jocelyn, and her voice and the different tone she used when speaking to me—or not speaking to me. I've only met her a few times and each time she's looked down on me with snide comments and sideways glances.

But Damien...he's so different from how I remember him. Like night and day. He used to be tall and lanky with pimples and messy, chin length hair. The first time I met him was at Jocelyn's wedding. I was sitting on some tires in their garage, fooling around with a boy I liked, Craig Shaeffer. He'd hounded me for weeks before then until I let him see my boobs. He wanted in my pants and I considered it, but when it came down to it that day in the garage, I said no. He didn't like that and he kept trying to sneak his hands down into my pants, even though I gripped his arm and told him to stop.

Damien walked in on us and I'm not sure what would have happened if he didn't. He gawked at us, but not in a way that made me feel as if he was judging me. I think he was just surprised to find us there and perhaps to see my chest. He stood there, gawking, before walking backward and stumbling over some golf clubs. Craig yelled at him and called him a loser, told him to fuck off.

I elbowed Craig and called him a dick. When Damien took off running, I followed. I don't even know why. Maybe to explain? I don't know. I never felt the need to explain myself to anyone, but somehow I did to him. I never did find him that night, though. Not at the dinner, or the dance after. He just vanished.

I'm conflicted as I watch him talk with his mother, because it's hard not to identify him with the awkward, shy boy he used to be that never seemed to fit in with anyone at school. The boy who ate in a corner while studying.

A big part of me wants to run out there and get in his face and scream at him for lying to me, while the other part of me feels a touch of gratitude and compassion. He couldn't know what he walked in on that night of his mother's wedding. He couldn't know that he might have saved me from something ugly.

But I can't forgive a lie. He needs to answer for that.

It doesn't matter that he's trying to keep me hidden. The truth is that Jocelyn almost found us. She would have turned us in without a second thought. He put us at risk, and this thought tips me over the edge between anger and compassion. So I bide my time, watch closely, pay attention to their conversation while I think about what I want to say to him and how I'll say it.

If only she'd fucking leave!

I lean my head against the wall and roll my eyes. Jocelyn rapes my ears with talk of her emotional distress. *I'll give her fucking emotional distress.* When the conversation shifts and Damien starts to talk about something other than her, she bores quickly and decides it's time to leave. In one breath, she talks about how she can't live without her husband, and the next she whines about needing a mani and pedi appointment because she desperately needs to be cheered up. All this while her husband rots in jail.

I'm so thankful Jimmy has such an amazing wife. They deserve each other, and I hope she makes him as miserable as he's made me.

Jocelyn finally quits her whining and makes her way to Damien's apartment door. He follows her, his hands on his hips and his head bowed slightly. It seems I'm not the only one she exhausts. She kisses him good-bye, pecking each cheek like she's some posh girl in a movie. No one does that shit around here. He practically pushes her out the door and when she's gone, he shuts and locks it before heaving a sigh.

I emerge from my hiding spot, creep down the hallway with the gun still in my hand and at my thigh. The floorboards creak, signaling my approach. His back is to me and he hesitates to turn. I can only imagine why. He's a liar and he knows he's been caught.

I wait for him to explain.

When he turns, he looks defeated. I'm a few feet away, sporting a scowl on my face. His eyes lower to the gun and he shakes his head. He surprises me by letting out a frustrated laugh. Then runs his hands down his face and groans.

"You're Jocelyn's son?" I ask.

He strolls to the kitchen, seemingly unfazed by the gun in my hand. Perhaps he knows I won't shoot it.

"Put the gun away, Beth. You're not going to use it."

"Maybe I will, maybe I won't," I say, keeping my chin up.

He pulls a glass down from the cupboard and opens the freezer, bending the ice tray before picking up some cubes and dropping them in his glass. He raises it up to me. "You want one?" He pulls a bottle of whiskey out from the back of the counter.

"What I want is a fucking explanation!"

He pours himself a glass. "My mother married into that family. I didn't really have a choice."

"You're one of them."

He grimaces at me. "Really? You think I'm one of them? Do you even *remember* me?"

I swallow a lump building in my throat. "Yes. Of course."

"Hmm." He takes another drink after swirling the liquid around his glass, making the shrinking cubes clank together. "I don't believe you. I was practically invisible in high school."

"No, I do. It just took me a moment to see through...your... your..." I wave my hands up and down in the shape of his body. "Your new look."

He chuckles.

"And that's not what's important here. What's important is that you lied to me, and if your mother had found Mickey, he and I would be dead right now."

"She couldn't have told them about you without involving me and regardless of her flaws, she's still my mother. She wouldn't have put me at risk."

"I think you're wrong."

He growls in frustration. "You needed help, and I gave it to you. Mickey's best chance was to go to a hospital, but you wouldn't do that. I knew if he had any chance at all then I needed to fix him up the best I could. You wouldn't have let me touch him if I told you about my connection to the Dantes."

"You're damn right I wouldn't have."

"Then I was right to stay quiet."

"So better to lie to me and take away my right to choose?"

"Take away your right to choose?" He laughs. "Like I could ever change your mind. You're as hard-headed as Mona."

"Why do you care?" Ugh! I feel like pulling my hair out. Like I'm banging my head against a wall, over and over again. "You know, people sometimes give money to guys singing on a street corner. They donate money to give to the homeless kids in Africa. Maybe they volunteer their time at a soup kitchen. They don't lie to people so they can take in a man with a gunshot wound to make sure they'll live. I think that's a little above and beyond a simple act of kindness. You're leaving things out. And I know you have an angle, so please, tell me before I completely lose my mind."

He takes a drink, looking at me from over the rim of the glass.

My frustration peaks and I raise the gun, point it at his heart. "Answer me!"

His face changes and becomes harder, his eyes darkening from chocolate brown to black. "Don't ever point a gun at me unless you intend to pull the trigger."

"I don't think you get to tell me what to do right now. I'm the one holding the gun."

"Then pull the trigger! You think I give a shit if you do?" he huffs at me. "Three tours in Afghanistan, each day waking up wondering if I'll live to see tomorrow. There is scarier shit than you in this world, Beth. And I ain't afraid to die."

"Fuck you!" I scream at him.

"Again with the language." He rolls his eyes.

My hands start to shake as I actually debate pulling the trigger. I don't even know why I want to. Because he doesn't think I will? I know how ridiculous that is and yet I'm still aiming the gun at him. I imagine what it would feel like to take a life, to watch blood drain from a body until a person's eyes go lifeless. The thought chokes me up...especially when I see his solemn face looking back at me, like he's in as much pain as I am right now.

Slowly I lower the gun but I don't loosen my grip. "My uncle and I are leaving."

"And how do you plan to leave? Your uncle is still unconscious in the spare bedroom. I would love to see how you plan to accomplish that."

I raise the gun again. "You're going to help me."

"No. *I'm not.*" He chuckles lightly before his face changes.

Tipping his head to the side, his eyes crinkle at the corners as he frowns. "He's going to die, Beth. Moving him will not help his situation."

"Don't say that. He's the toughest man I know. He'll survive this."

He frowns as he leans over the kitchen island to rest on his elbows. "I know this is the last thing you want to hear after losing Mona, but I've got to be real with you so it doesn't come as a complete shock. And since I'm being real, I have to tell you that I can't let you leave. I don't want you to be alone when he takes his last breath."

I close my eyes and breathe in and out. Steel myself to hold back the threat of tears.

"You want to know why I give a shit? Why I'm more involved and interested than I should be?"

I nod, relieved at the promise of clarity.

He groans and shakes his head. "You walked into the lunch room in junior high with a striped shirt on and tight jeans. You spoke with an accent. I never knew where you were from, only that you were around my age and you swore like a sailor while almost falling over your poorly pronounced words."

My head snaps back like I've been slapped. I thought he had an ulterior motive like he was a spy for the Dantes and was fishing for information. Or he's an undercover cop, also looking for information. I wasn't prepared for him giving me a play by play of my first day in junior high. "How...how could you possibly remember that?"

He smiles and as seconds pass, it seems to spread over his entire face.

"The first time you talked to me was in English. You said The Great Gatsby was trash and you weren't reading it. The teacher asked you to read a passage out loud and you refused. You said your English wasn't great and he believed you. When we wrote that test on it, you handed yours in without a name on it. I put mine on it instead. Put yours on mine."

"Why would you do that?"

"You were struggling and I wanted to offer to help but I couldn't talk to you." He shakes his head. "I tried to talk to you so many times and I never could."

"I have dyslexia," I tell him, though I don't know why. I've never volunteered that to anyone before. Not even Carrie.

"I know. I could tell by your writing."

"My teachers never picked up on it."

"They weren't paying attention."

"But you were?"

"I always was."

I take a step forward and gently put the gun on the kitchen island. As I work through what he's telling me, I return to the living room and lower myself into a chair. He's trying to tell me something without actually telling me. That he, what? Liked me? Had a crush on me? That he still does? Ten years later? Is that even possible? Is that creepy? Am I creeped out? I don't even know. I'm too shocked to work through my emotions.

"Look, I know you've got more on your plate now than you can handle. I don't want to do or say anything to overwhelm you. And I don't expect anything from you at all. It's just that in school you were the only reason I looked forward to going."

"Me?"

"Yeah."

"Because you'd do things that no one else would do. Like lie in the grass at lunch and stare up at the sky. Or wear clothes that no one else would dare wear."

"I was fashionable."

"I don't know about fashionable. Colorful, maybe."

He scratches his chin as he approaches me. "And your laugh.

Not that giggle you sometimes let out, but that full-on belly laugh
that sounds as if you're about to fall down and roll on the floor. I
heard it once in chemistry and I think you got detention for it."

"Mr. Burns told me I was disruptive."

He grins. "You stood out—at least to me."

"You could have said something."

"I did. I got up the courage to ask you to prom. You told me you
already said yes to Chad Taylor."

I frown, remembering that night that's always made me question my worth. I can't even remember Damien asking me. How
could I have been so oblivious to him? If I'd gone with him, things
would be different now. *I* would be different.

Just as I start to let my guard down, I throw my walls back up.
Warning flags scream in my head that he's a liar and he's trying to
trick me. Trying to force me to open up to him to take advantage.
But that doesn't make sense. Every memory he has rings true to me.
The details he remembers are too specific for them to be lies. I
mean, how could he remember what I wore to school my first day
at Sterling Junior High?

"So you what…have a thing for me? Still?"

He licks his lips and takes a moment. "I did. And when I left, I
dated and had relationships and I moved on. But then your aunt…
she pulled me right back in, right where I was when I was in high
school. All I had to do was ask once, about how you were. And that
was it. Every letter she sent had something about you. Something
you did or said or wanted. The smallest details."

"My head is spinning," I say, as I work through his words. I don't
know what to say or if I should say anything at all.

"I'm not the enemy, Beth," he says, softly. "I never have been."

I nod. "Because you want me." As the words come out I immediately regret them. They make me sound full of myself, which I
definitely am not. I couldn't be more shocked that he had a thing

for me in high school. That he watched me and thought I was... different...special...or whatever he wants to call it. Heat rises to my cheeks and I look down to focus on my fidgeting hands.

"I did. You don't even know how much."

"And now?"

"I don't know what I feel now. But I know I don't want you to leave yet and that's something."

"Yet?" That's the keyword. Crushing on me is one thing, but that's not what I suck at. Keeping men interested is my problem. And the more he talks the more I don't want him to be just like the other guys who've walked in and out of my life. He's making me feel special, like I matter. *"He's perfect for you,"* Mona said. Why couldn't she have just told me he had this fucking lifelong crush on me? But I know why she didn't. I would have run away. Faster than lightning.

I look over at Damien and his confidence seems to have dissipated. Now I see the boy I remember, in his shifty eyes and his fidgeting fingers. He's just as vulnerable as I am. Maybe more. It makes me want to throw down my walls. In fact, I can't stop myself from taking the plunge.

I hold my breath, reach out, and touch my hand to his. "I don't know what to think about all of this," I say. "But...I don't think you're my enemy. I...want...to trust you. And I don't want to go anywhere either."

His fingers intertwine with mine and the look he gives me... soft...sweet...intense...is something I've only ever seen in movies or fairy tales and it thaws the walls of ice I've strategically drawn around the real me. I like this look. I like it so much I fear I will crave it over and over again.

If only he'd looked at me like this when we were kids.

If only I'd paid attention.

CHAPTER SEVEN

Damien leads me to where Mickey still sleeps. He checks on his bandages and gives him some more medication through a needle to the back of his arm. After I tuck Mickey in, Damien takes my hand again—this time without asking. He gently tugs me out of the room and toward his bedroom. He opens the window and there's a ledge there with a railing around it for safety. He helps me out and then hops over the sill, urging me to climb the black metal railing against the building.

I reluctantly go first, hand over hand, foot over foot, until I reach the roof. When I get there I halt and my mouth drops open. "What is this?"

I climb over the lip of the building and hop onto the roof.

Damien stands beside me now, scratching his chin. "Mona found this place. I...uh...wanted to find a place with a backyard, but she took me here instead."

"It's gorgeous. How could anyone leave here?" I take a few steps forward, scan the roof. There's a wooded deck in the center with lawn furniture strewn across it and surrounding it are pots upon pots of shrubs and flowers. On the far side of where we stand there's even a layer of grass with a hammock resting on it.

"What I wouldn't give for a place like this." And I have to wonder why she never mentioned it to me. Why she never told me she was apartment hunting with Damien. In death, she seems more and more a mystery to me.

"Come on," Damien says, nudging me forward with his shoulder.

He takes a seat on an Adirondack chair and I lower myself into the one beside him. I note the telescope in the far corner and turn to him. "Astronomy?"

"Yeah. I'm not really into it or anything, but sometimes I like to look at the stars. In Afghanistan, I felt peace when I looked up at them at night. I could have been anywhere looking up at the sky and seen virtually the same thing."

"Hmph," I say, taking in what he's saying. We sit in silence, looking up at those stars for a few minutes. I hadn't expected him to surprise me like he did and it throws me off balance— but in a good way. I needed something like this to remind myself to breathe again, that life goes on, even if it'll never be the same.

He leans his head against the back of his chair and rolls his head over to face me. I do the same, my stomach fluttering as warmth spreads throughout my body.

"I could live up here," I say.

"Might get cold in the winter."

I chuckle. "I'd wear a coat."

"I'm sure you would."

I turn in my chair toward him. "I'm kind of pissed Mona didn't tell me about this place."

"She liked me better."

I frown, and his words hit home as I think about everything she kept from me. He may be joking but I can't help but wonder if he's right. Was I really as important to her as she was to me?

"Hey," he says, reaching out to tuck a strand of my hair behind my ear. "Mona adored you."

"Maybe."

"No maybes about it. One day...if you want...I'll let you read her letters. I kept some of them and I think seeing the side of her that she kept for me might help you understand her a little more."

"You'd let me read them?"

He shrugs. "If you want them, they're yours."

"Thank you, Damien. I want to read them."

"Just say when."

"Are you really this amazing? Like, am I going to find out in a few weeks that you're really a woman? Or a robot or...an asshole?"

He laughs out loud, the noise echoing around us. "I'm just a regular guy."

"No, you're not," I say softly. "There is nothing regular about you, Damien Mendes."

He takes my hand and turns it over, pressing his soft lips to the inside of my palm. "Ditto."

I pull my hand away, forcing a smile. I like Damien. And I'm in danger of liking him more than what's good for me. He could ruin me with his sad eyes and his gentle touch. He could end me. If he were any other guy, I would assume I had a week or two before he walked away and trampled my heart into the ground. My head tells me he'll do the same. I'm foolish for trusting him even a little, but my heart tells me something completely different. I can trust him. I can open up and feel safe. I just have to take a breath and jump.

But I can't.

Not yet.

"I need to focus," I say, switching gears.

Smirking, he says, "Okay."

"Now I know who you are, maybe you can help me fill in the gaps."

He puckers his eyebrows.

"Are you able to find out what really happened that night Mona died?"

He scratches at his chin and pauses a beat. "I already know."

"What? You know? You were keeping that from me too?"

"I assumed you knew more than I did so why tell you things you already knew?"

"I want to know everything," I say. "Until Mickey wakes up I'm completely in the dark and though I know I need to be afraid of the Dantes, I don't know why."

"What *do* you know?"

I shake my head, recalling the night I last saw Mona, and I tell him everything without leaving out a single detail.

"This Sam guy from the pub? He was the serial killer headlining the newspapers?"

"He was the guy who attacked my friend, Evie. And they say that she was attacked by the Night Walker." The Night Walker, the fantastic name given to the sick fuck by the media.

"I don't know why, but Sam was being protected by the Hills, *and* the Dantes," Damien says. "Jimmy told Declan not to retaliate for what Sam did to his girlfriend."

"There's no way Declan would have let that go. Jimmy had to have known that."

"Well, there you have it. Declan got his revenge. Or Jimmy thought he did because someone blew up Sam's apartment building the same night your aunt got shot. The same night Declan and Evie went into police custody."

"How do you know all this?"

"I have friends."

"Okay...friends like who? Because you can't always trust the information people in this city give you."

"I got a close friend on the police force. When Carrie called me to tell me she was bringing a wounded Mickey Bilski over, I started asking questions."

"To the cops? Are you kidding me?"

He holds up his hands and shushes me. "Just hang on a minute before you fly off the rails. I called a buddy of mine who served with me years ago. If I ask him for a favor, he'll deliver and he'll keep his mouth shut. We look out for each other."

"Well, I don't trust cops."

"I never asked you to trust him. I'm asking you to trust me." He studies my reaction but I hold my cards tight against my chest. "Besides," he adds, "I never told him about Mickey. I just asked if there was anything I should know about. That's when he told me my step-dad was in jail for a number of charges including ordering his men to kill your aunt."

I lower my head and take a deep breath. I want so much to believe it didn't happen, but there it is. And when he says it, it's a glaring reminder.

"Hey." He touches his fingers to my chin and forces me to look at him. "Jimmy didn't make bail. These charges are going to stick and he's going away for a long time."

"I don't want him in jail. I want him dead."

Damien tips his head to the side and the look he gives me is something akin to pity. I don't want any of it. I slap his hand away from my chin and he grips my wrist as I try to pull it away.

"You don't know what it's like to kill. You don't get over it, even if you think the person you kill deserves it. It haunts you, Beth. *Changes* you."

"I don't care; I just...want to feel something...something other than this crushing pain in my chest. No matter how hard I want to believe she's still alive, this pain reminds me I'll never see her again. I'll never tell her I..." I take a breath and try to collect myself as emotions bubble up inside of me.

"There are a lot of ways to deal with this—healthier ways."

"Like what? Tell me, because I can't think of a single one."

"Focus on what you still have. What's right in front of you."

Right in front of me? Like Damien? How easy would it be to forget all the noise in my life? To let myself have a moment's peace? I need it more than I need to breathe right now, because the tension inside me has my stomach in knots and my muscles sore.

I reach out and take his hand while staring into his eyes. He stills and his Adam's apple bobs as he swallows. I stand and release his fingers, letting mine trail along his forearm as I walk away. I can feel his eyes on my back and the delicate space between my legs starts to burn and my nerve endings flutter. I grab the hem of my sweater and pull it up and over my head, tossing it on the roof. Shyly, I look over my shoulder to watch him push out of his seat and adjust himself before stalking toward me as if he's about to pounce. It gets me hot, makes my breasts swell and my pulse race. His hooded eyes connect with mine and I can see his desire as he licks his lips. My muscles clench, anticipating his touch.

What will it feel like to have someone like him drive deep inside of me? Someone who sees me as more than a quick fuck? When I reach the grass, I bend over and slowly slide my pants down over my legs. His hands caress my curves as I straighten and step out of my pants, kicking them aside. His breath is in my ear, his now-bare chest pressing at my back. The small patch of his chest hairs tickles me and makes me shiver.

"You don't know how long I've waited to touch you like this." With the back of his hand, he marks a path from the side of my chest to my waist. I let out a quiet moan and lean my head back to rest on his shoulder.

He unclasps my bra and his hands palm my breasts, squeezing them to hit the delicious point between pleasure and pain. And if he wasn't getting me hot enough, he slowly moves his left hand over my stomach to dip under my panties and slide between my lips. "Shh," he says, his voice almost a purr, and I bite my lip to hold back my moans. I've never come without penetration before, but with Damien I'm hopeful. Other men I've been intimate with are all about me touching them and pleasuring them, but he's focusing on me.

He's unselfish. Sensual.

His breath is in my ear and his nose is against my cheek and I raise a hand to cradle the side of his face. He kisses my hand and I lean my head back and sigh.

"What are you doing to me?" he asks, now planting soft kisses on my shoulder. "As if I didn't want you enough."

"You said to focus on what's in front of me." My voice is quiet and breathless. "And I don't want to feel or think about how messy things are right now."

His fingers move slowly, circling my clitoris and my slick entrance. With his other hand he grips my hip and pulls me back against him so his swollen cock is between my cheeks. I brace against him, moving just enough to force him to whisper my name. He pants and pushes harder while his fingers continue to work me. I imagined he'd be big and thick and he's certainly delivering. I'm going to be sore in the morning—sated but sore.

"Damien," I breathe.

He slides a finger inside of me and then another. He moves them in and out with ease. His fingers are electric. They send waves of sensations from between my legs to spread through the rest of my body. Every inch of me wants him—all of him. I beg him to work faster, to plunge deeper. I beg for release, but he won't give it to me. And when I utter the word, "please," he stops and firmly says, "no."

I almost come right there. Getting me hot isn't enough, he wants to give me all he has, and perhaps more still.

"Not yet," he whispers.

He pulls his hand away and I spin around, unzipping his pants. His cock springs out and I wrap my hand around it, teasing him the same way he teased me, stopping just short of his release.

I lower myself to the grass, the cool blades pressing into my back. He lowers himself but I crawl away on my behind, trying to tease him and make him want me more. He clutches my ankle and yanks me forward, crawling on top of me to fist my panties and rip them free of my body in one swift motion. I swear I almost orgasm right there and I cry out into the night, my sounds echoing off the brick buildings.

He covers me with his warm body and I expect him to take me then, to drive into me hard and fast and collapse when it's over, but he doesn't do that. No...he does something I'm not used to and something I'm not prepared for. He smoothes my hair out of my face and looks deep into my eyes as he smiles at me. "You're so beautiful," he says and I avert my eyes. I've been told this before but never in this exact way...like he's admiring me for something much deeper than my looks. It makes me blush.

"No, don't," he says, forcing me to look back into his eyes. "Stay with me."

He rolls on a condom before pushing inside of me. I wrap my legs around his middle and pull him close. He pulls out, almost to the tip and pushes in again...slow and steady and it's so intense I explode in his arms. Over and over, slower and slower, like he's savoring every minute. It's like...he's making love to me as he presses sweet kisses to my nose and to my forehead and cheeks.

I've never been made love to before. Fucked? Always. But made love to? Never. I don't even know what to do with myself. Because sex with Damien is different. It's not about rushing and getting off; it's deeper because every touch feels personal. Like his body is speaking to mine.

"Damien," I whisper. "I...don't..."

"Shh," he says, pressing his forehead to mine. "It's okay to be scared."

I swallow a hard lump in my throat. He sees me. Totally sees me and it's the single most amazing experience I've ever felt. Not because of the sex—which is amazing—but because I've never had this level of closeness with anyone.

"You don't understand," I say.

"Then you'll tell me, but not now. Right now I just need to be inside of you."

Sighing, I nod and he pulls me in tight.

DAMIEN LAYS on the grass naked with his arm outstretched, my head on his bicep. He snatched a blanket off the hammock to keep us warm, but next to his body, I'm anything but cold.

"That was..."

"Yeah..." he says.

We sigh in unison and then chuckle together. Sex with Damien was nothing short of all-consuming. The way he touched me, looked at me, savored me...it was as if I was the only person on the planet, like the rest of the world fell away into nothingness. For as long as it lasted, I was able to forget about Mona and Mickey and just breathe.

He reaches over with his free hand and caresses my stomach and I close my eyes and enjoy his touch. Even with calloused hands, it's delicate and soft, like he might break me.

"We should go and check on Mickey," I say.

"Soon. I'm not certain I can move right now. My whole body feels like Jell-O."

His cheeks are still flushed and he has a glaze over his eyes that comes with the euphoria of satisfying sex. I can only imagine my eyes look the exact same and it makes me smile. Then it hits me. I'm developing a little bit of a crush. And it scares the living shit out of me. All my life I wanted something to feel like this—to feel right. But the timing is all wrong. It couldn't be worse. My life might be in danger and his, too, if I continue to let him help us.

He knows the risks and he doesn't care, but I do. More than I'd like to.

And what if this is it? What if the reality of me doesn't compete with the fantasy?

"Where are you?" he asks, leaning up and onto his elbow.

"I'm here. I'm just thinking."

"About?"

"About...I don't know. I guess I was just thinking this was nice. But..."

"I'm going to stop you right there," he says.

"*Damien*."

"Look, I know things are complicated right now. We don't need a label or to talk about our feelings."

I tuck my hair behind my ears and bite my lip. Stay. Run away. Tell him how I feel. I don't even know how to navigate myself with him because I haven't felt this way toward anyone else. My feelings are raw but they're new and they're fragile. The trust I've managed to give him extends to my safety and Mickey's. But trusting him with my heart? Well, that's something else entirely and it's too soon for me to know if I can give him that as well.

"Does anything scare you?" I ask, looking at him from my peripheral.

He laughs. "I'm not afraid of guns or bombs or men twice my

size. I've seen death on a daily basis and some of it was horrific. I've no phobias. And I have dreams sometimes that jar me awake screaming. But I ain't afraid of any of that. Now you?" He nods. "You frighten me."

"Why?"

"I've wanted you since I had my first wet dream—which coincidentally might have involved you in a pair of Daisy Dukes."

I grin at him.

"Now I've had you I'm not sure one night will be enough."

"Your timing stinks."

"It always has."

"Jimmy wants Mickey dead and I can't know if Jimmy's anger extends to me, but if it does, that means being near me is going to put you in whole lot of trouble."

"I suspect Jimmy wants Mickey out of the picture because he's afraid of what he'll do. I've heard rumors about Mickey and he's not someone you want to make an enemy of. But you? I don't know if anyone could see you as a threat."

"Maybe I could talk to him and get him to see reason," I say.

"I'm not sure that'll change anything. Mickey's a liability. With these people, a potential threat is enough to act upon, whether he's injured or not."

"So there are only two ways this plays out," I say. "Mickey gets better and takes his revenge and we both end up dead one way or another...or Mickey leaves and I go with him."

"You'd go with him?" Damien asks with a raised brow.

"How could I let him go alone?"

"Hmm."

"And this..." I wave back and forth between us. "Whatever this is?" I sigh.

"Bad timing?" he says, quoting me.

"Yeah." I lean over and peck him on the cheek and when I pull away, his hands grip my face. He pulls me back in for a long, lingering kiss. His tongue dances with mine and my eyes roll back as I melt into him. Oh, God. Why does he have to make me feel like this? Why does he have to be so understanding? And why is he making me want him now, when everything is falling apart?

CHAPTER EIGHT

Damien holds out his hand as I crawl back in through the window. Taking it, I hop over the sill, but lose my footing and stumble. His arms encircle my waist, saving me from falling on my face. He leans in, close to me, and gives me an intense look that reminds me how amazing it felt to have him touch me and how amazing it would be to let him have me again.

"I'll help you figure this out," he says. His look...oh God...that look...there it is again. And the sincerity in it makes it hard for me to doubt him. But doubting him isn't the problem right now. Figuring out how to unfuck my life and Mickey's is.

I nod in agreement, unable to do anything else, because my only other option is to push him down and wrap my legs around him again.

The sound of a throat clearing startles me.

I almost jump out of my skin. Damien and I turn our heads in unison to spy Carrie at the bedroom door. She raises her eyebrows at us while folding her arms across her chest and flashing me a shit-eating grin.

"Don't say a word," I say quietly.

She shrugs. "I'm not sure I know what *to* say."

"I really need to get a better lock," Damien says with a groan.

"I'm glad you're here," I say to Carrie as I brush by her. She follows me down the hall and into Mickey's room. After I take a seat on the bed beside him, I touch his forehead to see if he's warm. He is, but not terribly so. It concerns me to find him still slick with sweat.

"So..." Carrie begins.

I give her a look of warning.

"All right. I won't ask."

"Why did you bring me here?" I ask her. "How in the world could you think it was a good idea to bring me here of all places? To Jimmy's stepson's place?"

"I'd say it worked out well, wouldn't you?"

"That's not the point. What if he'd turned us in?"

She takes a seat on the chair beside the bed. "I didn't have a lot of choices, you know? And I trust him. From the looks of it, you seem to trust him too." She waggles her eyebrows at me, but I ignore her probing. Even though she's my best friend, and has been since I was nineteen, I don't kiss and tell, especially when it comes to dating relatives. That's just all kinds of uncomfortable.

"There's something about him," I begin. "Something...*good?* Does that make sense?"

"Well, he did spend six years as a corpsman. A guy devoted to helping others, in the worst of circumstances, can't be all that bad. And if we're being honest, the guys you date are absolute pricks."

I ignore the dig. "I remember him. Not really well, but I remember him. And I remember thinking—even back then—that when he smiled he really meant it. I wanted to smile like that one day."

"I know what you mean. He made me smile like I meant it, too."

"You were close?" I ask because I honestly have no idea. Carrie's a few years younger than me and I never started hanging around with her until after I graduated. We met at party, introduced by one of the many guys I used to date.

"He was good to me," Carrie says. "He used to take me out on dates with him."

"What? Why would he do that?"

"I don't know. He liked having me around—or so he said—which given my mother and father meant a lot. In the summers, he'd take me to the beach with him and his friends. No one else did that for me as a kid. My mother was too busy working and my dad... well, he was too busy with his other family."

"I'm glad you had that, Care."

She nods. "It was nice. It ruined me when he left. I didn't talk to him for a long time, but now I get why he left. If Jimmy had got his hands on him he'd probably be a completely different person right now."

I turn to face her while keeping a hand on Mickey's arm. Absentmindedly, I stroke his freckled skin, hoping to give him comfort, or just to reassure him that I'm here for him and never leaving.

What she says about Damien is true. Jimmy wouldn't have let him stray outside of the family business. He'd have dragged him in no matter how much he protested and Jimmy would have ruined him—taken all of the goodness out of him.

"Did you know Mona helped him leave?"

She tips her head to the side. "No, I didn't."

"She gave him the money he needed to leave town."

"Huh. Well, that's interesting."

"Why do you say that?" I ask.

"When he came back to town I saw him out with Mona and it seemed weird to me. I didn't ask him about it. It wasn't my business, but I just couldn't understand why they'd be out together. I didn't even know they knew each other—more than casual acquaintances."

"She helped him find this apartment."

"Seriously?"

I nod. "Apparently."

"Huh." She chews on that nugget of information for a moment. "She gives him money and then six years later he comes back and they're the best of friends?"

"I don't know about the best of friends, but...they were close. Pen pals, even." I sigh. "How is that possible? There was a lot I didn't know about her, but why keep something like that from me?"

"Wait. What? Mona had a fucking pen pal?"

"I know, right? How out of character is that?"

Beth shakes her head as she drums her fingers on the wooden arm of the chair. "Well, I guess it makes sense that Mona kept that to herself. Having a pen pal doesn't exactly give you street cred, if you know what I mean."

"But hiding it from *me*? What else did she hide from me? It makes me think I didn't know her at all."

Mickey moans and his eyes flutter. I give him my undivided attention, holding his hand in mine and leaning in, eager to hear him say something...anything.

"Mickey? Can you hear me?"

"Ugh..." he moans. "I feel like I've been shot."

I find it hard to hold in my excitement. He's finally awake! I feel as if my heart has leapt from my stomach to find its home back in my chest. Chuckling, I wrap my arms around him and squeeze until he moans again.

"Sorry," I say. "Did I hurt you?"

"How long have I been out?"

"Not too long. A day."

He tries to sit up but I push him back down. "No, not yet."

Mickey's face tightens and he stills at the sound of a drill bit fighting its way into a wall somewhere. The apartment shakes lightly, the only picture on the wall tipping to the left. "What the hell was that?"

"I'm not exactly sure," I say, looking over to Carrie.

She rolls her eyes and leaves the room. "I'll look into it."

"You have no idea how worried I was," I say, heaving in a deep breath. "I thought you were..."

"Going to die?"

Silently, I nod.

He shakes his head, his eyes full of rage. "Kid, they need to be taken care of. You understand, right?"

"There's lots of time for that and I'll tie you to the bed if you try to move before you're ready."

"You and me kid. We're going to kill every last one of them."

I bite my lip, letting his words sink in. I want them dead, too, but pulling the trigger? I'm not sure I have that in me.

"Promise me we'll do that. Every last one. And if I don't pull through..."

"Mickey, don't talk like that."

"Promise me!" he says, his voice straining. "There is nothing more important than respect. This is how we fix what Mona did. You got me?"

I lower my head and avoid his eyes. "I promise, Mickey." I want revenge as much as he does, but Damien's words spring to my head. I've never seriously hurt anyone before and hadn't thought about it until recently. Do I really have what it takes to take a life? I don't know. No matter how much I want to see Jimmy and his men pay. And it hits me hard that he's focused on fixing what Mona broke and not actually caring that she's gone and never coming back. Can he really be this cold?

"But first...rest, okay?"

"Not yet...we need to talk."

I swallow hard. I've been waiting for this conversation since he the cops told me Mona was dead. Damien's filled in some blanks, but now I have a chance to find out everything. The whole story. I settle into my chair and I give him my full attention.

"So Jimmy had Declan and Mona called the cops to save him?" I say, summarizing what Mickey's told me.

Mickey scowls at me, his face a brilliant shade of crimson. "Jimmy wanted to punish Declan because he thought Declan went after Sam for attacking Evie. Sam and Jimmy had some deal...not sure what, but I'm pretty sure it was drug-related and he told Declan that Sam was off limits."

"So Declan didn't listen and he killed Sam?"

He shakes his head. "Nope, Mona did."

I scratch at my head. This woman who I love more than anyone has killed at least two people—that I know of. I'm not even sure how to feel about that. The only thing—for me—that makes it less deplorable is knowing in my heart that she did it to protect someone else. Evie? Declan? Maybe both. And Sam was a bad person who not only hurt Evie but came to the pub just to torment her. What would he have done to her if he got his hands on her again?

"Okay...so why did Jimmy have Declan?" I ask.

"Because he thought Declan didn't listen."

"And then Mona got in bed with the cops to save Declan?" I pause and consider this. "So Mona wasn't a rat. Not really." Here I thought she'd been working with the cops for a while rather than once, as a last ditch effort to save a life.

"Yes, she fucking was. It doesn't matter *why* she did it. Bilskis don't rat!"

"Did you try to talk her out of it?"

He narrows his eyes. "She called me before she went in. Said good-bye. I think she knew how it would end. I raced over there to try to stop her, but by then the cops were already raiding the place and she was dead."

"Did you know she killed Uncle Ralph?"

He stares at me and doesn't offer an answer. Okay, then. I guess that's a yes.

He tries to adjust his position. His muscles tense and his face tightens, and I quickly reach out to help move him over and get comfortable again. "Do you need more meds?" I ask.

"Nah, they fucking knock me out. And I like pain. It motivates me."

I nod, following along, but I'm confident that's not the main reason why Declan would have gone after Sam. He loves Evie. Sure, hurting him was revenge, but it was also a way to keep her safe. Mickey might not see that because love doesn't come easy for him, but I can.

"I still can't believe she'd go to the cops," I say softly.

"It was that bitch, Evie. From what I heard, she'd gone to them before. She's in protective custody right now and I swear if I see her again, I'll put a fucking bullet in her head, too."

"Don't say that, Mick."

"I'm speaking the truth, kid. Wasn't for her none of this would have happened. Declan would be safe and so would Mona. Behind every ruined man sits a smiling woman."

"No, if it wasn't for me..."

"What are you talking about?"

"Nothing. Forget I said anything." He doesn't need to know about how my actions created a domino effect that landed us in our current predicament. And explaining won't help. He'll still blame Evie because he doesn't like her. He doesn't like many people—especially women. I don't think he's ever been in love. He's always thought women were the root of all evil and yet he's allowed himself to care for Mona and me and perhaps no one else. I want to yell at him for it, but then...I love him. Unconditionally. The way family's supposed to.

He looks around the room and grips my hand. "Now, do you mind telling me where the fuck we are?"

"Um...well...I..."

"Spit it out, will ya?"

"Wow, you're certainly as cranky as ever."

"What can I say? Getting shot doesn't put me in the brightest mood."

"We're at Carrie's cousin's place. He's a medic."

"A stranger?"

"No, he's not a stranger. I trust him."

He looks at me through narrowed eyes. "I taught you better than that."

"Oh, for crying out loud, Mickey. He saved your life. Now get some sleep."

"Not until I meet my savior. Get him the fuck in here."

When I find Damien, he's crouched by the door, a drill in one hand and a long screw in the other. He's installed a deadbolt at the top of the door and now it appears he's adding one to the bottom. I'd ask if this is necessary but then, I know it is, especially after his mother picked her way in and Carrie... How the hell did Carrie get in?

"Mickey wants to see you," I say to Damien.

He turns to glance at me and then drills the final screw into the bottom deadbolt. Carrie is leaned against the wall, rolling her eyes. "How will I get in now?" she says, smiling.

"You knock on the door like a normal person," I say.

"I only picked the lock because Damien didn't answer when I knocked. I thought something was wrong."

"Does everyone know how to pick a lock except me?" I ask.

They both shrug their shoulders. "I learned when I was eight," Damien says.

"Ten," Carrie adds.

"Fantastic." Apparently, I missed some lessons in criminality from my aunt and uncle.

"Does Mickey need more pain medication?" Damien asks as he drops the drill onto the kitchen island.

"No. He wants to talk to you."

"Why do I get the feeling that's not a good thing?" He puts his hand on his hips and his expression seems guarded.

"Well," I whisper. "How about if we don't tell him who you're related to, just yet."

Carrie smiles at me. "Look who's keeping secrets now."

I glare at her. Sarcasm is the last thing I need right now.

"Do I need a bodyguard?" Damien touches his hand to my waist when he reaches me.

"I don't know," I say. "Just be honest."

"Except for talking about my family?"

"Except that," I agree.

When he goes into Mickey's room, I hear Mickey tell him to shut the door. I bite my lip as Carrie's and my eyes lock. Maybe him going in alone isn't such a good idea.

"It's not like he has a gun or anything," she says. "Right?"

"No, of course not," I say, but then I really think about that for a minute to make sure it's true.

Carrie sits with me while I wait for Mickey to talk to Damien. I know she's tired from working earlier and I should tell her to get some sleep, but I can't bring myself to say good-bye. I'm waiting for the other shoe to drop, for Damien to slip and tell Mickey who he is and for Mickey to attempt to kill him. It's a crazy thought, but then, my Uncle Mickey doesn't think like a normal person.

"Should you maybe go in and check on them?" Carrie asks, pointing to the room.

"I don't know." I chew at my nails.

"They've been in there an hour."

"You're right. I can't sit here any longer."

I knock on the door and neither of them tell me to come in. Or maybe I don't wait to give them the opportunity. I open the door and peer in, looking back and forth between them. Mickey's dripping in sweat, even more than earlier. His eyes are glossy and he gives me a half smile.

"Everything okay?"

"I just gave him some drugs. He was having a lot of pain."

Mickey coughs and Damien hands him a tissue. I gasp at the crimson stain on the white paper. "Oh my God."

Damien gives me a look that silences me.

"He needs to rest. Let his body work on healing."

"Of course," I say. "Mickey, do you need anything else?"

"No, kid. I'm just going to sleep awhile."

"I'll be here when you wake up."

"You keep that promise, kid," he says before his eyes roll into the back of his head. "Whatever you do, you keep that promise."

"I will."

Carrie leaves shortly after. She wanted to stay but has to work in the morning and there really isn't anything she can do here, anyway. I sit in the chair beside Mickey, reading a magazine I found in the bathroom. It's a men's magazine, with half-naked women interspersed with thoughtful articles about cars and electronics. Not my kind of thing, but then, I'm sure it's everything a guy could want and more.

I'm unfolding the centerfold with wide eyes when Damien comes in to check on us.

I let out a low whistle. "Well, Aria Fillion certainly has a lot of assets," I say as I stare at her tits.

He peeks over my shoulder. "I've seen better."

He smirks at me and he only lets me wonder a moment about who he's referring to before he sticks his finger in the neck of my shirt and pulls it out to get an eyeful. "Yeah, much better."

With hot cheeks and a goofy smile, I bat his hand away. "Too bad you won't see them again."

His eyebrows knit together. "Serious?"

I'm still smiling. "I haven't decided."

"Hmm. Well, that isn't a no."

"What happened to you to change from this shy loner guy to a guy who has the balls to look down my shirt in front of my very scary uncle?"

"A prostitute in Singapore."

"What?" I sit up a little straighter. "Serious?"

He chuckles. "No." He takes a seat on the window and the radiator rattles as he accidentally kicks it with his feet. He tenses, his nose crinkling as his eyes flash to Mickey. Luckily, he's out cold.

"Are you going to leave me in suspense?"

He shrugs. "I don't know what happened or when things changed. The military helped a lot, I suppose. They tore me down, almost to the point of breaking and then...they built me back up, only I wasn't the same. I was bigger, stronger, faster. Girls looked at me then. I didn't have to go to them because they came to me."

A pang of jealousy hits me and I frown. Jealousy is something I'm familiar with. It's something you learn to live with when you never feel good enough. Everyone has something or someone that you want, that just might make everything better in your life.

"There were girls in my unit too. The shit they talked about would make the men blush—me included. And they seemed to want to talk to me. They said I was easy to talk to. Maybe because I listened more than I talked—I had years of practice, remember?" He winks at me. "More listening to conversations instead of being a part of them."

I drop the magazine into my lap and tuck my feet under me as I try and get comfy. God, this seat. He should toss it out the window. "I think it's sad you didn't talk in school."

"Yeah, why's that?"

"They all missed out on getting to know you."

"You think you know me?" he asks.

"No. But I think I know enough to want to."

He holds my eyes and I feel the butterflies again.

Mickey moans and his eyes go wide. I spring to my feet and stand over the bed but Damien pushes me aside. At his back, I can't see what he's doing so I hold my breath and wait for Damien to tell me what's happening. But then he stands tall and his hands drop to his sides and there's silence.

"Is he gone?" I whisper.

"No, but his pulse is weak and..."

I push him out of the way and drop to my knees.

"I'll get some morphine."

Mickey's breathing is irregular. He takes one breath and then pauses for a few seconds and then takes two and pauses for another ten seconds. As the time between his inhalations grows longer and longer I worry he's left us, but then he gasps and breathes in again. His eyes are rolled back and his mouth is open wide. The bandage to his gut is stained, but not like before. I thought because he was bleeding less that maybe he'd pull through. That maybe Damien was wrong. Sure, he knows what he's doing, but he doesn't know how determined or stubborn my uncle is.

Damien is at my shoulder, moving Mickey's arm across his chest so he can jab a needle into his flesh. Seconds later, Mickey sighs and his eyelids flutter. He squeezes my hand.

"Mickey?" I choke out. When he doesn't answer, I say his name again.

"You promised," he says, his voice weak. "You promised," he repeats.

And then without warning it's like his whole body sighs as his final breath escapes his lips. I don't need Damien to feel his pulse or tell me the obvious as his eyes go blank and the color drains from his body.

My Uncle Mickey is gone.

I'M AWARE OF VOICES, though it takes me a moment to recognize who they belong to. At some point I must have fallen asleep, bent over the bed where Mickey still lies. My trembling hands lift from his chest and I hold them up to look at them. They're as pale as his skin.

I push myself back to sit on my feet.

"Beth?" Carrie says, kneeling beside me. She lays a hand on my shoulder and I turn to her, make sense of her blurred image through the fog of my tears.

"He's gone," I say quietly and without emotion.

"I know, honey. I know."

She pulls me into a hug and I rest my head on her shoulder. I don't cry anymore though. I'll never cry again. I have no one left to cry over. I look up to Damien, who leans against the far wall with his hands hanging at his sides. His face is expressionless. I glance away from him, feeling bare and exposed as I sit here. I don't want him to see me like this. Weak. Vulnerable. Messy. The last thing I need is for people to think of me this way.

Carrie holds me tight, her hand gently stroking my back. At some point, she guides me to the living room. I sit there by myself, alone with my thoughts. I don't even know what I'm to do next. I don't know who I am anymore. My life with never be the same without Mickey and Mona.

"Mickey and I won't always be around to take care of you." Mona's words hit me like a dart to the chest. I told her I could take care of myself but how can I? I'm a mess. She didn't believe me when I said it, and deep down I know she was right. Ready or not, it's up to me now. I need to step up and fix my messy life.

I hear noise in the other room, ripping...grunting. It continues awhile longer and when all is silent Damien and Beth emerge from Mickey's room to stand in front of me.

"I should have taken him to the hospital," I say taking a break from biting at my nails. "You said he could have survived. I could have..."

"You did what you thought was right. You listened to what he wanted."

"Because he always knew best. So did Mona. I knew it was a bad idea but I refused to trust my own instincts. I didn't want him to feel the same way about me as he felt about Mona when she died."

"How did he feel about Mona?"

"Betrayed! He thought she made people lose respect for our family."

"That's ridiculous."

I shrug. "So now he's dead, but he doesn't *hate* me. So, essentially, to keep his love I helped kill him. You warned me and I still refused to see reason. First Mona and now Mickey." The blood of each of them forever staining my hands.

"How could you think any of this is your fault?" Damien asks.

"Because it is, directly or indirectly. Does it even matter?" I shake my head.

Damien sighs in frustration as he approaches me but I take a few steps back, making it clear I don't want to be touched.

"We can't change what's happened. And unless you fired the gun that put a bullet in his gut, you're not responsible for his death. Understand?"

I do understand. The problem is that Damien doesn't. He couldn't. And I know he won't approve of what I need to do next: carry out my uncle's last wish. I'll do it because I owe it to him. And because his blood *is* on my hands and I feel as if he won't rest if I don't do what I promised.

Hours pass. I sit on the windowsill, staring out, my mind completely blank. When I found out about Mona I was so upset; I felt like I was falling apart. I should feel this way about Mickey and I don't. I think I'm numb. If I have any emotions left inside of me, I don't feel a single one, not even anger.

But numb is better. It's what I need right now to do what I need to do. Because I can't let my emotions deter me.

"We need to get rid of Mickey's body," Damien says softly as the day turns into night.

"Body?" I scoff. "Is that what we're calling him now?"

Carrie elbows her cousin and he turns away from us to walk to the window. He moves the curtains aside, looking down onto the street below. It's sunset now. Where did the time go?

"I'm going to suggest something and you're not going to like it," Damien says.

"Damien, shut your mouth. We talked about this," Carrie warns.

"You talked about what?" I've been left out of a conversation that seems to involve me. "Tell me," I say, when no one talks immediately

"Your uncle is gone. His body is just a shell. If the Dantes could see for themselves that Mickey is dead...then they may just forget about you."

I can't believe what they're suggesting and it makes me want to start throwing things at them. How can they be so cold?

Damien hold up his hands. "Hear me out. They want Mickey because they think he played a part in the death of Mona's husband. Or maybe they think Mickey will retaliate or who the fuck knows why. Show them his body and they won't have an issue with you anymore. You can still have a life."

"A life?" I chuckle without humor. What will my life look like now?

Carrie takes a seat beside me and lays a hand on my knee.

"I can't deal with this right now," I say.

"He has a point, Beth."

I glare at her. My best friend, siding against me.

Even if I could bring myself to do this, I don't think it would make a lick of a difference. "I was there when they shot Mickey. You think anyone wants me alive? A witness? My aunt ratted so what makes you think they won't assume I'll do the same? Not to mention the fact that they killed my aunt *and* my uncle and I promised—"

"You promised what?" Damien interrupts.

"Nothing. Nothing at all. Maybe I just want revenge. Maybe I want to make them pay for what they did."

"That's your uncle talking, Beth. Not you."

"Don't tell me what I want. You barely know me." The moment I spit those words out—even if there's truth to them—I regret them. That soft, intense look he likes to give me is gone and is replaced with something that makes me feel dirty and ugly. Disappointment? Sadness? Pity?

"What did you promise?" Damien asks.

"I..." Looking down, I focus on the grain in the faux wood floor. His expression is killing me, ripping me apart piece by piece.

"He wants you to do what he couldn't?" Carrie offers so I don't have to.

When I refuse to answer, she gasps and curses before storming out of the room.

Damien approaches but I shake my head and he backs off. He paces for a moment and I brace myself for a lecture. We've already had this talk—the one about taking a life. I don't want to hear it again.

"Your aunt wouldn't want this."

"How would I know? Turns out I barely knew her at all." Hypocrite. She wouldn't want this and yet, how many people did she kill?

"Beth, she knew her days were numbered. She wanted you to leave here so you could have a normal life. She's wanted that for years, but you were all she had and she couldn't let you go."

"I don't believe you."

He storms toward me, grabs me by the arms, and shakes me to get my undivided attention. I look up at him with malice, afraid to look to him for comfort.

"I swear it's true. And you'll know it soon enough."

"What do you mean?"

He bites his lip and considers my question before shaking his head and letting me go.

"Are you keeping more secrets?" I ask, a single eyebrow raised.

He growls in frustration, pulling his hair at the roots before returning to pacing. "Look, regardless of what you're going to do— because I'm confident you'll do what you want no matter what Carrie or I say—showing the Dantes the body is your best option. It takes the heat off you. Understand?"

I run my finger across my bottom lip. My stomach is rolling and aching and the veins in my head are throbbing so hard I can feel them. It's hard to think but I try my best to see through this, to think like my aunt or my uncle would. What would they do? Damien makes sense, I suppose. How can I plan my revenge if the Dantes are focused on Mickey and me? The only way to have him forget all about me is show him that Mickey is no longer a threat to him. And me? No one fears me. I'm five foot nothing and I barely weigh a hundred pounds. His assumption will help me when I'm ready.

"What will they do with him? Cut him up? Feed him to the pigs?" God, the image that flashes through my mind is too much to bear. I hug my stomach and swallow bile. I don't care what they say. He isn't just a shell.

"Your uncle isn't in that body anymore. He'd want you to live and this is how you do it."

Keep living. Nope. I'm pretty sure that's not what my uncle wanted, unless by living Damien means live long enough to make good on my promise. I need to keep living so I can be a hitman like my uncle.

Is that who I am now? Cold and numb and able to kill?

Carrie stays with me for a few more hours. We sit together, not saying a word. This is how I know she's a friend. Being together in silence is enough, and it's comfortable. Damien leaves us be, and I'm sure it's because he's upset with me. I try not to care, though it's a lie. His opinion suddenly means something to me and it amazes me how quickly he's managed that. I feel a connection to him regardless of how little I know him or how scary the thought may be.

At some point, he leaves the apartment and the slam of the door makes me jump. I watch through the window as he storms out into the alley with his hands gripping his hair. He hauls off and kicks a dumpster before hitting it with his fists. The noise echoes through the alleyway, the clamor loud enough to resonate through the closed windows. I press my hand against the pane. *I'm sorry*. I'm doing this to him. Making him crazy.

This is yet another thing I have to add to my conscience.

"He'll be okay," Carrie says. "He wants to protect you, but he can't protect you from yourself."

"You think I need protection from myself?"

She shrugs. "We're not on the same level as the Dantes," Carrie says. "No matter how much you want to believe you can be. You'll never be Mona and I kind of think that's a good thing. We don't think like she did. If you want to get through this, you need to listen to Damien. He's not the guy you went to school with anymore. He might seem sweet and reserved, but he's killed people. A lot of people. If anyone can help you through this, it's him."

"Maybe I don't want him to help me. Maybe I want to do this alone."

"Why? To prove a point? Will that be satisfying for you when you're dead?"

I grimace at her. Everything she's saying makes sense, but it doesn't remove the hurt and anger that continues to swell inside of me or quiet the little voice in my ear that encourages me to take revenge. It's stupid, I know it. Going after the Dantes alone will no doubt get me killed. Especially if I continue on this path alone. But can I ask for help? Or accept it? I'm not sure I can. Pride is an awful and stubborn thing and it doesn't listen to reason.

Carrie gets a few phone calls while we sit together and she ignores them. The next time her phone rings, I snatch if from her and read the name attached to the number. Donatelli's Italian Bistro. "Are you supposed to be working right now?"

She shrugs.

"Carrie, the last thing I need right now is to feel guilty about you losing your job."

"You just lost your uncle and you're my best friend."

"There's nothing you can do right now," I say, holding her hand.

"I can be here for you."

I wrap my arms around her shoulders and hug her tight. "I'll be fine. Maybe some time alone will help."

"Or maybe you'll do something stupid."

"Is that why you're skipping work?"

I practically push her out the door when she says, "No," because she's an awful liar.

When she's gone, I tiptoe back to the spare bedroom, to where Mickey's body still lies. The door is shut and I put my hand on the thin wooden barrier and stay there. I want to go in and stay at his side. I know he's dead, but Damien and Carrie are wrong. That's my uncle. Not just a body. Being near him might help me feel less empty. But as I put my hand on the doorknob, I can't turn it. I don't want to remember him like this. Pale. Cold. Lifeless. So I take a step back and lean against the wall behind me, lowering myself to the floor.

The door opens and I hear footfalls on the stairs before the door unlocks and Damien appears at the end of the hall. He props his hands on his hips when he sees me, tipping his head to the side. The long hair on top of his head falls over his right eye.

He says nothing. Just walks forward to lower himself onto the floor beside me. He takes my hand. Doesn't ask, doesn't hesitate, just takes it like it belongs to him. And we sit in silence with my head resting on his shoulder.

I have a feeling he'd stay like this with me forever if I asked him. Seconds, minutes, hours, days. I don't think it would matter. What did I do so right to deserve even a moment of my life with him? Amid all my mistakes, I must have done something right.

I flip his hands over and note his cut up knuckles. They've already started to bruise. His other hand is the same, only he has a deep cut to the side of his thumb. I lift our joined hands to my lips and kiss his knuckles, each of them.

He sighs and leans in to me a little harder. Like he can't get close enough.

"You need to decide," Damien says quietly. "Sooner, rather than later. The longer he stays, the harder it will be for us to...*hide* him."

He's referring to the smell. The thought makes my stomach turn. The rotting body of my uncle is not something I would soon forget. In fact, I'm pretty sure it would give me nightmares for the rest of my life. Plus, he's right. I need to make a choice, not just about Mickey but about what to do next. I've already decided, but I need to commit, so with closed eyes I nod. We'll take Mickey's lifeless body to the Dantes and then, when the time is right, I'll do what I promised.

CHAPTER NINE

Damien hefts my uncle over his shoulder. Mickey's wrapped in an olive green shower curtain, the ends tied with gray duct tape. Seeing him this way...lifeless...encased in a manner that makes him look like yesterday's trash...hits me hard and instinctively my hands go to my stomach, as if holding it will stop the nausea and ease my nerves.

"It's for the best," Damien says.

"Yeah," I say, not fully believing it.

I step aside so Damien can pass me in the hallway. He walks to the door but stops to offer me a look of sympathy before descending. I grab one of his sweaters and follow after him.

"Lock the door behind me," he says after opening the outside door and walking through.

Confused, I stop on the stairs. The door slams shut. Does he really think I'm going to let him do this without me? I bound down the stairs, fling the door open and find him by his SUV, the back door open wide, Mickey still resting over his shoulder. The moon is full and gray and shines a light on his solemn face. I glance around, trying to make sure no one hides in the shadows to witness him carrying a body. When I'm sure we're safe, I say, "Do you seriously think I'll let you leave without me?"

"That was the plan, wasn't it?"

"No," I snap. "I agreed to take him to the Dantes. I never agreed to let you go while I stay here with my thumb up my ass!"

He frowns at me. "Not sure I've heard that expression before, but...okay. If that's what you want to do while you wait."

I feel like I'm about to stomp my feet and take a tantrum in the alleyway. Could he be any more infuriating? "There are only two ways this is going to happen. We go together or I go alone."

He tosses Mickey into the truck, and he lands with a thud.

"That's my fucking uncle!"

"Wow. You got to stop with the language." His eyes glance all around and up to the lit up windows floors above us. "And keep your voice down."

"Why the *fuck* would I do that?" I whisper, my tone sharp.

"It's not ladylike."

"*Ladylike?* You're giving me grief for my mouth when there's a body in your truck? I think you need to adjust your priorities. I've got bigger flaws than a foul mouth."

"It's a pretty one, though," he says, a tiny smile claiming his lips.

I frown at his attempt to be cute. Yes, it worked. And yes, it pisses me off to no end that he almost made me smile back. I gasp as I notice Mickey's hand break free from the plastic. It flops out, hanging over the edge of the truck. Damien quickly takes Mickey's hand and tucks it under the curtain, but I still see it.

His white flesh and the blood under his chewed off nails.

"You could end up like him," I say before drawing my mouth into a straight line. My voice is shaky and I curse myself for it, not wanting to show my fear.

"And so could you, which is why I'm coming."

"I've already pulled you in too deep. There's no coming back from this once I show up at Jimmy's house with you."

"We're not going to Jimmy's."

"What? Of course we are."

"Jimmy's still in jail. Frankie's running the show now."

Frankie is Jimmy's slightest less sadistic brother—though not by much. Although I do recall my aunt saying he's more reasonable.

A clang rings out into the night. A rat scurries almost by my feet and I jump back, almost stumbling. Damien puts his hands out to steady me and I stare up at him as his arms surround me.

"Stop fighting me," he says. "Let me help you. You think I would have made it through Afghanistan without friends? Without brothers?"

"Are you addicted to risks? Maybe an adrenaline junkie?"

He snorts and shakes his head. "I'm addicted to you, maybe."

I sigh and push away, rolling my eyes at him and his smirking face.

"Damien, I know you have ties to them, but if they decide that they want me dead, they might just take you along with me. You mother won't be able to protect you."

"I can handle myself," he says, his tone serious. "Beth, you need to trust me. Can you do that?"

I sigh and close my eyes. "I'm trying."

His warm hand on my face stills me. When I open my eyes, he doesn't look hurt or pissed. "I can let you have your way on some things, most things even. But when it comes to your safety? I could care less what you want. So get the fuck in the truck. I'm done with this conversation."

He slams the back door shut and walks away from me. He climbs in and the engine purrs as he waits. It sits idle for a moment or two while I decide it's no use arguing with him anymore. And if I'm really being honest, I don't want to go there alone.

I climb in and glare at him, needing to give him at least one more sign of protest and one last chance to walk away.

"Belt," he says, gripping the wheel.

"Are you serious?"

"Safety first."

I want to hit him over the head.

He's nothing like the guy I imagined him to be when I first met him. He looks like your average handsome bad boy destined to break a million and one hearts. I've only known him a few days and he's none of those things, except maybe beautiful, even with the scar down his cheek that I'll one day ask him about when I'm sure he won't think me rude. He's been a good friend, someone I can talk to, someone who'll offer me comfort when I need it. He's someone who's dependable and loyal. He's someone that I want to know better—even if the timing is completely wrong.

He turns onto the main road and keeps to the flow of traffic, glancing often from his peripheral to check on me. It starts to get annoying. And then there's his taste in music. Country? He even hums and sings a few lines under his breath.

The heated seats are a nice treat, especially after sleeping in that awful chair in his apartment. I sink into the leather, my eyes growing heavy. I should be amped up right now and preparing for a possible fight. Or death. That might come too. But beside Damien, I'm oddly at ease, and I'm thinking about this as he asks me, "Are you scared?"

I roll my head on the head rest to face him. "Not right now."

"Hmm."

"You?" I ask.

He grins and I guess I have my answer.

There's no talking him out of this, and I'm done trying. I close my eyes but feel his gaze still on my face. Then the warmth of his body radiates up my arm as he gently takes my hand in his. And I'm too selfish too pull away.

The wind is strong and whips against the car, rattling the metal. Black walls of trees zip by, and the night grows darker as slate grey clouds block out the moon. I see the sign to Brockhurst, the small suburb where Frankie lives. We make a left and he picks up speed. We're almost there and tension builds in my chest as I wonder if today is the day I die, just like Damien said he wondered each day when he was deployed. Is this what he felt like?

I clutch his hand a little tighter and he squeezes mine right back.

"I don't deserve you," I say.

"I'm no angel, Beth. I've made mistakes, too."

"But...I've never been a very good person."

"I don't believe that."

"Believe it. I'm a taker. I *use* people. I take what I need and then I leave them in the dust when I decide it's time to move on. If you're helping me because you think you can save me...*don't*. There is nothing left to save."

"If you believed that, then you wouldn't be making the trade."

I sigh and tilt my head back in the seat as he turns the corner and accelerates down the street, swerving every now and then to avoid the divots in the road that never seem important enough for the town to fix.

Nothing left to save? Nothing worthwhile, maybe. But I'm not doing this for me; I'm doing it for Mickey. I'm saving my life so I can keep my promise. And so I can keep Carrie and maybe Damien safe, especially when he seems to care so little about his own life. If I die today, then at least I know I did all I could. I didn't back down or run away like a coward. Aunt Mona and Uncle Mickey would be proud of me for that. I know they would.

"You know...Mona thought the exact opposite of you."

"What do you mean?"

"You think you're a taker?" He shakes his head. "She told me about all the times her inventory would be lower than expected and she'd catch you giving free food to some of the homeless people who came into the pub, even after she told you to keep them out."

I blush at his words, not wanting to put any faith in them. "Lots of people would have done the same."

"She told me you practically begged her to hire a girl down on her luck even though Mona was already set to hire someone else—because the girl needed the job more."

"Evie," I say quietly. "She's in protective custody now, by the way. So I'm not sure how much she appreciates what I did for her. Then there's the other girl I screwed over. Who knows what her circumstances were? She could have been a single mother with four kids to feed."

"Your heart is in the right place. It always is. Even if you don't recognize that." He shifts in his seat and grips the wheel with one hand. "I remember in high school you came between these two girls fighting behind the gym. God, what were their names?" He strokes the growing hair on his chin.

"Amy Clover and Mia Boone," I say quietly.

"Man, Amy was a fighter. I think she could have taken on most of the guys at school without a problem."

I shrug.

"What was that about?"

"What do girls normally fight about? Boys."

"I was almost at the path leading behind the baseball field and I stopped to see what all the noise was about. There was a crowd around them as Amy kept punching her over and over. And then you sauntered up with a stick the size of my arm and you smacked the ground with it. Everyone stopped and stared and Amy laughed. And then I don't know what you said but the crowd was gone and Amy was off Mia. No one else stood up to Amy in high school. And it didn't have to be you to break up that fight, but it didn't matter. You did it."

"Please. It wasn't that big of a deal."

"I'm sure it was to Mia."

I frown at him.

"Why'd you break it up? I've always wondered."

"Mia was nice and she tutored me for a while. I'm not sure I would have graduated without her."

"Bad people don't walk into a crowd alone and try to save someone."

I fidget in my seat, unwilling to hear him. He's wrong. Sometimes bad people do good things. My uncle was bad most of the time, but sometimes he was my hero. Helping Mia didn't make me a better person. I was just standing up for someone who was outnumbered. And it pissed me off that everyone crowded around and watched and cheered. That situation got me angry. "I couldn't just stand by and watch."

"Because you're good."

I groan.

"I knew it. And so does Carrie...and Mona did too."

"Mona," I breathe.

"She said so."

My gaze darts over in his direction, hopeful.

"She thought you were amazing and the best thing that ever happened to her."

"She wouldn't say that."

"She didn't have to."

I pull our intertwined hands up to my lips and kiss the back of his hand, as if to tell him thank you. If only she could have told me herself.

Damien drives slowly, obeying the speed limit and observing the lights and stop signs. I'm not so careful. He almost reminds me of Declan. And not just the way he drives either...it's that quiet, thoughtful look on his face that doesn't seem to dissipate, not even when he smiles.

"If you change your mind...about coming..." I say.

"I won't."

He turns down a lane, the road morphs from pavement to gravel. Near the end there is a gate with a man out front, his arms cross across his chest. He approaches us as the SUV slows to a stop. Damien lowers his window and the guy eyes him and then me. I'm pretty sure I've seen him around The Pipeline. I might have fooled around with him once or twice. Not that I was ever really interested in him or anything. It was just something I did. Go to bars, get drunk, party, find a guy and have some fun. I don't even know his name. Before, none of this would have bothered me, but I have to say, it bothers me now, especially when he's looking at me like he wants to put his fist through my head.

"You got business here?" the guy asks. He puts his hands on his hips, pushing back his jacket to expose the gun in a holster at his side.

"Damien Mendes. I'm Jocelyn's son."

He leans in, takes a closer look. "You got ID?"

Damien sighs and reaches into his back pocket, pulling out his wallet. The guard's eyes never leave my face. "I don't need to see yours," he says to me.

Damien glances at me and I give him nothing.

The guard studies Damien's ID. "Haven't seen you around in a while. Aren't you some kind of a war hero?"

Damien doesn't respond and I can tell, even while facing his back, that the connection makes him uncomfortable. Or maybe it's the reference to him serving. He sits up a little straighter and grips the wheel a little harder. I guess he hates compliments about as much as I do.

The guard lifts a radio up to his mouth. "I got two visitors for the boss." Static crackles from the radio speaker as he lets go of the button. Another voice asks for names. "Jocelyn's boy. And..." his voice changes. "Beth Bilski."

A large buzzing noise sounds before the gates slowly recede along the fence.

"Go straight up to the house. No detours."

Damien puts the car in drive and accelerates up the slight slope, driving through the canopy of trees around us. The road forks and to the left Frankie's house is a quarter of a mile up the driveway. A barn is to the right. We follow the road to the left and stop outside of the house. I've only been here once. Even in the moonlight, the white pillars glow like I remember from when I first saw them as a young girl. Three men stand on the porch and they march toward us, guns drawn and gripped at their sides. One of them opens the door and motions with his head for me to get out. I do as he says. He holds the gun—for now—so I'll play ball.

They let Damien get out on his own and when he rounds the car he glowers at the guy who puts his free hand out to death grip my upper arm.

"Let go of her arm," he says, firmly, clearly not intimidated by the men's guns or their thick, muscular appearances.

The guy holding me scoffs at him, and refuses to let go. So Damien does something unexpected. He retracts his arm and faster than I can process he smashes his fist into the guy's nose. He certainly lets go then, bending to cough and sputter as blood pours from his nose to stain the dirt at his feet. Another guard raises his gun and presses it to Damien's temple. But Damien doesn't hold his hands up or try to talk the guy out of hurting him. I swear he wants to die—here and now. He pushes back with his head, the metal biting into his flesh.

"Stop!" I scream.

Jocelyn barges out through the double doors and starts yelling at the guards. "That's my son, goddamn it. Don't treat him like the enemy." She pulls her son into a hug and her eyes shift to me and back to him. "What the hell are you doing here with her?"

"Not now, Mother."

She leans in and whispers something to him and I hear him give her a firm "no", though I can't be sure what she's said. Probably something heinous.

"I want to speak with Frankie," I say.

She glances at me from the corner of her eye. "Good for you. And I want a black Rolls Royce, but that doesn't mean I'm going to get one, does it?

"He'll want to see me."

"Oh, I doubt that."

She gawks at me, like a doting mother would a scantily dressed hussy about to climb aboard her son. The wheels spin in that old head of hers, but after she considers her options, she sees reason. Or maybe she thinks Frankie will kill me and she'd like to see that happen. Who the hell knows with her? And how the hell did a woman so awful give birth to someone like Damien?

"Follow me," she says with a sneer.

With a sideways glance at the back of the truck I start forward, following in her wake. She takes her son's arm and though he's reluctant, he allows it. Inside the house, I ignore all the fine pretty things they have. Like the art on the wall, or the random white, faceless sculptures along the far wall. We go into a library with a large wooden desk in the center. Frankie sits behind it and when he sees me, a confused look crosses his narrow face. He scratches his head and leans back in his chair.

"Well, this is unexpected," he says. "Damien, it's good to see you."

"Is it?" he says under his breath.

Frankie ignores him, focusing on me with narrowed eyes as he smirks. "And Beth Bilski. Yes. Very unexpected."

"Well, no one's ever called me predictable," I say.

"Hmm." He gestures to the seats in front of him. Damien waits for me to sit before he drops into the one beside me. I lean back, fold my hands in my lap, and try to keep my cool. Though now I sit in front of a beast, my nerves are firing and my pulse is racing. I hold up my chin and keep my face straight. No one ever said I can't act when I put my mind to it. Meanwhile, Damien is on guard. He leans over to rest his elbows on his knees.

"You came together?" Frankie asks.

I shrug.

"Jocelyn, leave us alone. And shut the door behind you."

"Frankie, my boy doesn't belong in here, in *this* conversation."

"Don't tell me what to think, Jocelyn. I don't have the patience for you tonight." He dismisses her with a wave and though she hesitates, a line of worry streaking her otherwise botox-ed forehead, she does as she's told.

"You have the floor, Miss Bilski."

I let my bottom lip fall and draw in a long, slow breath. "You wanted my uncle dead?"

"Is it that simple?" He leans back a little farther in his chair. He hums and haws for a moment. "No, I don't think it is."

"The cops came to my apartment and told me about Mona, and they also told me she...that she..." I can't form the words.

"Turned on her family?"

"Yes," I mumble. "They thought you might retaliate against my uncle and me. Which turns out to be true since some of your men showed up at my apartment and ended up shooting Mickey."

"Sometimes cops aren't as stupid as they seem."

"You want to know if my uncle knew about Ralph's murder?" I wait for him to nod. "He did. And I wouldn't be surprised if he was the one to pull the trigger."

Frankie licks his lips and his fingers curl into fists on the armrest of his chair. Then he pushes out of his seat and paces the length of the picture window on the opposite side of the room. The branches from a nearby tree tap at the glass as the wind picks up. The noise crawls up my spine and makes me shiver.

I give him a moment to process what I've said. I might not like him, but he lost a brother and I'm not completely heartless.

"And now you're wondering if I knew? Well, the answer is no— at least, not until yesterday I didn't. Like you, I believed Ralph disappeared. I knew my aunt wasn't all that sad about it, but he wasn't all that nice to her and I figured she was just happy to be free of him."

"I'm curious why you feel the need to tell me all of this."

"Because I'm a survivor, Mr. Dante," I say. "I don't want to run away. I don't want to have to constantly look over my shoulder. I just want to move past this. I understand you want blood for blood, and I want you to know that you've got it." I take a breath. "My uncle is dead and in the back of Damien's SUV."

He faces me, his eyebrows puckered. "Excuse me?"

"He's dead...in Damien's truck. You can go and see for yourself."

"Just like that?"

"Just like that." I repeat.

At this, Frankie laughs out loud, outrageous-like, as if he's never heard anything funnier. "You are Mona's Bilski's blood, I'll give you that."

"You took my aunt and now my uncle. Nothing can take away

the pain of that, but I don't want a war—especially one I know I can't win. I just want my life back."

He leans over his desk, staring at me like a collector appraising a piece of art. He tries to understand me, tries to see through me, to my intentions, but I hold my cards tight against my chest. I won't let him see.

"Okay."

"Okay?" I glance at Damien who continues to stare at Frankie.

"Blood for blood," he says, repeating me.

I stumble, looking for the right words but realize I have none. There is no appropriate thing to say right now.

"Oh, well...thank you." I start to rise but he raises his hand to stop me and I reclaim my seat.

"This conversation isn't over yet. Not until I say it is."

"What more could we have to say to one another?"

"Careful. I'm an important man and I deserve your respect—if not your fear."

I swallow hard and sit up straighter. His arrogance and the smug look on his face is enough to make me want to shoot him right here...in the throat or maybe in the forehead.

"Have you read her will yet?"

"Excuse me?" I say, a touch confused.

"It's a simple question."

"No. I guess I haven't had time, what with running for my life and all," I say, my voice sour.

"I suspect she'll have left everything to you and so she should. However, that pub was built on my brother's money and she didn't deserve to keep it after she..." He pauses and pinches the bridge of his nose while attempting to calm himself. "None the less, I don't want any of it. But...you will continue to pay for operating in Jimmy's domain."

"I don't know anything about that."

"Well, now you do. I expect my payment weekly. Friday afternoons at four p.m. One thousand dollars. I will come to you. Do not seek me out. I'll expect you to be at the pub waiting for me, envelope in hand, all one hundred dollar bills—unless we make prior arrangements."

"A thousand dollars? I don't have that kind of money."

"Good thing I'm a reasonable guy. Given the recent loss of your family, I'll give you a few weeks to get your affairs settled. Tomorrow is Friday so you have three weeks from tomorrow." He leans back in his chair, steepling his hands.

"Are we done?"

"Not quite."

I stare at him, expressionless, unable to imagine what he'll throw at me now.

"Tell me, Beth, can I trust you? Like I trusted your uncle before all of this mess?"

No, absolutely not, is what I should say, but I don't. I hold my head up high, look him straight in the eye, and hope to God he doesn't see the sweat building in a thin layer over my whole body. "You can trust me," I say.

"Hmm. We shall see."

"Can I go now?"

A wicked smile consumes his face as he holds up his hands as if to say "be my guest."

I push out of my seat and stand. Damien follows my lead.

I turn away from Frankie and am nearly at the door to the library when he calls out my name. "For what it's worth, I *am* sorry about your uncle."

"For what it's worth, I don't care."

He glares at me momentarily before chuckling. "In another life, Beth, I might have liked you, perhaps more than was good for me."

"Well, aren't we lucky we're living this one."

I push through the doors, never looking back, but when I get to the car, I finally let out the breath I was holding, my air coming out in raspy, shaking breaths.

The guards round the car, open the back door and drag my uncle out. I close my eyes and say a quiet good-bye.

CHAPTER TEN

"A thousand dollars?" I whisper to myself, though I know Damien hears me.

"It's a lot of money," he agrees.

I turn to him. "How long has she been paying him that? Do you know?"

"Mona and I didn't talk about things like that." He turns onto the highway before asking me, "Do you have the money?"

"You've done enough."

"I wasn't offering."

My lips form a perfect circle as he tosses his comment out and I feel like the biggest idiot until he starts to smile and then I want to hit him.

"I don't have it, but I could get it if you need it."

"I appreciate the offer. I'm amazed that you continue to be one of the two people I can count on the most right now. I shouldn't trust you as much as I do, and I wouldn't if Mona hadn't."

"So you trust me now?"

"I'm starting to," I say quietly. "I *want* to."

He reaches out to squeeze my hand and my body tenses. He seems to notice because he takes it away just as quickly as he offered it.

"It's not you," I say. It's the thought of letting my guard down, of opening up and trusting, and of getting burned. Everything inside of me tells me to stay cautious.

He scoffs at me.

"I know that's what people say when they're not interested and need an excuse. I've used it myself a few times and I can't even tell you how many times it's been used on me."

"Who would give you up?" he says, his voice as serious as a heart attack.

A small smile crashes through my defenses, before I realize I'm doing it.

"You've got a beautiful smile."

"Damien..." I bow my head and feel the heat of embarrassment in my cheeks.

"I won't push you. I told you before, I'll be whatever you need, and if that's a friend, then I'm cool with that."

"Whatever I need?" I ask.

"Anything," he agrees.

I bite my lip and stare out the window. When he says this, I imagine there is a short list of things he assumes I'll ask for. He can't imagine what comes to mind, other than the obvious.

"Just spit it out."

"I need...I need..."

"Yes?"

"I need you to teach me how to shoot a gun and make it count."

He blows air out through pursed lips. "Beth, I told you before that killing a person isn't something you'll ever get over. It'll ruin someone like you."

"It didn't ruin my aunt or my uncle."

"I think we can agree you're not like them."

"What if I'm exactly like them?" I retort.

He scratches his head, shakes it, and starts to speak, but then snaps his mouth shut. "Your aunt wanted something different for you. I told you that already."

"Well, my uncle didn't," I snap. "And I promised him I'd take revenge for my aunt."

"At what cost? Your life?"

I refuse to answer. Instead, I wrap my arms around my middle and hug myself for comfort.

"Think about that. How much could he really care about you if he asked you for that? People who love you protect you at all costs. They don't put you in danger. And you're willing to die for someone like that?"

"You're right. My uncle didn't love me the way I loved him. Do you feel better for making that obvious to me?"

"Beth, I'm trying to get you to see reason."

"Because you care about what Mona wanted?"

"Because I give a shit about you!" he snaps.

"You'd get bored of me if I let you in."

He groans and lets out a breath. "So better not to try?"

"Damien, I told you before, your timing—"

"I know it sucks," he agrees. "Doesn't make me want you any less."

I gulp and my heart thuds. There's the look. I can't even think when he gives it to me. It would be so easy to forget about my life right now and to focus on getting to know his mind and, better, his body. I could fall...hard. It would be easy. And yet, I can't let myself.

"Damien, you'll find someone else. They'll be amazing and I'll hate them. But I want that for you because you deserve it. You don't deserve to come home from war to fight another battle that's not your own. You don't deserve a girl who's never quite been able to get her shit together."

"The fact that you're pushing me away only makes me want you more. Do you get that?"

I bite my lip before sighing. He doesn't give up easily and it's a quality I find attractive. Another one to add to the list, I suppose. "You're so persistent."

"I can be."

"I don't need a boyfriend right now. I need someone who can help me hit a target and you don't want to do that."

Lines of worry crease his forehead. He reduces his speed until we're crawling, prolonging the drive. "I'll make you a deal," he says, finally. "If you give me a good reason why you need to keep your promise—and not that 'I promised' bullshit—I'll help you. If I can understand why, then yeah, I'll help you."

I don't like to be put on the spot, especially when it comes to sharing my feelings. Opening up makes me feel so naked and vulnerable and I worry about being judged, about saying the wrong thing and seeing a look on his face that screams disgust or disappointment. Could I say anything to him that would make him understand my motivation? Do I even know it myself? I give it thought as we continue to drive. I shouldn't care what he thinks—what anyone thinks. For the longest time I've let people believe I don't care, but that couldn't be further from the truth. I want to be accepted. I want people to like me even if I don't like them. I don't want to look foolish or stupid. And I care about what Damien thinks more than I've cared about many other opinions.

"You wouldn't understand," I say, in an attempt to blow him off.

He doesn't bite. "Whenever you're ready."

I groan, shifting in my seat so I'm leaning toward the passenger-side window. The condensation wets the fine hair on my forearm and chills me. Shivers crawl through my body from my toes to my head. I snatch his sweater from the seat between us and pull it on over his T-shirt.

"They took everything from me," I say. "Yes, Mickey made me promise and I didn't want to. I hesitated when he first asked me, but then he died and I felt like maybe I wanted revenge, too. My Uncle Ralph used to beat my aunt. He'd call her down, push her to the floor, and basically tell her to kiss his feet. She'd fight him and he'd just ride her harder. He was a bad man who deserved to die. All the Dantes are. And even if it's hard for me to pull the trigger, and even if I get nightmares forever from what I'm going to do, I'll feel some comfort in knowing that the world is a better place without them." I clear my throat and take a slow breath. Then, I bow my head and wait for his judgment, but he says nothing. Just keeps his eyes on the road, with an occasional sideways glance. I'm sure he's not to going to respond at all until his soft voice draws me from my thoughts.

"Okay."

"Okay?" I ask, unsure if I've heard him correctly.

He nods. "But I want you to think about it some more. And you don't act until I say you're ready. Can you listen to me and do what I say?"

"Probably not," I say.

He scoffs. "Well, at least you're honest. But that's the deal. You think about it and let me know."

"Thank you." This has always been hard for me to say and I seem to say it an awful lot to him.

"And I'll get you the money for Frankie," he says.

"What? No, not a chance. I'm sure Mona has money in her safe —I think. She usually keeps a week's worth of profits in there so..."

"You have the combination?"

I nod and sink deeper into my seat.

A thousand dollars. *A week*. Can I keep giving him that? Fuck. I don't even know if I want to keep the bar going. If I do, it's because it meant a lot to my aunt. Not that I'll be any good at it. I was a mediocre waitress and I'm now manager and owner. Ugh. I wince in pain as I feel immense weight in my shoulders along with a tightness in my chest. *Trapped*. Handcuffed to a business I have no idea how to run and chained to a man who thinks he's owed something he absolutely has no right to.

"Fuck!" I scream, slamming my open hand onto the dash.

Damien isn't fazed at all by my outburst. He's relaxed in his seat as we crawl along the coastline back to the city. And he's thoughtful enough to be silent, as if he can sense it's what I need right now. He seems like a straight and narrow guy, so I can only imagine how much he hates what I've dragged him into. No matter how willingly he came, it doesn't escape me that he ran from this life and these people. How curious is it that he's at my side right now?

When Damien nears the turnoff to my apartment complex, I clear my throat and am grateful to find that my voice isn't shaky, an incredible feat since I've been near tears since Frankie's thugs dragged my uncle into the darkness.

"Could you drop me home?" I ask. "I just live down on Mayfield."

"Are you sure you should be alone?"

I *am* alone. "I'll be fine."

"I don't know. Frankie might say you're safe, but who knows if he meant what he said? These people can't always be trusted to be true to their word."

"No, that's where you're wrong. All they have is their word." My voice is quiet, emotionless, like a robot relaying information without any trace of emotion.

"Would you bet your life on it?"

I force a smile. "What choice do I have?"

"Stay with me, just until you feel safe again. You never know what those assholes might do."

"I think I'm rubbing off on you."

"How do you mean?"

"You just swore, Sergeant."

He shakes his head. "I do swear, Beth, just not like a sailor." He pauses. "And how did you know I was a sergeant?"

"Good guess."

"Hmm."

"Or maybe it was on a piece of fabric in one of your drawers."

He glances at me, his face full of indignation, but then he just sort of shakes it off. "I guess I should have figured you went through my things when you came out of my bedroom with my gun."

"I suppose I should apologize for that."

"Wasn't looking for an apology."

He drives his car down the dark alleyway to park in a tight space behind his building. I never did agree to stay with him but I suppose he took my changing the topic as complacence. I'm too tired to argue, and well...I don't want to be alone. If I'm being honest, I feel better with Damien nearby.

We walk to his door and after he unlocks it, he opens it and lets me go in first. A gentleman. I like that. Not too many guys in my life have that particular quality and it's a good one.

He turns on the lights to the living room and kitchen and I slowly make my way to the spare bedroom, my breath catching in my chest. Mickey's blood remains on the covers with some hand-print smears on the walls. I swallow a lump in my throat and let out my breath, jumping almost out of my skin when Damien's hand rests on my shoulder.

"Take my room," he says, "I'll take the couch."

"If you're sure."

"I'll just get some clothes," he says as he passes by me in the hall. He takes a pair of underwear and pants from his dresser and then goes to the kitchen where he picks his gun up off the kitchen counter. "Just in case," he says.

When the apartment is quiet, I lay in bed, my heart aching for the people I've lost. I don't know what I'll do without them. My chest constricts, making it hard to get my fill of air, and no matter how much I toss and turn, I can't fall asleep. I don't want to grieve; to think about Mickey and Mona. I just want this deep-seated pain to go away. In the past, whenever I've been sad I've found ways to distract myself: men, alcohol, pot. Whatever I can do to numb myself. I need something like that. And as I lay here, thinking of Damien in the next room, I know exactly how to forget about my pain.

I sit up and lower my feet to the cold floor. In one of his over-sized shirts and underwear I tiptoe out to the living room. He sleeps on the sofa, the moonlight streaming in to highlight his cheekbones. His eyes are closed, his breathing just loud enough to hear him sleeping peacefully. I envy him that. I take a step closer, then another. I look down at him one last time before I make my move. I notice a scar on his chin and his neck that I never noticed before. His leg sticks out from under a ratty old afghan and I see an old scar on his shin, like his flesh had been gouged out. It's pink; old but still new. I've run my hands over most of his body and yet I never noticed this mark. I lower myself to the couch, sitting on the edge beside him.

He is nothing like the guys I fuck and forget. He's the kind of guy that slips inside of you and takes up roots. Now I've had him I'm not willing to let him go, even though I know I'll ruin him. He will never have a happy, normal life with me because he's nothing like me. He's not a guy to play the field, I can tell that easily. There is a sort of cocky quality about those guys, the ones who know another girl is waiting for them if you dare to say no. But not this guy.

It makes me hesitate. I don't want to hurt him. I really, *really* don't.

But I need something—or someone—to get me through the night. And I want him. Can I do that to him after all he's done for me? Sleep with him again and still refuse a relationship with him that's meaningful? Would he care if I have nothing else to offer? Which makes me wonder why he's still even with me, insisting I stay with him. I bite my lip and hate myself—want to scream at myself—as a single tear rolls down my cheek. For Mona, for Mickey, for the life I will never get back. I bat it away and Damien's eyes flutter open.

"Hey," he says. He adjusts himself, sitting up just enough to reach his hand out and touch my cheek. "It'll be okay."

"Will it?" I ask.

"Yeah." He puts his hands on my shoulders and pulls me down on the couch to lay beside him, his front facing my back. I don't cuddle. I'm not sure I've ever cuddled like this. I mean, perhaps for a moment after sex, but it was never comfortable and it was a very far cry from comforting. Not with a boyfriend and not with family. Let's be honest. The most affection I got from Mickey or Mona was a high five. And boys only want to fuck me and roll over and have a cigarette or get dressed and leave—or I do the leaving. But I as I lay here, enveloped by his strong arms, his warm breath a sweet caress against my ear, my eyelids grow heavy and I let them fall as the pain in my heart dulls.

～

I WAKE UP COVERED in sweat. Damien's arms are around me, his leg hiked up and dangling over my hip. His body is like a furnace and his heat surrounds me. It's comforting, and yet stifling at the same time. I wiggle away from him, stopping momentarily when I feel his cock stir against my back. Wow. It feels like he has another leg pressed up against me and I have to look over my shoulder to make sure but no, his other leg is straight and it reaches past the arm at the other end of the couch.

If I wasn't so hot right now, I might wake him up with morning sex. I sit up and smile to myself, my gaze traveling from his middle to his face. His eyelids flutter and his full lips blow out small puffs of air. His chest rises and the sparse hair that covers it tickles my thigh.

He's peaceful like this. Handsome. The more I'm near him, the more he grabs a hold of me. The me from a week ago would have stripped bare and climbed on top of him, using him to satisfy myself and my hunger. The me from today still wants that, but considers what will happen if I do. We've had sex and it was amazing. One time and I think I could walk away. Maybe he could, too. But more than that...I think we're in danger of finding something more.

Ah, who am I kidding? He's made it clear he wants as much as I can give, which is why I need to be so careful.

I won't hurt him like others have hurt me. I don't want to. If I fuck this up, he might never forgive me. He'll never look at me the same and that thought stings a little.

His eyes slowly open and now it's his turn to smile. His sleepy, doe-eyed smile has my stomach dancing. He reaches out and his hand touches my shoulder while his other takes my hand. "Come here," he says.

I lay down, this time facing him as he caresses my cheek. "Can't sleep?" he asks.

"I have a lot on my mind."

"Such as?"

I let out a breath. "You."

"My favorite topic," he says with a grin.

I bury my head into the crook of his neck and lightly shake my head. He excels in relaxing me and making me forget about everyone and everything else. "Don't go anywhere," I say. "Give me time."

He grips my hip and pulls me close, my leg resting on top of his. His cock twitches and rests between my legs. I close my eyes and sigh.

"I've been into you since you were fourteen. Do you really think I'll get bored so easily?"

"Maybe. Everyone else has before you."

"Then they were morons."

Lightly, I hit his chest. "When it happens constantly, I have to face the facts. It must be me."

"Or the guys you pick."

"Funny, that's what my aunt said."

With a lazy finger, he strokes up and down my leg and over the curve of my ass. He detours and moves through the short hair between my legs, sending chills through me. I lose my breath and let out a moan. I can't have a serious conversation with him while he continues to touch me like this.

"The guys you dated in high school were pricks. I hated the way I'd hear them talk about you."

This stills me. He's not telling me anything I don't know. I'd see some of it in writing under the bleachers or as graffiti in the girl's bathroom. Popular, yep. With girls, I suppose. But not like I was with boys. Chad took my virginity without a second thought for my feelings, knowing he didn't want anything more from me. But before that, I never said no to other things. To any boy who wanted attention. I might have refused sex a lot, but I'm sure the guys who used me for other things talked about it, and maybe embellished. It's probably why Chad thought he could treat me like that. Because when I told him I was a virgin, he laughed at me.

"Why did you let them treat you like that?" he asks.

"I don't know."

His hands move to my back, tracing a line down my spine, and I tense from the delicious feeling deep within. "My mother was the same. She'd have boyfriends at the house all the time. She didn't care if I was there or if I could see. I guess that's what I knew. That's how men treated girls like her and me.

"That's when Mona stepped in. We came to visit and Mona paid for everything. Mom had a bad relationship and she'd been beaten pretty badly, but when we came, she just fell into the same pattern and took up with a guy that was no better. Mona came home one night to my mother naked with a boyfriend in the living room. Mona lost her mind. I was in my room, with headphones on, trying to drown them out. Mona told Sasha—my mother—she had to go back and she agreed after a long fight that thankfully Ralph wasn't there for. I can't even imagine if he'd been involved or saw my mother having sex in his house." I shudder at the thought. "She left and Mona asked me if I wanted to stay. I said yes. My mother's not a bad person, I think she was just lonely. I know that now because..."

"That's how you feel?" he asks.

"Sometimes," I say quietly. "I never meant to be like her; it just kind of happened."

"You're not like her. I don't think you would do what she did. You wouldn't ignore your child to get off. I just don't see that about you."

"I think your opinion of me is skewed. If I let myself be with you, you'll see everything. And I kind of like knowing that someone sees me as you do right now."

He wraps his arms around my shoulder and pulls me in close. I find it hard to breathe against the heat of his chest but I turn my head and let him hold me. I love every minute of it. When he tries to pull away, I resist and he gives me my way. Soon, it's not enough. I want more, and I tilt my head up and search for his lips. The moment our mouths touch, my whole body relaxes and I feel as if I'm falling. Only he's waiting to catch me.

I lower my hand to his boxers, slide my hand underneath the waistband, and encircle his long, thick cock. His breath hitches as I stroke the length of him faster, moving from the base to the tip and covering him with his wetness. It gets me hot and I pull down his boxers while he fumbles to pull down my panties. After tossing them to the floor the barrier between us is gone. He grips me and rolls me onto my back. I open my legs wide for him to settle in tight against me. His dog tags dangle in my face and he tosses them over his shoulder. "You're so beautiful," he says, his voice husky.

I look away and he takes my chin in his hand, forcing me to look back at him. He tells me again and this time I can't look away. "I'm going to keep saying it until you believe it." He captures my lip between his, nibbles lightly before kissing me deeply, his tongue diving in to dance with mine. He presses his cock against me and pushes in tight to reach the sweet spot between my lips. I let out a moan. He moves back and forward to give me delicious tingles between my legs. I want more. I want everything. I grip him and guide him to my swollen entrance.

"Condom?" I ask.

He presses against me again, the tip rimming my entrance and I want desperately for him to dive in, but it's not smart and I can't create any more drama in my life. I've had my fill.

He kisses me quickly and rolls off me, strutting over to the counter in the kitchen and pulling out a roll of condoms. The sight of his naked back and tight ass makes me impatient. Then he turns and I see the thickness of his cock as he stands at full attention. It's enough for me to tell him to hurry the hell up.

He smiles at me as the roll of condoms fall. There must be at least ten. "You're optimistic," I say with a small smile.

"Power of positive thinking."

He stands over me, his cock inches from my face and I move to a sitting position. I take one of the condoms and open it with my teeth before rolling it snugly down his shaft. I lick the tip for good measure and it's enough for him to push me down and crawl on top of me with impatience. He reaches in between us to grip my shirt and I wiggle as he pulls it over my head. He drives inside of me and I call out his name in pleasure as he pauses to pay attention to my breasts. His tongue circles my nipples. He sucks and flicks them until they're hard and erect and I'm almost embarrassed to say I've left a wet spot on his couch.

"Damien, this is all I can give for right now. Until I figure some things out."

"This is enough," he says, breathless. "But I don't share."

"Damien," I say softly.

"I mean it." He holds my face in his hands. His face and eyes are serious and his voice is firm. "I won't share you. But I won't push you into anything either."

"I have nothing to give you."

"I'll be the judge of that." He pushes into me, thrusts to the hilt, and I gasp as he pulls out and drives in again. He rocks on top of me, alternating speeds between fast and slow and shallow and deep and I've come more than once but I swear he's not even close. When I feel as if I might pass out, I beg him, "Please, I can't take anymore. It's too much."

"No, I want you to remember what this feels like. I want you to crave it. And when you think about sex I want you to think of only me." He slams into me again.

I gasp. "Only you," I agree as I come again and scream out his name.

CHAPTER ELEVEN

I stand, stretching up on my tiptoes as I yawn. It's freezing in here and my toes are cold. I search the floor for my clothes and slide into my panties and shirt, the floorboards creaking slightly under my weight. The noise makes him stir and he rolls forward, cuddling deeper into the crevice of the old faded couch. His face is relaxed; his lips open just an inch as he breathes deeply.

I cover my face with my hands. What the hell am I doing? Letting myself live in the moment, as always? What I should really be doing is planning a funeral and getting my shit together. I chastise myself for this, telling myself I'm avoiding responsibility—as usual. Though this time I feel like it's different. Last night with Damien doesn't feel self-destructive. He's perhaps the best thing that's ever happened to me. I thought our timing was off, but maybe it's exactly right. Maybe he's what I need to help me get through all of this.

After a quiet sigh, I creep to the kitchen and pour myself a glass of tepid water. The pipes groan and rattle as water falls out, first a leak and then a stream. I cringe from the sound and look over my shoulder to make sure I didn't wake him.

He's still sleeping soundly, only now with lines of worry on his forehead as he makes the smallest of movements with his nose.

The water goes down smoothly, but it's not enough to fill my growling stomach. That will have to wait, though. I don't want to disturb him. I wash up in the bathroom, helping myself to another one of his T-shirts and some massive jogging pants—which I suspect are even too big for him—that I find in one of his drawers.

When I open his bedroom door, he's in the hallway, hair messy, his cheeks wrinkled from sleep. And shirtless. He shouldn't be allowed to wear nothing on his chest, because it hits me in all the right places and I have to say over and over in my mind how little time I have for throwing him down right now. He makes it worse by scratching the small patch of hair trailing from his navel to below his underwear. He has that amazing v-shaped cut of muscles by his pelvis that makes me want to fan myself. Couple that with the definition in his tatted arms and legs and I feel like I have to wipe the drool off my chin.

"Everything okay?" he asks, as he stares at me with his sleepy, bedroom eyes.

I almost forget who I am and look away to distract myself.

"I'm fine," I say, a little too quickly. My voice sounds squeaky and it brings a smile to his delicious face.

So I think about clowns—I fucking hate those scary bastards. And wrinkled old penises on old men. And getting a pap test or an enema. "I'm fine. I just have a lot to do and I need to get going. I've got to meet with Mona's lawyer, plan her funeral, and figure out what I'm going to do with the pub, and...yeah—a bunch of other shit. I'm fine. I just...I need to go. There is so much I need to do."

"Okay," he says. "Let me get dressed. I'll take you wherever you need to go."

"Damien, you've done enough. More than enough."

"And your point?"

I chuckle, partly from his sense of humor and partly from frustration. "Can you take me home? I need some new clothes. I can't really go out in these."

He approaches me, his hands reaching out to touch my waist, but I take a step back and his hands return to his sides. If he touches me again I'll be naked on my back before he can count to three.

He frowns and I feel as if I've offended him. I punch his chest to get his attention. Not hard, just enough for him to break free from whatever he's thinking.

"I'm not running. I just need to get back to life. You're... distracting," I say with a smile.

He reaches out to grab the drawstring of my pants and pulls on it slowly so the bow comes undone and my pants fall to my ankles. "Whoops," he says, deadpan.

Sighing, I pull them back up. I don't just want him, I like him. As a person. I can just relax around him and let the real me out. Usually, I act confident and in control even when I don't feel like I am. But with him, I feel like a silly girl with a crush. I'm all blushing cheeks and butterflies.

"Why are you single?" I ask, shaking my head. "How has no girl dug her hooks into you so deep that you can't get them out?"

"Well, one girl did a few years ago."

I remember Mona telling me about a bad breakup. "What happened? You break up with her? Maybe you lost interest while you were deployed?"

He frowns at me. "Why do you want so badly to find something wrong with me?"

"I don't...I just think that everyone has flaws. I have yet to find yours."

"You've only just met me. I'm far from perfect." After he takes my hand in his, he leads me to his bed where we sit down next to one another. He's so close our arms are touching. He's warm, like a well-lit fire and, without meaning to, I find myself leaning against him.

"I thought I was in love with my ex. She was the first girl I felt any sort of emotional connection to. She laughed at my jokes—and I never found myself particularly funny. And we had a lot of the same interests. I gave her all I had and I thought she felt the same. When I was in Afghanistan the last time, she told me she was pregnant. I was so excited. I couldn't wait to get back to her, but then I did the math when a buddy asked me how far along she was. "Kid wasn't mine."

"Wow. I'm sorry."

He forces a smile. "I got leave, went back to our apartment and I thought I'd surprise her. I needed to confront her...I don't know...maybe see if there was anything worth saving. But she was gone." He squeezes my hand just enough for me to notice. "She left a note. She was eloping with some other guy."

"Here I thought all guys were jerks. Turns out us females can be just as wicked."

"Not all."

"She didn't deserve you. And it's a good thing that happened so you were able to get away from her."

"Maybe."

"You need a nice girl...with an easy life. Have kids and get a fucking white house with an even whiter fence."

He chuckles. "My mother is Jocelyn Dante. I have cousins and aunts that make her look like mother of the year. I've dated the kind of girls you're describing and they're nice...for a while. But I need a little sass in my life, and I need a girl who can keep my attention. Someone strong and sweet all at once."

"That's a tall order," I say.

"It is," he agrees. Shaking his head, he sighs. "I could get hooked on you again, Beth. It would be so easy."

It would be easy. For me, too. But I don't say this, instead I tell him his ex was a moron, earning me a wide smile. Then wordlessly I tell him I'll try my hardest not to hurt him, too.

He takes a quick shower while I sit and wait in the living room. It doesn't take him long to get dressed and for us to be out of the door. In the car I am surrounded by his fresh, clean scent and I want him again. Will I never be satisfied? I've only just had him.

In ten minutes, we're outside my apartment complex and the car is in park, idling by the curb. I linger in my seat, staring at the tall, brick building. It surprises me to find I don't want to get out—leaving him is like trying to pull duct tape off my skin. I fear it will hurt. And I fear that he and I will be over after I get out. That somehow the magic between us will be gone.

How can I be equally scared of losing and keeping him? I'm more fucked up than I thought.

"I'll see you," I say quietly, before jumping out and running to my building. As I reach the doors, I slow and look over my shoulder. He's staring at me, a confused expression etched on his face. Why couldn't I have asked for his number? Or given him mine. No. I just ran away like a frightened dog.

He pulls away and I tip my head back and stifle a scream. Good one, Beth. Smooth, real smooth. But there is nothing I can do about it now and I'll only feel pathetic if I try. I'll see him again. I know it. Even if I have to orchestrate something. Because I want to see him again.

Soon.

I pull open the double doors in front of me and am hit with a gust of warm air. They always keep the lobby warm and it makes coming home really welcoming. Fresh roses and carnations sit on the desk by the doorman. Carl, I think his name is. He smiles when he sees me, stands, and nods.

"Morning," he says, his voice garbled as he chews on something.

I return his sentiment and approach the elevator. Two shrubs in tall clay pots stand on either side of the doors. Their scent cuts through the sweet scent of the flowers.

My eyes grow heavy from lack of sleep while I wait for the elevator to sound off. I close them, giving them a minute to rest, though I fear I might fall asleep on my feet. I almost think I have when Carl's voice startles me. Only then do I notice he now stands beside me.

"Ms. Bilski?" he says. "I'm sorry, I didn't mean to startle you."

"That's okay. I'm just a little tired."

"I thought you might want to know some people were around here, looking for you."

My pulse kicks up a notch and my lethargy dissipates. What if Frankie really didn't mean what he said?

"The police were here again yesterday....and I wasn't supposed to tell you about the other visitors. They said...they'd...it doesn't matter what they said. I just wanted you to know some people were looking for you. I wouldn't forgive myself if something happened to you. You've always been so nice to me. And I know you're probably going through a tough time right now."

I raise my hand and set it on his shoulder, squeezing ever so slightly. He's shorter than me, but much rounder and as I look down at his serious, sweating face, I feel thankful to have someone else left in this world who seems to give a shit about me. I bend at the waist and give him a little peck on the cheek.

"Who were the other visitors?"

He clears his throat and glances all around like he worries they might be watching.

"Big guys. And they had guns. I couldn't be sure, but I thought maybe they work for you know who."

"Hmm. Okay. Thanks, Carl. I really appreciate you telling me."

The elevator dings and the doors slide open. I step inside but then as the doors begin to close, I jut my hand out to stop them. The doors rattle before opening wide again and the alarm sounds for a beat, like a ringing bell.

"Hey, Carl?"

He stops, turning to face me.

"When did those *other* visitors come by?"

"Yesterday morning and then one was across the street in a truck all afternoon. He must have left in the evening sometime. I didn't see him go. I was trying my best not to look like I was watching him."

I nod and drop my hands, offering him another sincere thank you until the doors block him from my view.

This is good. Or, better than I feared. They left before I had my chat with Frankie. If they'd stayed after that, I would have had to change my plans because I would know Frankie wasn't completely committed to our deal. But this small detail gives me confidence that I'm safe—at least for now.

My body aches to shower and sleep but I don't let myself right now. I have too many things to do. After going through a dozen or so voice mail messages on my home phone, I start to do callbacks. Most of the calls are from the police so after a heavy sigh I elect to call them last. They want to speak to me in person—big surprise there. I really don't want to be seen going into the police station, so I'll get Detective Russell to meet me outside of the city, where people won't recognize me.

Mona's lawyer is first on my list of people to call. Thankfully, he left a message for me so I copy his number down quickly and call him back. It's early, probably before business hours, but he did say on his message that this number is his cell and I could call him at any hour.

"At your convenience," he says when I ask to meet him.

"How about now?"

He cancels another appointment to fit me in and I'm amazed at how accommodating he is. But then, my aunt just died and she was my guardian for a long while.

I call the cops next, but thankfully I get voicemail and I hang up. I have no intention of leaving a message. I don't want to talk to them in the first place. They're part of the reason my aunt is dead. And if she went to them, she must have felt that they would protect her. Clearly, they didn't do their job. They're as high up on my hit list as Jimmy right now. I have no doubt if they want to get a hold of me that badly they'll track me down.

Mona's lawyer, Fitch Moby, asks me to meet him at his favorite coffee shop. The bell above the door startles me when I walk inside. I keep waiting for someone to point a gun at me and tell me that Frankie lied and he'd rather get rid of me than risk me avenging my family. But then, deep down I believe what I said: he's a man of his word. Besides, what kind of threat do I pose to him? I'm sure he sees me as this short blonde girl who relies on her looks a little too much. He has to know I've called on Declan and Mickey and Mona more times than I count because of my ability to get myself in sticky situations that I can't get out of. I look weak to him, even if I tried to be like Mona when I went to his house. He had to see through me. See that it was an act and I was about to fall apart at any moment. Didn't he?

Of course he did. I don't believe I'm strong, so why should he? And Mickey thinks I can do what he couldn't? I could kill the Dantes and everyone responsible for Mona's death? God, I don't even know if I have it in me. But I'll try.

I shake off the thought as I enter the coffee shop and search for

Mr. Moby. It's afternoon and the crowd is small. Maybe a half dozen people, drinking or talking. Their voices mix with a Muse song playing quietly on the speakers tucked into the ceiling.

Mr. Moby stands when our eyes meet and his solemn face hits me harder than I expect. He cared for Mona and that common bond between us chokes me up. I wade through the tables and chairs and stumble as my foot connects with a heavy purse sitting on the ground.

"I'm sorry," the woman says, pulling it away and hanging it on the back of her chair.

"Don't worry about it," I say politely.

Mr. Moby opens his arms when I reach him. He locks them around my back and holds me tight, like I imagine a father would. "It's really good to see you."

"Same to you."

He pats my back, and when I break away, he holds out my chair. Always a gentleman.

"How're you holding up?"

I cross my arms over my chest and shake my head. "I'll be fine," I lie. "Eventually."

"What would you like? Coffee? Tea?"

"Vodka?" I suggest.

He frowns at me, but it feels like there's affection hidden in there somewhere.

"Coffee, it is," he says.

He pushes out from the table and stands, headed for the counter where he patiently waits in line while reading something on his phone. When he returns he places a muffin with butter and a black coffee on the table.

I wasn't hungry when he asked but now I'm digging into the muffin like it's the last meal I'll ever eat.

He raises his eyebrows. "Are you not taking care of yourself?"

I nod. As best I can, I suppose. I mean, I can't remember what I've eaten in the last few days or if I've slept longer than a few hours but I *have* been busy.

"The first few weeks will be the hardest and then with time the pain will fade. It may never go away, but you'll learn to live with it."

"Live with it," I repeat. "I'm not sure I want to."

"What choice do you have?"

I raise an eyebrow. The alternative to sadness is anger. *Revenge.* Ugh. When Mickey asked me to take his revenge, I agreed. I didn't know if I could take a life but I was willing to try because I was angry. Hell, I'm angry still. My emotions are real and raw and I'm not sure they will ever heal. But now I'm back to my life and the dust is settling, part of me doesn't want that anymore. I know it will only cause more chaos and destruction and maybe hurt the people I have left.

I've had a glimpse of happiness with Damien and I think about what life could be like and I want it. When the time is right, I really want it. But if I do what I promised my Uncle Mickey, I might forever ruin the possibility of Damien and me. He won't look at me the same, and I love the way he looks at me. I wish he was looking at me right now. In that quiet, intense way.

Hours later and I miss him. Is that even possible? I have to give myself a little shake and Moby assumes it's because I'm cold because he offers me his jacket.

"No, I'm fine. Just had a chill," I say. "Now, what was it that you wanted to talk to me about?"

"Mona's will, for starters. She left clear instructions that everything be left to you." He reaches down to the floor to grab his briefcase and after a quick snap of the lock he opens it and removes some papers. "You can look over the details. I've marked where you need to sign."

"She left everything to me?"

"Yes. The pub, her apartment upstairs, her savings, and her life insurance, which totals over half a million dollars."

I cough, almost choking on the coffee scented air. "Excuse me?"

"She wanted you to have some security after she...passed on. This should help you achieve that."

"I don't need money," I say sadly. I'd give it all back just to see her one more time, have her growl at me or just tease me. Or stroke my hair as I fall asleep like she did when I was still young enough to appreciate it. But at least the money will help keep Frankie happy until I can decide what to do about him and his brother.

I go through the stack of paperwork, signing and dating everything labeled with yellow arrows. It takes much longer than I imagined and when I glance up at the clock, I realize I've been here almost two hours. Not that I have anywhere pressing to be.

When I sign the last piece of paper, I gently put the pen on the table and feel a sense of finality. This *really* is happening. She *really* is gone. Never again will I see her flame-red hair, or her small smile that she always fought to hide.

Fitch flips through the paperwork and, when satisfied, he tucks it back away in his briefcase. "I can organize the transfer of her remains to a funeral home, and if you're not up to it we can pay someone to coordinate the details."

"Yeah, that would be great. But I don't want a funeral for her."

His posture stiffens as he tips his head to the side. "No?"

I laugh without humor. "Everyone she knew is connected to the Dantes. The moment she went to the cops she lost every relationship she had except for me and her brother." And perhaps even him... "No one will go to her funeral, Fitch. No one."

"Maybe. Or maybe you'll come to realize more people cared about her—and you—than you think."

"Maybe." Or maybe not.

"I know this is hard..."

"Do you?" I hug myself tighter. "My aunt was a rat. Life for me won't be easy now. And the pub? It won't survive. No one will eat there—maybe not even the regulars. And...I'm not sure if you knew that Mona was paying off the Dantes for 'protection' of her pub, whatever that means. Mona didn't need protection." But as soon as that last statement comes out of my mouth I realize how foolish it sounds. The only person she needed protection from was the person who ended up finishing her off. It's almost ironic.

"I was aware," he says sadly. "She asked me to bring it up to you if anything happened, although she hoped she could eliminate the fee before she passed." He clears his throat and changes direction. "It may take a few weeks to get all the paperwork resolved and for you to receive your inheritance. Will you be okay until then?"

"She has a safe. I never went into it unless she asked me to get something for her, but I know the combination. I imagine there's money in there."

"Perhaps some other things, too."

"What do you mean?"

He shrugs and forces a smile. "Nothing. Nothing at all." He shifts in his seat. "So you'll keep the pub running?"

"I suppose so, not that I know the first thing about running it. Mona did everything and she wasn't keen on letting anyone in on what she did behind the scenes. I don't know a thing about what I need to do to keep it afloat."

He cups his drink in his hands and steam rises from the liquid. After a slow drink, he says, "I can refer you to a recruitment agency. They may be able to find someone for you, at a cost."

I scoff. There's always a cost. "No, thanks. I'll manage. Besides, it hardly matters. Closing is inevitable."

"I hope that's not true. She wanted you to keep it running."

"I can try, but to what end? To see it bankrupt after people boycott it? To run it to the ground because I don't know the first thing about managing a business?"

"I don't know the right answer. I can only tell you what she told me."

"Right." I down my hot coffee and warmth trails down my chest. The mug is hot, almost too hot to hold and I put it back down on the table, keeping my hands in my lap.

"You could always ask your uncle to help with the pub."

I open my mouth to tell him Mickey's already dead but then I close my mouth and decide that's information I can't entrust, even to him. I don't need anyone asking me questions about him, especially the cops. I'm already on their radar. I don't believe that shit about them wanting to protect me.

"He's...missing."

"Convenient," he says, eyeing me.

I look away. I know I'm giving away too much but I can't help myself. His death is so fresh and, unlike Mona, I saw him die. I saw his cold, pale body, and the blood on his stomach and all over the bed. His face will haunt my dreams.

"And I can't turn to Declan either," I say.

"I heard he's in custody."

"No chance of talking to him?"

Fitch laughs without humor. "Not a chance. They'll be well guarded until after the trial. And then...they'll just disappear. New identities, new home, new life..."

"Everyone...gone."

He touches my shoulder and squeezes ever so gently. "You're not alone," he says. "Think of me as family. Whatever you need, I'm happy to help you with. Legal or not. And there are others who would offer the same."

"But can I trust them?" I say, with a frustrated sigh. "Who isn't on the Dantes' payroll?"

"Your concern is valid, for sure. You'll have to be careful. Trust your gut and it shouldn't steer you wrong. And..." He reaches into the breast pocket of his jacket and pulls out a business card.

I take it from him and furrow my brow. "The Velvet Sands Hotel? Is this your idea of helping?"

He frowns and holds up his left hand to show me his wedding band. "Flip it over."

I take the paper and run my thumb across the messy cursive writing, written in black ink. It's so messy I can barely read it.

Hamish Allen, 5 Duff Street.

I say the name out loud. It's one I've never heard before. "Am I supposed to know who this is?"

"I have no idea. Your guess is as good as mine. Your aunt gave that to me eight months ago. Said if things got bad to give you that, and I'd say her death qualifies as bad."

"Eight months ago? Is that a coincidence?"

He takes a drink of his coffee and after he sets it down, he shrugs his shoulders. "When it came to your aunt, I never asked questions. If she knew what was coming, she didn't say."

"Fantastic," I say, more to myself. Now I have another thing to add to my monster to-do list: find out who the fuck Hamish Allen is.

CHAPTER TWELVE

The next few days are a blur of dealing with Mona's finances, getting paperwork finalized, and planning Mona's burial. I want to cremate her and maybe scatter her ashes in the ocean, but I thought about what Moby said and I changed my mind. If no one wants to celebrate her life or mourn her death, that's fine. But I will. And that's enough.

Turns out Fitch was right. I'm not alone. I have friends, even if they aren't as obvious to me as Carrie. When the people who work at Mona's pub find out about her funeral, everyone is all too eager to help. I decide to keep it small, not bothering to put an announcement in the paper or anything. And I tell my mom. She doesn't recognize my voice when I call.

I close my eyes and sigh after she says, "Who is this?" in Polish for the second time. I'm hit with the same familiar ache in my chest she always caused me when she disappointed me as a child. But I steel myself and brush it off, unwilling to let her affect me anymore. "Mona's died," I tell her plainly.

Her response, "At least it was quick."

I guess she still has hurt feelings over how they said good-bye all those years ago because she doesn't even sound sad. I hear music in the background and a man calling out her name. I roll my eyes and imagine what he looks like. Who he is... Another deadbeat, I imagine. Someone who treats her like garbage.

"I got to go," Mom says. "If you...if you need anything..."

I scoff and hear my breath as static in the phone. "No, I'll be fine." As usual.

"Right. Well, take care of yourself, kid."

"You, too." I hold the phone for a while, sit down, and take a breath. Then I bury my feelings down deep to consider them later when I'm alone and have the time. That usually happens at night when the world is still and quiet, when I feel the most vulnerable.

We have the funeral at a church. Mona wasn't religious. In fact, you could see how uncomfortable religious talk made her. She'd pretend to stab herself in the ear whenever anyone brought up the names God or Jesus. But she didn't say how she wanted this to go so I choose my way. I'm not so religious either. Not even sure I believe in organized religion—or religion at all. But, now she's gone, I'd rather believe she's gone somewhere nice, where I might see her again, as opposed to the alternative.

When the ceremony is over, we take her ashes to the beach.

The ocean roars as the tide makes it way to the rocky shore. It's sunset, my favorite time of the day. The sun is on the horizon, coloring the edge of the ocean with shades of pink and lavender. It's beautiful. When I was younger, my aunt would bring me here in the summer—I guess that's why I chose to scatter her ashes here. The water is never warm, even in the summers. The Atlantic Ocean never is, but it never bothered me as a kid. I used to strip to my bathing suit and run against the waves and duck my head under, jumping up and out of the water to run back to shore, my skin prickled with goosebumps. Then I'd do it all over again. Aunt Mona would read on the beach while sitting on a towel.

At the time, Mona's actions didn't strike me as odd or out of character. Thinking back, it makes me chuckle and feel a pang of sadness. She must have been so bored. And yet, she always took me when I asked, without putting up much of a fight. She pretended to be like the other kids' mothers and tried to act normal. She did it for years until I was old enough to handle the real her—or maybe she just couldn't take it anymore. Then, the flood gates opened and I saw her for who she really was. Foul-mouthed and chain smoking, with leathery skin and hard features. She was perfect and had a heart of gold or maybe brass—unless you pissed her off.

Seeing her true self made me love her more. Not because I liked that version of her better, but I liked her more because she worked so hard to keep me innocent and sheltered when I needed it. I can't imagine how hard that must have been for her. If I'm honest, I liked colorful Mona more than I ever liked the pretending-to-be-domesticated Mona. It just didn't suit her. Not one bit.

I hold the urn close to my chest, the thought of her inside of it confounding me. Bigger than life, and now every piece of her in this small metal vessel. Nothing could contain her in life, and it just doesn't seem right to let her sit inside this cold, lifeless jar.

I remove the lid. The ocean roars a little louder, as if angry. It reminds me of her spirit. The water circles my ankles and I walk farther, avoiding the large rocks and stepping over shells and seaweed.

"Until we meet again, Aunt Mona." I tip the urn on its side just enough for a steady stream of her ash to slip out. Some falls and mixes with the water while more of her ashes catch the wind and scatter like dust motes in the sunlight. I close my eyes and let the final strands escape. When I feel enough of a difference in the weight, I open my eyes and tip the rest of it over.

Quietly, I say good-bye as a thin a layer of ashes works through the foamy water's edge. A hand touches my shoulder and I turn my head to see Carrie. Her eyes are red and her makeup is streaked. She's so soft sometimes.

"Come on, Beth," she says, blubbering. "Let's go."

I wrap my arm around her shoulders to comfort her and pull a crumpled tissue from my pocket. She blows her nose and glances at me with her red nose and puffy eyes. "She was bad ass," Carrie says.

"Yeah," I say softly. "Definitely bad ass."

When we reach Carrie's car I offer to drive since she's kind of a mess. We climb into the car and I leave the music on low. Carrie turns on the heat and warm air blows in my face and it smells of burning dust.

We drive back to Mona's pub—my pub now, I guess.

I pull around the back, into the small space where Mona usually parked, tucked between her shed and the big garbage bins. The back door is unlocked. I caved and—though it pained me—gave the keys to Henry to open up so he and the staff could put something together to celebrate. Mona never gave her keys to anyone but me and it felt wrong to hand them off, but I'm coming to realize I'm not her and I won't ever be. And I couldn't have pulled today off without Carrie and the staff. I used to think asking for help was a bad thing—even though I did it often. Mostly for attention. But it's okay to accept help sometimes. It doesn't have to be a bad thing.

The lights are on in the kitchen and there are trays of food on the counter and soup cooking on the stove. I even smell baking bread and that chokes me up a bit. It reminds me of her, and our late night talks while she baked. I can also smell cooked beef and onions and potatoes. Beef stew? I peer over the tall pot, put my face in the cloud of steam, and inhale deeply.

"I'm so hungry," Carrie says, snatching a roll and eating it plain.

I force a smile. I can almost see Mona by the far wall, giving

Carrie a look of irritation for touching food in the kitchen. She would slap her hand away if she were here right now. Tell her to go out front and eat at a table like a normal person.

"Are you okay?" Carrie says, bringing me back to reality.

"Yeah. Great."

The music calls to us. Acoustic guitar with a hint of drums, but not loud and obnoxious. It's soft, like background noise. I push through the swinging doors and see Collin Smith, a man who often comes here to play and sing on the weekends. He winks at me when our eyes meet. Beth links arms with me, pulling me along and I match my pace to hers.

There are a few dozen people here, more than I expected. The whole staff, Mona's lawyer, her accountant, and some regular customers who raise their beers as if to toast Mona. I smile and I mean it. Here I thought no one would come. I'm overwhelmed with emotion to see so many people proving me wrong.

"To Mona," Henry says, raising his glass.

Damien's sweet face appears in the crowd. He saunters forward, his eyes never leaving mine, and he hands me a glass of champagne. "To Mona," he says, tapping his glass against mine.

"To Mona," I say softly.

I down my glass and the cool, sparkling liquid helps me relax.

I mingle with everyone for the next few hours. Everyone takes a turn going to the dance floor to tell a story about Mona. I expect to feel sad, to miss her, and yet, most of the stories have me laughing. Colorful Mona. No one will ever hold a candle to her.

A few hours later, when everyone is buzzed and feeling good, people start to file out. It's only when the crowd thins that I notice a man I've never seen before sitting in the corner of the room. I try and place him but I come up empty. So, naturally I jump the gun, and assume he's a spy for the Dantes. If I were dead sober I would bite my tongue and talk to him privately, away from the crowd. But

I'm not dead sober and this is not the time or place for the Dantes to make their presence known.

I stalk over to him, my heels clicking angrily on the floor. He raises an eyebrow at me as he takes a drink of whatever is in his Collins glass. He watches me over the edge, his brown eyes dark and hooded. He licks his lips when he sets his drink back down and wipes his hand over his beard.

I want to swat his drink away. Drinking for free here at Mona's celebration!

"You've got some nerve!" I snap at him.

The bastard has the nerve to grin at me. Without thinking, I haul off and my arm flies toward his face. He catches it and before I know it, I'm being bear hugged from behind. I fight against Damien. I know it's him. I recognize his scent and the tattoos on his arms. "Let me go!" I scream. But he won't and I elbow him hard as my anger gets the better of me.

He lets out a loud curse and immediately I feel bad. I glance back and forward between him and the mystery man, torn between comforting Damien and smashing a broken beer bottle over the head of the latter.

Damien wins.

"Shit! Damien, I'm so sorry. I didn't mean to hurt you."

He raises an eyebrow and smiles as if to tell me he's okay, but then his nose starts to bleed. "Did I do that?" I don't know how I could have. Did my head hit his face? I don't even remember.

Carrie hands him a cloth and he presses it to his nose. And all the while, this mother fucker is laughing at me.

"You certainly have Mona's temper, I'll give you that."

"Who the hell are you? You here to spy for the Dantes? Ruin Mona's celebration?"

"Not at all. I think you've got things wrong." He leans forward, pushing out of his seat. He holds out his hand. "Hamish Allen."

"Hamish?"

"You've heard of me?"

I nod.

"Who is this guy?" Damien asks.

"Nnn...no one," I mumble.

"Really?"

"Carrie, can you take care of things down here?" I ask.

She shrugs and backs away, turning her focus on the people left, who now watch us with their complete attention.

"We need to talk," I say to Hamish, as I usher him to the kitchen.

He has a swagger to his walk, like he's big and bulky and wants everyone to notice. I eye him, noting everything about him, as I try to figure him out. His flesh is clean. Not a single tattoo. But he looks hard with a crooked nose and some scars on his forehead. He's seen more than his fair share of fights. I even see a pink line across his arm that's probably the length of one of my fingers, with dots on the side that suggest stitches. Stab wound? Maybe. His hair is long and braided down the back, highlighted with streaks of gray.

Damien grabs my elbow and forces me to stop. "Beth, do you even know him? And you're going off to talk to him alone?"

"It'll be okay," I say, and stretch up on my tiptoes to peck him on his cheek.

His loosens his grip around my arm and his hands fall to his sides. Frowning, he shakes his head at me. "I don't like this."

"Trust me," I say quietly. "And don't go anywhere."

CHAPTER THIRTEEN

I offer Hamish another drink as we sit at Mona's kitchen island staring at one another.

"You wanted to talk," he says, taking a sip of his whiskey.

"Who are you?"

"I told you." His voice is gravelly and deep, the voice of a man who's probably smoked a pack a day since he came out of diapers.

"Not your name. I want to know who you were to my aunt."

"I'm offended she never mentioned me."

"Well, it seems she kept a lot from me, so I wouldn't take it personally."

"What about Mickey?" he asks.

"You knew my uncle, too?"

"Knew?"

I bite my lip, cursing myself for giving too much away, but it's too late to put the cat back in the bag now.

He swirls the ice around his glass. "How'd he die?"

"Oh, no. You tell me who you are first and then I'll decide if I wanna share."

He tugs on his ear. "You really do look like her. Or like she used to." He sets his glass down and reaches into a deep pocket on the inside of his leather jacket. "This is for you."

I take the envelope he hands me and tap it against my other hand, eyeing him like he's the enemy. But then my curiosity wins out. I rip through the sealed end and open it wide to find two passports inside. "Passports?" I pull them out and hold them up. When I open the first I see my picture, the same one I have on my current passport, only it's not my name typed neatly below. "Clara Emily Brightmore?"

He shrugs. "I didn't pick the name."

"Who did?"

"Your aunt, of course."

I pull out the other passport. "Why do I need two?" Again, no answer. I open it up and make a face. This one doesn't have my picture; it has Damien's. "Lucas Arthur Simon?"

"I didn't pick that one either, in case you were curious."

"I'm so confused. Why did she have passports made for me and Damien?"

"So you could fly far away from here, Little Bird."

"What did you call me?" My voice is a whisper. I never thought anyone would call me that again, that the name would be buried with Mona. On his lips, it should feel wrong, but there is something tender about his words. And his tone is the same as Mona's was whenever she said it. I swallow a lump in my throat and though I want to respond, I have no words. I don't even know what to say. He's rendered me speechless.

"Your aunt knew her days were numbered and she wanted you to be able to make a clean break. Especially if things got bad."

"But Damien? Why make a passport for Damien? Why not Declan? Or Mickey?"

"Well, it's a good thing she chose who she chose or you'd be flying solo."

"I'm not going anywhere," I say, tossing the passports on the counter.

"That's unfortunate."

"You still haven't told me who you are."

His jaw widens as he clenches his teeth. "I'm the man who taught your uncle everything he knew. The man your aunt ran to when her prick husband beat her for doing stupid shit. And the man who helped her bury that same prick husband."

"You were there when she killed him?"

He makes a face. "That what she said?"

"She never told me anything. I had to hear it from Mickey." Something in the way he glances at me sideways as he takes another drink...brings me to a surprising revelation. Mona didn't kill Ralph. It was Hamish.

"You loved her?" I ask quietly.

He shrugs. "As much as a guy like me can love anyone."

"I thought you were here because of the Dantes."

"Don't worry about it, kid. Takes a lot to offend me and I ain't in the habit of killing women if I don't have to."

"Um...thank you?"

He laughs out loud now.

"You said she knew her days were numbered. How could she have known what was going to happen?"

"Because of the cancer," he says, throwing it out like it's the most obvious thing in the world. But as the words hang in the air, he quickly realizes his misstep. "You didn't know?"

I pull my head back like I've been slapped. "No. I didn't."

"Ugh...I'm sorry, kid. I thought she would have told you above anyone else."

"I'll just add it to the growing list of things she kept from me."

"She had maybe a year, if that. Didn't surprise me much to hear she told the Dantes she killed her husband. I suspect she did it to make sure I never got thrown into the mix. She always did feel guilty about what we did, even though the guy was an asshole."

"How is that you've been...close...to her this long and I knew nothing about you?"

"The Dantes and I go way back. They wouldn't have liked her hanging around me, especially after her husband died. And before that, I needed to stay away so Ralph didn't get suspicious. He was always looking for a reason to take me on. But his brother Jimmy and I were friends, once upon a time, so I think he kept Ralph in check."

"Hmm. I'm really glad you could make it today. She would have wanted you here."

"I suppose so." He takes another drink. "And what will you do now? You going to take those passports and fly off into the sunset?"

I scoff at him. "No. I have things to do first."

"Is that so?"

I refuse to look at him, and yet he knows.

"Hope you're not planning on taking revenge."

"How...?"

"That's who we are, isn't it? We don't let things go. We want retribution." He sighs. "Your aunt wanted something different for you, but we can't run from who we are, can we?"

"I promised."

"Mickey?" he chuckles at me. "Mickey was a selfish bastard who only helped others when it served his purposes. And you're going to honor a promise to him? When your aunt clearly wanted something different for you?"

That's the crux of it, isn't it? I loved them both. One wanted me to leave and the other wanted me to stay. I force a smile and change topics. I don't want to have this conversation right now and I don't intend on having it with a stranger, even if we both loved Mona. "Thank you for everything. Especially for helping me know my aunt a little better."

"Kid, I don't know why she never told you about the cancer. Maybe she found it hard to be honest about it. She wouldn't even take the damn treatments. I don't know if she thought she was strong enough to beat it without help." He scratches his head. "Or maybe she was too stubborn to admit she wasn't invincible. Who knows? We all got to go sometime, right?"

Hmm. I nod in agreement and show him to the door, hugging the passports close to my chest. They're the last gift she'll ever give me. I watch him thump down the stairs and as he reaches the bottom, Damien appears. Hamish waits as Damien steps out of the way and when Hamish is gone, Damien climbs up the stairs to meet me.

"She had cancer," I say quietly.

He reaches out to steady me, putting his arm around my waist while the other rises to rest against the side of my neck. I could turn away from him and be alone with my thoughts and sadness, but I don't want that.

I want him.

He rubs my back, soothing me with a shushing sound that an adult would make to calm a baby. "What do you need?"

I look down and choke out the word, "You."

He reaches up a hand to caress my cheek. "I need you, too," he says, before leaning in to press a soft kiss on my nose. Still holding each other, we walk inside the apartment, shutting the door behind us.

We break away from each other, but hold hands. I lead him to the same room I used to sleep in before I moved out a few years back. It's the same as I left it, pop star posters on the wall and all. I let go as I reach my bed, shedding my top and skirt. When I turn, he appraises me. He explores every inch of me with his eyes and then presses his hand to my heart before his fingers trace a line between my breasts and down my stomach. His touch is feather-fine, just faint enough for me to recognize it and yearn for more.

I gasp at his delicate touch and my head falls back. I try to steal a kiss from him but he pulls away each time I try. His resistance infuriates me and makes me want him more. I try again, more forcefully this time, but it makes him more determined. He pushes me back and I fall on the bed, bouncing lightly.

I crawl backward, working my way to the head of the bed, but he grips my ankle and yanks me back down, closer. He takes my hand in his and with his other, he unzips his pants, urging me to touch him.

I do as he wants. In fact, I couldn't be more eager. If only life could be like this. Touching...teasing...pleasing. I could spend every moment like this, absorbed by him and nothing else.

I slide my hand up and down his shaft, first slow, then fast. He groans and when I look up, his eyes are closed and his head has fallen forward, enjoying my easy strokes. I slide his pants down with my other hand and let go with the other as he steps out of them.

He pushes on my shoulders, climbing on top of me as he forces me onto my back. "I can't get enough of you," he whispers in my ear, his breath like a warm caress, tickling me. The hairs on my back stand on end as he rubs against me. I push back, and he's hard against my nub. He breaks away just long enough to slide on a condom. Then he lowers his hand between us to guide himself to my entrance. My eyes roll back and my whole body sighs as he slides inside of me.

I sink into the bed, my muscles relaxing with the feel of him moving on top of me. Closeness. I love this feeling, of someone joined with me, loving me, if only my body. But as he looks down at me, refusing to let me look away, I feel that it's more than that. I mean, I know it is, but I can actually feel it as he pushes deeper. This isn't just sex. It's not love—not yet. But I'm in danger of it. And the thought brings tears to my eyes.

But I don't let them fall.

Try as I may, I can't hide their presence on the tips of my lashes and he lowers his head to press his forehead against mine. "We'll get past this," he says, reassuring me.

"I just don't know if it's possible."

"I love proving people wrong."

"Prove me wrong, Damien," I say before I find myself reaching my sweet release. "Please."

WE LAY SIDE BY SIDE, warm and sated. The smell of sex is in the air and it makes me dizzy—but in a good way. I could have him again. And again. But then I fear I might be in danger of never stopping. Sex with Damien is unforgettable. I'm not sure if there's anything better.

"Hungry?" he asks.

"Starved."

"Hang on." He tosses the covers aside and stands, crossing the room in nothing except what he was born with.

"Impressive," I say, teasing him as I stare at his cock.

He raises an eyebrow. "I've been told that before."

"I bet."

When he returns, he has a small tub of ice cream in hand and a couple of spoons. He pulls off the lid and we dive in. Heavenly hash. And it's exactly as advertised.

"This is good," he says.

"It's my favorite." I swallow a mouthful and lick my spoon clean, making sure he watches me as I try to be seductive. If he were any other guy, I would feel confident about creating a mood and turning him on. It would be a game of cat and mouse. I would be on my toes and constantly fighting for the man's attention. But with Damien...my cheeks are on fire and I'm trying hard not to laugh at myself. I don't have to be *that* person anymore.

"Do that again?" he teases.

I shake my head. "What about you?" I ask. "What's your favorite?"

"Vanilla."

"That's kind of boring," I say.

"You think? Vanilla can be sexy," he says, winking at me.

"Don't you like to switch it up?" I ask.

"Offer me another flavor and I promise I'll enjoy it."

Now, I laugh out loud. I pick up a pillow and hit him in the chest. Clearly, we've abandoned the topic of ice cream.

"Sometimes I like to let it melt a little before I attack it."

I roll my eyes. "Personally, I like it hard."

He raises an eyebrow and then his cheeks turn crimson before he looks away and breaks out into a laugh. I swear I've never seen anything more endearing on a man than a smile that's so big his eyes practically disappear. "Enough about ice cream," he says.

He repositions himself, covering his middle with the floral sheets but still leaving his leg exposed. It's the one that's both tattooed and scarred. I never did ask him about it and when he catches me staring, I can't look away quick enough. I wanted to ask him about it when I first saw it and now, I feel comfortable enough to ask without feeling awkward.

His eyes gloss over, as he gets this faraway stare. "IED," he says. "We were in a convoy and the vehicle in front of us got blown up. I took some shrapnel to the leg and some to the face."

I touch the pink line on his face with the tips of my fingers. "Oh my God."

He rolls his leg to the side enough for me to see the entire now-healed wound. "An inch to the right and it would have severed an artery. Took me months of rehab."

"Is that why you came back?"

"Yeah, that and Mona asked me to. She got pretty upset when I told her. Said she didn't build a friendship with me for me to die in 'butt fuck nowhere' without family."

I smile as I imagine what her facial and hand gestures would be like as she delivered these words.

"You remember when I said Mona didn't like anyone?"

He nods.

"I get it now. She couldn't help but love you. At first, I'm sure she just wanted to help you. But then she got to know you and she didn't stand a chance. You would thaw even the coldest heart."

He takes his thumb and presses it to my lips. I kiss it and then he strokes them, making me sigh and tingle just about everywhere. I drape my arm over his middle and cuddle up against him.

"I saw her a couple of weeks ago—when I first came back—she came at me like she meant to hug me. I didn't expect that."

"And did she?"

"No, I think she changed her mind. Punched me in the stomach instead."

I chuckle with him and reach over for the ice cream, dunking my spoon to search for some of the marshmallow.

"It'll never be the same without her," he says.

"No," I say with a sigh. "Or without Mickey."

He clears his throat and takes another bite.

"Did Mona ever talk about Mickey with you?"

He steals my spoon and puts a scoop in his mouth.

I elbow him.

He swallows and pauses for a beat. "She didn't say much, but I got the feeling that…they were blood and that was it. I don't know if she had a lot of love for him."

"I'm starting to wonder, myself."

"She told me if something happened to you that I might need to protect you from him. And I think she was right because…"

"Because of what he made me promise?" I ask.

"Yeah."

I hug him a little tighter.

"You don't owe him anything."

I bite at my lip and close my eyes. He runs his hand through my hair. I'm sure it's tangled and a mess but I'm beyond caring right now. My makeup is probably all over the place, too. Any other guy and I'd excuse myself and freshen up. But not Damien.

"He saved me more times than I can count," I say.

"He was family. He was supposed to be there for you. And he should have done it without expecting anything in return."

I know what he says is true, but it doesn't lessen the guilt I carry in my heart. I had one chance to save him, like he'd done for me, and instead of doing what I knew was right, I listened to him and I let his poor judgment cloud my own. I could have saved him. But I let him die. Like Mona, he believed he didn't need a doctor to help him live. He thought he was invincible and he could pull through.

Why the hell wasn't I stronger? Why did I let him sway me?

Both of them. Stubborn and reckless right up until the end.

"Are you still planning on taking revenge?"

Sighing, I tip my head back to look up at him. "Yes. But it's not just about him. I've told you already, I want to do this because everyone in that family is poison. The world is better off without them." I take a breath and softly ask, "Will you still help me?"

"I'm not sure I'm capable of saying no to you."

"Can you get me the names of the people arrested the night Mona was killed?"

He breaks free from my embrace and sits up on the side of the bed with his back to me. His shoulders are slumped as his head hangs.

"Damien?"

"You do this, and you won't be the same. And I...don't know if you'll still be the person who..."

"Who what?" I grab his shoulder and force him to face me.

"You won't be the person I thought you were."

"You barely know me at all."

He scoffs at me, stands, and starts to get dressed. "Yeah, my mistake."

"That's it? You're done? That's all it took?"

"Are you kidding me?" he says, his voice rising. "You want to kill multiple people and I'm supposed to say, *yeah, okay, cool*? No."

"You've killed before."

"For a cause."

"And this isn't one?" I snap.

He pulls at his hair and starts to walk away, but then he storms back to my side of the bed, where he stands over me. I look up, watch his jaw widen as he clenches his teeth. "What I did wasn't a crime. *This*...this is revenge."

"I've told you, that's not the reason I'm doing this."

"Maybe not entirely, but it's part of it. If you want to make them pay, let the cops handle them. Jimmy's in jail and the others are out on bail. The cops can take care of this. The evidence is solid and they know it."

I push the sheets off and slide into my panties and a T-shirt. I pull my hair back and out of my face, securing it with an elastic. He makes sense. I know it. But I can't let it go and I don't know why. There's something inside of me that knows something will happen and they'll end up walking. Whether it's evidence getting lost or tampered with or some small detail that makes evidence inadmissible. I bite my lip and shake my head. No, I don't trust the cops to make sure Jimmy and his friends stay behind bars forever.

"Please, just think about what you're doing," he says.

"I'm sorry I'm not the person you thought I was—or maybe who you wanted me to be. This is who I am, take me or leave me. I'm done bending for men."

"You're being stubborn and ridiculous. Think about what we're talking about here. We're not talking about a personality flaw, or snoring or leaving the toilet seat up. We're talking about taking lives. You want to ruin your life and get yourself killed I'm not going to sit around and watch. Because I give a shit about you, Beth."

"I never asked you to."

He shakes his head. "No, I guess you didn't."

He storms out of the room, leaving me practically shaking with anger. A unicorn figurine sits on my dresser and I pick it up and toss it. It hits my mirror on the opposite side of the room and it smashes. Splinters of glass rain onto the carpet as I heave deep breaths in and out. Tears spring from my lashes.

"Beth?"

I turn and he's by the door. When our eyes meet, he sighs and lowers his head. I swallow hard and hate myself for losing my temper and for letting myself cry. But if I'm being honest, that's not the only reason I'm crying. I worried he might not ever come back. My feelings for him hit me hard, to the point where I feel as if the wind has been pounded out of my chest.

He marches toward me and folds his arms around me and I rest my head against his chest, sniffling.

"I'm sorry," he says, his lips against my neck and hair. "You're hurting and I'm not helping."

"Don't apologize," I say. "I understand what you're saying. You should leave and you should never come back. But I need to do this, Damien. I don't want to, but I need to. My aunt didn't want this for me, but you know what? This is exactly what she would have done, and for the exact same reasons. Can you understand that?"

He pulls back to look at me and I feel the desperation in my voice and my face and I know he can see it too. It's probably why he's so willing to give in. And I hate myself for showing this side of me. It makes me feel pathetic and yet instead of running, he's here, at my side and he wants more.

"I'll get your list, Beth," he says. "But we do this my way. Understand?"

I nod, hugging him tighter.

"You'll feel empty when it's over. But if this is what you want, I'll give it to you. I promise. Anything for you."

CHAPTER FOURTEEN

Bang, bang! The gun recoils and my hands lift as the bullet races to the target on the other side of the forest clearing.

"No, not like that," Damien says. "Loosen your arms at the elbows a little."

"Why can't I shoot like this?" I hold my gun out with one hand and tilt it to the side and close one eye.

"Because you're not a gangster," he deadpans.

I make a face at him. After putting my ear defenders back on, I shoot anyway; my arm flies up.

Damien shakes his head his muffled words have me yelling, "What?" I remove my ear defenders again and quirk an eyebrow as I wait for him to repeat himself. I can't hear a damn thing with them on.

"Two hands. It gives you more control." Bravely, he walks forward on his makeshift range deep in the woods of Norton, a small rural community a few miles outside of Sterling.

"You sure you want to be walking in front of me while I'm holding a gun?"

"You just used your last round, or I wouldn't have considered it."

"Ha ha," I say, without a trace of humor.

Damien made this elaborate wooden board in the shape of a human silhouette. He layered it with a piece of paper that he keeps replacing each time I empty a magazine. My shooting is pretty awful and sometimes I don't even hit the stupid target. My uncle might have been a crack shot but I didn't inherit his talent. I fucking suck. I might have more luck chucking the gun at the Dantes instead of firing it.

He rips the paper off the board and frowns as he stares at it. He moves his finger over the paper, searching for holes. His frown worries me because I'm certain my unlucky streak is continuing. I wonder why he's frowning. Shouldn't he be happy about it? That would make more sense.

In his black boots and jeans with a flannel shirt, he trudges across the overgrown grass, his footfalls making a swishing sound. His face is covered in coarse hair and as I tip my head to the side and study him, I feel a tugging sensation between my legs that makes me sigh. I like his new beard. I hope he lets it grow. There is something about his hair scratching at my face that drives me wild. And I love it especially when those coarse hairs are positioned snugly between my thighs. The delicate burn...

"What are you thinking about?" he asks, his eyebrows puckered.

"Nothing," I say a bit too quickly and I'm sure I've given myself away when his cheeks start to flame.

He runs a hand through his messy, wind-blown hair. There are a million and one things I want to do with him right now, and shooting guns—literally—is not one of them. I think that might be why continues to let himself look rough, when I know he prefers a more polished look. He's trying to distract me. But it won't work.

When he reaches me, he shakes his head and kisses me on the lips. The scar on his cheek moves into a wide V-shape as he smiles and I reach out to run my fingers across it. It must have hurt. I wonder if he cried; if he thought he'd died when the bomb went off that day.

"Focus," he says, gripping my hand.

I both love and hate this Soldier Damien. When he turns it on, there is little I can do to snap him out of it. He's a sergeant with a mission and he pushes me to succeed. He even yells at me. Not that I mind. The more time I spend with him, the more I find everything about him sexy, and that makes this even harder. I know how much he objects.

I drop my hand and take the paper from him. I count the bullet holes and jump up and down when I discover I connected with the target for every single shot! When I notice his solemn face, I calm myself and wrap my arms around his neck. "I couldn't have done this without you," I whisper.

"That makes it worse," he says.

He breaks away and starts packing up his stuff, shoving the leftover magazines in his backpack and rolling up the extra paper. I leave him to his thoughts because I'm pretty sure I can't fix the tension between us right now. *I'd like to*, but I know I can't. Not without changing my mind about the Dantes.

We ride back to town in silence. When Damien agreed to help me a few days ago, I happily accepted his help. Now I know it was a mistake. He still wants me, but how long before he decides I'm really not what he wants? I can see it now. And the look that I crave —that makes me feel like I'm loved and I'm home—has vanished. I should have kept him out of this. I should have learned to shoot on my own and kept everything about my plan to myself. I should have lied to him if I had to, and done anything to keep him happy. Because I've fallen hard for him and I'm in danger of losing him.

He drops me off at the pub. I moved into Mona's place permanently yesterday. I still have my apartment, but I've decided to live here now and it makes sense considering the pub is downstairs and I can be available if anyone needs me when it reopens.

I still haven't decided when that will be.

Tension fills the air when he pulls over to the curb. Usually, he turns off the car and gets out with me, and I know he's coming in. Not today, though. Today, he puts the car in park and lets it idle and I know I'm on my own tonight. I don't ask for an explanation. I figure he needs some time and I get that. Maybe more than most. I smile at him before gently shutting the door. As I back away, he lowers the window.

"I should have given this to you earlier," he says. He holds out a large manila envelope and I reach into the window and take it from him.

"What's this?"

"The names you wanted."

"Oh," is all I can manage. I'm hurting him. I can see it in his face and it kills me, eats away at my insides. I knew I was starting to fall for him, but I never felt it quite so sharply until this moment, when I can see what being with him is doing to him. I flash back to the night where he fucked up his hands in the alleyway outside his apartment. I saw a side of him that I'm pretty sure he doesn't often show, and it crushed me to know I caused it.

"Thank you," I say quietly.

"Sure," he says as the window rolls up. He drives off and I watch after him. Giving a shit and meaning it sucks sometimes.

I slide my finger through the end of the sealed envelope as I turn and walk to the pub door. When I get there, I put the key in the lock and open it wide. The lights are off and the place is in shadows. I reach out to turn on the light to the left of me, flick it on, and jump when I see someone sitting at the bar.

Jocelyn Dante. And she's helped herself to some of the champagne left over from the funeral.

Well, fuck me sideways. She certainly has a habit of breaking and entering.

I could try to tuck the envelope behind my back but I think it would make it obvious that it's something I really, really don't want her to see. I don't think I could do it quick enough for her not to catch it, and I can't risk it. She'd probably sell her own son to get ahead in this world.

"I'd say it's a pleasure, Jocelyn, but..."

"Feeling is mutual." She raises her flute and takes a long drink of the pink, bubbly liquid. I was saving that for a rainy day. I'm actually pretty pissed that she thought it was okay to steal it, more pissed than her breaking in, actually.

"To what do I owe the immense pleasure?"

"I heard you're spending an awful lot of time with my son."

"And?"

"And I don't like it," she says with a sneer.

I laugh at her as I stroll by, bending down to duck under the bar arm so I can stand on the other side of the counter and keep a safe distance. I snatch a bottle of opened tequila and pour it into a shot glass, spilling a drop or two on the bar. I slam it back and pour myself another, knowing a few more will help me navigate my conversation with this skank.

"Pour me one of those," she demands.

I give her the middle finger and she glares at me, a wicked smile on her red rose lips. I hate that she's practically fifty and yet looks like she could be my older sister. Botox? Plastic surgery? I do remember her disappearing for a month or two a few years ago. That would explain her absence. Or maybe an unplanned pregnancy to one of her many lovers?

I set the envelope on the table, too far away for her to snatch it, but she tries anyway. I grab it and hold it firmly in my hand. *Almost, bitch, but not quite.*

"You're a little jumpy. What are you hiding?"

"None of your fucking business," I say.

She grins at me, her white teeth like fangs under the florescent lights. I swear she'd bite me if she got close enough.

"You and I aren't so different, you know," she says.

"This ought to be good." I give her the biggest eye roll I can muster.

"Beautiful, smart, loved by men, but never for the right reasons. You want more than you have but you don't know how to get it. An easy life with a husband and kids would bore you. You want excitement, and I think secretly you like the drama that bad men bring to your life. You like having them burn you over and over because then you get to pretend you're the victim, when the truth is, if you had a good guy, someone like my son, you would crush him. Because happily ever after wouldn't suit you."

"You're so wrong, it's unbelievable." I laugh out loud and pour myself another shot. She thinks I love the way men treat me? That I love the drama? *Fuck you, bitch*. The only thing she had right was that her son is a good guy, one I intend to hold on to because I want to be loved, not treated like the piece of trash I've always felt like.

"Jocelyn, I've had a really bad week and you being here is the cherry on top, let me tell you. So why don't you do us both a favor —because you're looking a little tired yourself—and tell me what it is you want."

"I would think it's obvious."

"Nope. Spell it out for me."

"Stay away from my son."

I shake my head. "No, I don't think so. If your son wants to stay away from me then he'll have to tell me himself."

"I'm only going to tell you once."

"You think I'm afraid of you?"

I see a change in her as I laugh. It's like a switch has flipped inside her head. Her eyes darken to the color of asphalt and her face hardens, smoothing out all of her wrinkles. I'm not one to back down or fear women. Usually, they like to make a big production out of things and then they back off. But Jocelyn? I know what's coming even before she lunges over the bar like a fucking Olympian.

I jump back, out of her reach, and she topples to the floor. I'm no idiot and I know when I don't stand a chance. I've been in a few fights in my life and, as a girl, I'd fight anyway. I'd figure, what the hell and take the licks as they came. I would never run away. Not ever. But Jocelyn doesn't want to hurt me tonight. She wants to choke the life out of me with her bare hands, and she'll probably manage it if we duke it out like men.

So, I run. Back through the swinging doors and into Mona's office, slamming and locking the door behind me. I fall to the floor, crawling to the safe as Jocelyn kicks the living shit out of the door. *Bang. Bang. Bang.* One of the heels of her stilettos breaks through and I can see the long, red end.

Well, shit.

"Face me, you bitch! Come on! Going to run off like the scared cunt you are? I'll die before you ruin my son's life! He belongs with my family! In charge like his stepfather was! And if you think I'm going to let a whore like you take him away from me again, you're fucking mistaken!"

She's crazy. Flat out, needs-a-psych-evaluation crazy. How the hell does Damien share her DNA? I wonder if I should be worried.

Crack. The heel penetrates the door even deeper, the wood splintering around the point of impact. The safe cracks open and I snatch Mona's .40 caliber handgun and fumble with the magazine while trying to lock it in place. After I hear the click, I spring to my feet and turn to face the door. I fire once, twice, and then there's silence. No, it can't be that easy. She's on the other side, waiting to take me out when I unlock it. *But I can't stay in here forever*. The pub still hasn't reopened yet so it's not like anyone is going to come in here and find us. And people in this neighborhood don't call the cops when they hear gunshots. They look the other way and pretend it was some random fireworks.

"Playing possum?" I yell at her.

I strain my ears, hoping to hear something that might give her away. Tick tock, tick tock. The hand moves around the clock on the wall. Sighing, I tiptoe to the door, careful not to make any noise. My heart is racing and I start to sweat. I'd worried that I couldn't pull the trigger when I faced the people responsible for Mona's death, but now that I'm faced with the possibility of killing someone, I feel nothing. Even though I know if I kill her, it will hurt Damien. Okay, maybe I feel bad about that, but could I pull the trigger? Fucking right. Because this woman is poison. And he's better off without her. Just like the world is better off without the Dantes.

Plus, she's trying to kill me.

When I'm a few feet away from the door I still, wait and listen. I can hear a floorboard creak—ever so faintly—and I know she's still here. Wounded? Maybe. Then again, I don't know if bullets alone would take this witch down. She's probably like a cat with nine lives, a beast that keeps coming back.

I kick the door open and it slams into the wall in the hallway.

"Marco?" I whisper.

"Polo!" She lunges for me and I pull the trigger but I miss her as she struggles to rip the gun from my hands. Grunting and groaning, both of our hands around the black metal, we smash from one side of the wall to the other like a ball bouncing around in an arcade game. I take an elbow to the face and my head snaps back, blood spurting out of my nose. I let out a curse and try to knee her in the gut. We collapse on the tiled floor and the gun slides across the ceramic.

"Fucking bitch," she says as she punches me in the face. The blood comes harder now and I can feel it running down the back of my throat. I'm practically choking on it as I haul off and pop her in the eye. We keep it up like this, both of us hitting, neither of us blocking. When neither of us has an ounce of energy left we finally roll onto our backs on the floor, hefting breaths in and out.

"I hate you," I tell her.

"Right back at you, bitch. I'm fifty-one years old and you're what? Twenty-four? I almost had you. You should be ashamed of yourself."

"Go fuck yourself." I spit out blood and pinch my nose. When Jocelyn spits and her tooth clanks along the tile a wide smile claims my face. Serves her right. I cough up blood and wipe it from my chin with the back of my sleeve. The smell of it makes me dizzy. Or maybe that's my splitting headache. I reach down and tear a strip off my shirt. I ball it up to press it against my nose. I'm going to be in a lot of pain tomorrow. No doubt my nose is broken. I hope hers is too, though she'll probably just get it fixed. At least I'll always know I was responsible for *that* surgery. Maybe she'll die on the table. No, I'm not that lucky.

"Eight names," she says. "Eight men released on bail except for one. My husband."

I still and turn my head to face her. She's smiling wide, a black hole where one of her incisors used to be. I can't even be happy about it or gloat, because I know exactly what she's talking about. When I ran to the back room, I dropped my envelope on the floor.

And she read it.

"Jocelyn..."

"No, you don't get to speak now. I'm holding all the cards. You will end things with my son. You will make him believe you don't give a shit about him. Are we clear?"

"No."

She pushes up on her elbows to a half-sitting position. "Excuse me?"

"You won't understand this, so I don't know why I'm bothering to explain, but here goes. Damien deserves to be happy and if that's with me or someone else, then so be it. But I won't lie to him and push him away to save myself. I've made enough mistakes in my life and I won't be the reason he turns to you and a lifestyle he wants no part of."

"Well then, I guess there's nothing left to say, is there?" she says, glaring at me.

I haul off and smoke her in the chin, knocking her off her elbows to lay flat on the floor. "Yep, nothing left."

CHAPTER FIFTEEN

J ocelyn groans as she picks herself up from the floor and hobbles out the front door in one stiletto. The other hangs from her left hand. I sit on the cold floor, legs outstretched, watching her leave, wondering how long I have before Frankie and his goons come to get me.

I'm fucked. I know it. And now I have to deal with the most obvious question of "what now?" Problem is I have no fucking clue. My first urge is to disappear, to grab my passport and run and hope that by leaving Damien behind he'll move on and be happy without me—and hopefully his mother won't be able to drive her talons deeper into his flesh.

He cares for her. God knows why. Pushing a kid out of your vagina does not make a woman a mother, that's for damn sure. She hasn't got a motherly bone in her body. If she did, she would want Damien to be happy on his own terms. She wouldn't force what she wants on him. And I know him enough to know that his vision of happiness does not include running a criminal enterprise with his mother at his side. Crazy bitch.

This realization hits me hard. It makes me decide once and for all that Mickey couldn't have loved me. Perhaps not even a little. I always used to say, "he loves me in his own way" but I'm not sure he managed even that. So my decision to take down the Dantes should have nothing to do with him and his promise. Not that it matters now because Jocelyn is about five minutes away from ensuring Frankie puts a hit out on me.

I rise to my feet and the pain in my muscles and joints is sharp and consuming. Cursing, I rub my hip like an old lady as I hobble to the bar. I laugh out loud when I find my envelope missing.

Fucking Jocelyn Dante. What an asshole.

Now what? Sighing, I sit at the bar and slump forward to rest my elbows on counter. Do I sit and wait for them to come? Not likely. I could act quickly, take them out before they get to me? I have to laugh at that option. I've only just become a decent shot. *Decent*, not fantastic. She's left me with few options and I feel cheated. I guess I would have liked to take them down. I wanted to be the one to do it. Was it realistic? Probably not. I probably should be relieved and perhaps I am to an extent. But the choice should have been my own.

I hate her so much I want to scream.

There is only one thing to do now. Run. Ugh. I'm not a coward, but I'm a realist and I know it's the only choice I have. And Mona made it easier for me to accomplish. And for Damien too. Will he come with me? Do I want him to? Wow. I never thought I would be making permanent decisions that involve him so quickly and it should scare the hell out of me but I don't feel any fear at all. Somewhere, deep inside of me, I romanticize about what running off with him will be like...and I don't hate the idea.

I think I might actually like it. Escaping with him by my side might make me happy. Surprisingly, I feel as if heavy weights have been removed from my shoulders and I know what I need to do. I need to follow my heart and my instincts. I need to come clean to Damien about his mother and hope he doesn't hate me for trying to shoot her dead. I need to lay all my cards on the table and see where we end up.

I grab some ice and wrap it in a dishcloth before grabbing my emergency bag and heading out the back door. With one hand on the wheel and the other holding ice to my nose, I speed to Damien's in Mona's old sedan. It's late and traffic is light so it takes me mere minutes. Jocelyn's car isn't here.

Thankfully. So at least I'll get to him first. I can't imagine he'll be happy I got into a cat fight with his mother, though something tells me it probably isn't her first fight and it won't be her last. He might not expect that of me, though. He hasn't really seen me lose it, yet...though I have pulled a gun on him and he didn't seem to hold it against me.

Man, my life seriously is messed up.

The lights are off in his second-story apartment. I bite at my nails wondering if this is the best choice, but deep down I know it is—for him. He's been a good friend to me, and I need to return the favor. Nothing will ever repay him for all he's done, but this is a start.

Honesty. Like I've never been honest before.

I reach his metal door and—just in case—I reach out and try to open it. Of course, it's locked. I knock lightly, looking back and forth down the alley. A metal can somewhere clinks and rolls on the concrete and I jump back, staring down into the darkness. A black cat scurries across the alley to hide behind a dumpster.

I knock a little harder, deciding to give him another minute or two before I start blowing up his phone.

The lock clicks as he opens it from the other side, then the door scrapes as he frees it from the jamb. Damien is still sliding a shirt over his tattooed arms and over his chest when the door swings fully open. His hair is wild and his cheeks are rosy. As he pulls his shirt down to cover his stomach, he uses his other hand to wipe the sleep from his eyes. "Beth?" He shakes his head and his eyes go wide. "What the hell happened to you?" He takes my arm and pulls me inside, slamming the door shut behind us. After he's locked all his locks—and I notice there is another one now—he flicks on the light to the staircase. He surveys my wounds, gently taking the ice pack from me to look at my nose. "Jesus," he whispers.

"You should see the other guy," I joke without any trace of humor. I don't have the courage yet to tell him it's his mother. Baby steps.

Upstairs, he sits me down on a stool at his island counter. He grabs a medical kit and pulls out some gauze and a bottle of something or other. I read the label and it's says something like saline. He soaks the gauze and starts dabbing the cut above my eye and the dried blood on my upper lip, cheeks, and chin. I wince and jerk away and he apologizes and tries again. This time his touch is lighter.

"You going to tell me what happened?" he says.

"I'm afraid...you'll be upset."

He pauses for a beat and then continues. "Don't ever be afraid to tell the truth. I might not like it, but it's better than a lie. Lies have a way of destroying people."

"Yeah, I guess I can agree with that."

"Your nose is broken." He leans back, takes a good look. "I need to set it."

"Oh, God. It's going to hurt, isn't it?"

He nods. Then, without warning, he clutches my nose and snaps it back into place. I scream out his name, curse him to hell and back, and ball my hands up to rest against my thighs.

"It's better when you don't expect it."

"Fuck! I seriously doubt that."

He tosses my cloth and ice into the sink and grabs a real ice pack from his freezer. He holds it up to my nose, gently, and I still cringe.

"Better?" he asks.

"A little, but it still hurts." I swallow blood and almost retch at the sharp taste of metal.

He chuckles. "You look like you got dragged behind a car. I'd expect some pain for a good week or two."

"Damien...I...I'm in trouble."

He pulls up a chair and takes my free hand, patiently waiting for me to explain.

"Please don't hate me."

"Hate you? Why would I hate you?" he asks softly. "Just tell me what happened."

"I got into a fight with your mother."

He raises an eyebrow and then open his mouth to speak but snaps it shut. After a minute of consideration, he calmly repeats, "My mother?"

"She was in the pub when you dropped me off. She broke in somehow and she tried to take the envelope. We kind of started arguing and she jumped over the bar and I ran and then it just kind of escalated from there. But she...she saw what was inside the envelope, Damien. She knows and she's going to tell Frankie."

"No. She wouldn't do that."

"Are you kidding? She wants me to stay away from you and when I refused, she said she was going to Frankie."

He takes a moment to process the situation, standing, and pacing as he thinks. He runs a finger along his chin, mumbling under his breath.

"It's only a matter of time before they come for me."

"I'll call her. I'll tell her to keep it quiet."

"Damien, you don't understand. She wants you to be a part of that family—like a *big* part. And I'm in the way. She won't listen to what you say, even if it means upsetting you. She's like Uncle Mickey. Nothing will stop her from getting what she wants. Think, Damien. You *know* her."

"I'll kill her," he says, snatching his cell phone off the coffee table. He's quiet as the phone rings and then he pulls the phone away from his face and punches in her number again. "She's not answering."

"Damien, I wanted you to hear about what happened from me. And I want to know that when I'm gone, you'll stay away from all that." I bite my lip. This was not what I planned on suggesting before I got here, but now I'm here, I'm too chicken to ask. Because I fear he'll say no and I'll have to face rejection on top of all of this.

He stops and turns to me. "When you leave? Where are you going?"

I swallow a lump in my throat, feeling mighty choked up right now. "I don't know, but if I stay, I'm dead. And I might have lost pretty much everything, but I worry if I stay...I'll end up getting you killed too."

"I can take care of myself, Beth."

When he's in front of me, he takes my hands and looks deep into my eyes. "I promised you aunt I would look after when she left this world."

"You knew too, didn't you?"

He takes my hands and kisses them, avoiding the question.

I tip my head back and close my eyes. "Why couldn't she tell me? Why? I don't understand? What did I do wrong? Why couldn't she trust me?"

He shushes me and strokes my hair as I lean forward to rest my head on his chest.

"She knew you wouldn't let her die. She didn't want treatment and she knew you wouldn't accept that."

I sniffle and tap my head lightly against him. "So she dealt with this on her own? Do you know how that makes me feel? I could have been there for her. I could have...I could have..."

He kisses my head and gently palms my cheeks to push my head back so I am looking up at him. "You know her. Better than all of us did. Do you think she wanted to spend her last months watching you hurt? She loved you. I'm pretty sure she went out the way she did so you wouldn't have to stand over her in a hospital bed while she wasted away."

"I loved her," I say, my voice strangled.

"I know you did. And she loved you more than anyone."

I push away and rise to my feet. After spitting blood in the sink, I turn to face him. "Is that why you were so determined to help me when we came to you?"

"At first. And I honestly did have a massive crush on you in school."

"What about now?"

His face relaxes and his eyes gloss as he reaches out to pull me close. "I adore you. I want to be near you because of you, not her. But yeah, I promised her I'd look out for you. I promised I would be there for you no matter what. And I would have been, even if you decided you wanted nothing to do with me."

"I knew it couldn't just be me," I say as my insecurity creeps in. It had to be something more.

"Beth, listen to me. I want you. However you'll have me. I want *you*. I'm not sure I'll ever stop."

"I'm nothing special. And I'm..." Tears spring from my eyes and trail down my cheeks. "Look how fucked up I am! I have nothing to give you."

"If you're leaving, I'm coming with you. There's nothing left for me here now."

"I can't let you do that," I say, shaking my head.

"I'm not asking you."

"Damien, we haven't even been on a date!"

"We have something to look forward to then."

I groan at him. "I wasn't going to show you this. I wanted you to make your own choice. But..." I take the passports from my pocket and hand him his.

He opens it and looks up at me. "You got me a fake passport?"

"Mona did before she died. She had one made for me and one for you. Hamish gave them to me the night of Mona's celebration. I don't know if she meant for us both to leave together or separately, but I know she wanted us both to be free of this place."

He leans in and presses a kiss to my lips. "Then what are we waiting for?"

I nod, scared. But not scared that I'm tying myself to him. Oddly enough, that doesn't scare me in there slightest. It's the thought that taking him along might hurt him in the long run— that *I* will hurt him in the long run, as Jocelyn said earlier.

"No more thinking," he says. "We gotta move."

He snatches a packed bag from the closet. Seems I'm not the only one who has an emergency bag. Perhaps he and I have some things in common, after all. We were both raised by criminals, after all. After he grabs a few more things, we race out to his car. He flicks on the headlights and we peel off, his tires squealing. His phone rings not once but four times on the way to the airport. He doesn't answer it on Bluetooth and he doesn't pick it up to check the number. I'm not quite so dismissive. I snatch it and read the number, rhyming it off to him. He glances at me from his peripheral, his lips drawn in a straight line.

"Your mother?"

He doesn't answer and I know I'm right. I almost want to answer it the next time she calls, so I can hang up on her.

"She was wild at the pub. What's she gonna do when she finds out I stole you?"

He grins. "Is that what you're doing? Stealing me?"

I shrug. "Maybe."

"Then by definition I wouldn't be yours, and we both know that couldn't be further from the truth."

I reach over to touch his face, running my finger along his stubble. Just when I think he couldn't be any sweeter, he proves me wrong and pulls me in deeper.

"So," he says. "Where do we want to go?"

WE STAND in the security lineup at the airport. I fidget and chew on my nails. Every muscle in my body is tense and apparently, it's obvious.

"You need to relax," he whispers. "They can smell fear."

I frown at him. "That doesn't help me."

He's as cool as a cucumber. Pretending to text on his phone and looking up, bored, every minute or so. We move through the line and when it's my turn, I swear the big guy from border security is eyeing me. I'm positive I'm getting a gloved finger up my ass, but he waves me through. Damien, on the other hand, has to spread his legs and go through the x-ray machine.

"Who's cool as a cucumber now?" I tease when they finally let him through.

"Yeah, yeah." He puts his hands on my shoulders and guides me forward.

We board less than an hour later. Once I'm in my seat and my seat belt is fastened, I finally let out a long sigh. Damien is still staring at his phone. "How many times has she called now?" I ask.

"A few. And a few texts."

"What do they say?"

He pushes the button on the top of his phone to shut it off. Staring at me, he smiles. "It doesn't matter. None of it matters anymore."

I pull out my neck pillow and blow it up. Then I take out my eye mask and my earphones. I'm all situated and about to pull my mask down when I catch Damien laughing at me. "This is the only way to travel," I tell him.

He puts his hands up and shakes his head. "I believe you."

I pull my mask down and adjust to the darkness as I lay my head on his strong shoulder. Fuck, I love the smell of him. He's sweaty now, and his musky deodorant mixes with it and I swear it has me weak in the knees. I wonder if Mr. Calm and Cool was perspiring while security gave him a hard time.

I manage to sleep on the plane and when we land, I'm woken to a kiss on my forehead and a small shake of my shoulders. Embarrassed, I jostle awake and slide my mask up my forehead and wipe the drool from my chin. He's still smirking at me while we wait for our bags in the airport.

St. Kitts. It's beautiful here. The sun is out, shining down on us without a cloud in the sky. There's a smell here, similar to the one I remember from home: the ocean. But I also smell fresh fruit from the market nearby and the wild flowers waving in the wind.

A man directing non-existent traffic flags a cab for us and the driver pulls ahead. He gets out and opens the door for me. He takes us to a remote area on the other side of the island. I don't believe him when he tells me this because it doesn't take a really long time. There are cabins for rent here, colorful ones. The one we're staying in is a lovely shade of pink. It makes Damien do a double take, but when he sees the smile on my face, he says, "I like it."

"Liar," I say, hitting him in the stomach.

"All right, like might be a strong word. I could learn to like it, maybe?"

It's a one-story wooden structure with a covered front porch. There are a couple of wooden chairs on the porch with a hammock in the corner. I can't wait to rock myself to sleep on it. I practically skip to the door when I see the agent there waiting for us.

"This is gorgeous," I tell him.

"So glad you like it. We received your online payment so enjoy your month's stay. If you need longer, please get in touch."

"How much did this cost?" Damien whispers in my ear as I unlock the door and step inside.

"Don't ask. Mona left me enough money to keep us comfortable for a while."

"We need to be careful. The money has to be untraceable or it could lead them to us."

I frown at him. "Please let me enjoy this for a minute. I've never been anywhere except Poland and America. I've never had a vacation."

He takes my hands in his and sighs, finally allowing himself to smile. After a quick peck on the cheek, I take the place in. Yeah, I could *really* live here. Open floor plan, big kitchen with stone countertops and solid wood cabinets. There are two doors, one leading to a big bedroom painted canary yellow and a bathroom as bright as the bedroom, though it's painted lime green.

"I'm going to have to get some sunglasses," he says as he comes in the bathroom behind me.

He wraps his arms around my waist, starts kissing my neck and I tip my head back to rest on his. "You promised me a date," I say, my voice quiet and dreamy.

"I did, didn't I?" He draws a line from my collarbone to my ear with his tongue, nipping and sucking my lobe. I'm so wet and I've never wanted him more than I do now.

He lifts up my dress, sliding one hand into my panties to part my lips and slip a single finger inside of me. "I think you'd prefer this to a date."

"Maybe..." I say, closing my eyes. "As long as one comes later."

"Oh, it'll come all right."

I laugh at his attempt to be sexy. He hasn't talked to me like this before and I kind of like it, especially now I'm hot and definitely bothered.

"Too bad the neighbors can see the hammock."

"Only during the day," I retort.

He whips me around, claiming my mouth with his. His tongue dives in my mouth, dancing in perfect unison with mine. I reach for him, glide my hand up and down his shaft, and his breath hitches. Without warning, he scoops me up, still kissing me as he carries me to the bed—to our bed—with my legs wrapped around his waist.

He throws me down, crossing his arms over his torso to grip the edge of his shirt. He yanks it off and I crawl back on the bed as he follows me. The movement from his legs hitches up my skirt. After a long, lingering kiss, he reaches between us and pulls down my underwear as I pull down his. Then he's deep inside of me.

"This isn't a good idea," he says.

But I don't care. I grip his hips and pull him deeper. No man has ever been inside of me without a condom before and I want him to be the first. He groans in delight and starts to pull out but I push against him, refusing. "Beth, I won't be able to stop."

"Then don't," I whisper.

I'm not an idiot and I know a baby will only make my situation worse but I'm on the pill and right now my hormones refuse to let him pull out. I wrap my legs around his waist and press my heels into his back. He drives into me, first slow and then fast, always bracing himself when he's close. He wants to please me, to let me come first and it only makes me want him more. It puts me over the edge, to have such an unselfish lover. He wants me to feel every inch of him, to come as he comes and only when I say those delicious words, "I'm coming," does he work harder and harder until I cry out in ecstasy. And only then, as my breathing hitches and a ripple crawls through my body, does he find his release, collapsing on top of me as his cock spasms inside of me.

"It feels different like this," I say as I rub his back.

"You have no idea."

"Have you...?"

"Just that one girl."

"Do you trust me?" I ask, biting my lip because I hope to God that's what he means.

"Yeah, I trust you. I...I...trust you."

I get the feeling he meant to say something else. With glossy eyes and a sincere, solemn face, he holds my eyes and I tenderly kiss his lips. I want to think he meant to say he's falling for me, like I've fallen for him, but I can't let myself hope for that because the disappointment would be severe. He traveled all this way and left his life behind to be with me. That says a lot in itself and that's more than enough. More than I've ever had. And I'm okay with that. I would be okay if that's all it will ever be. He doesn't have to love me, he just has to care about me and treat me with respect. And Damien will always do that because that's who he is.

CHAPTER SIXTEEN

"So happy to hear you're staying," Mr. Nero says when I hand him cash for another month's rent. He escorts me to the door of his office with one of his hands lightly touching my back. "You must be enjoying yourselves."

I smile so hard my cheeks hurt. I swear I've smiled more in the last month than I did in the last twenty-four years before combined. A shit-eating grin, is what my aunt would call it if she could see me now.

Sigh. I wish she could. This is what she wanted, and she wanted it for me with Damien.

Damien.

My smile widens even more and Mr. Nero shakes his head at me, making me blush. Who knew someone could have this effect on me? Certainly not me. But Damien is...I don't even know what to say about Damien. There aren't enough words: thoughtful, intense, attentive, sweet and sexy. *Perfect.* Or maybe just perfect *for me.* Everything he does makes me feel warm all over. Whether he's staring at me with his big warm eyes or smiling at me, or just lying next to me on the hammock while he strokes the back of my head to put me to sleep while we watch the sun set. He does it all in a way that gives me butterflies in my stomach.

I shake Mr. Nero's hand and say good-bye as I walk out with a skip to my step. It's a beautiful day today, warm but with a nice breeze. I shrug out of my sweater and pull down my shades before gripping my bike that's leaned against one of Mr. Nero's yellow exterior walls. I have no other plans for today and when I smell fresh bread from the market I decide to spend some time there. I buy some rolls, some fresh vegetables, and herbs. The seller and I barter a little bit until I get the price that I want. When he hands me the bags, I take in the scent of the bread. Nothing reminds me more of home, or of Mona, than the warm scent of yeast.

On the way home, I spy some coconuts in the trees and one magically falls down, rolling along the dirt road to stop a few feet away. I tucking it in the basket of my bike and plan on eating it later in the hammock. I don't ride home today. I walk alongside of my bike, taking in the sights. The small volcano in the distance; I never thought I'd see one of those. The coastline never ends, with its white sands that merge with the rain forest that spreads up the mountain. From here, I can even see Damien on the docks as the boat he works on comes in.

He's a fisherman now. Paid under the table, since we're not supposed to work here—but what the government doesn't know won't hurt them, and his boss, Gus, isn't about to tell anyone. Pretty sure he's an illegal himself.

I make a fresh salad at home and cook the fish Damien brought home last night. Dill and lemon waft throughout the space as the wind blows through the open windows and it has me salivating. I'm about to taste test the sauce when my cell phone rings. I jog to the living room to find it. It's slipped in between the cushions and I have to dig it out.

Phone calls sometimes put me on edge, but there are only two people that ever call me. One is a number from a burner phone Carrie bought. She checks on us every few days and lets me know if there is anything we need to worry about. The other caller—also from a burner phone—is Mr. Moby. Damien makes enough for food and living expenses but the rent is pricey and we need Mona's money to sustain ourselves. Fitch moves money around for us and he also keeps an eye on things that Carrie can't see. *Like Jimmy.* Last time I heard he's still in jail. Rot away, asshole. Rot away.

The number on the phone is Carrie's. "Hey!" I say, tucking the phone into the crook of my neck.

"How's it going?"

"Fantastic."

"I wish I could visit," she says with a whine.

"You have no idea. I'm enjoying Damien, but sometimes I just need my best friend."

"It's lonely here without you."

"Everything good?"

"Y...yeah."

"What? You hesitated."

She clears her throat and sighs and I take a seat on the stool by the counter while I wait for her to elaborate. The thought of trouble makes my whole body tense.

"It's nothing, Beth. Just the usual. Jocelyn is on the war path and of course she assumes I know where you guys are."

"Did she hurt you?"

"No, but she threatens to. She even came to work today and caused a scene in a way that only she can. I swear Tony is going to fire me if she keeps it up."

I clench my fist and mean to slam it on the stone countertop but I steel myself and set it down under control. "I'm so sorry, Carrie. We left you with a mess."

"Don't worry about it. My two favorite people are living it up in paradise. I'm good."

"Thanks, buddy."

"Don't mention it."

The timer on the oven goes off and I shut it off and the oven too.

"You're busy?"

I chuckle. "As busy as I can be, I suppose. I'm going to have to find a hobby or a job or something. I can occupy myself most of the time but I get a little lonely when Damien is working."

"Oh, no."

"What?"

"That dreamy, faraway voice. The way your tone changes when you say his name. You've fallen hard."

I bite my lip, my grin consuming me yet again. "Oh my God, Carrie. I never thought it could be this good. Never thought someone could make me feel...cherished." I roll my eyes and laugh. "I know how stupid that sounds. I want to smack myself right now."

"You and me both."

"I don't know what I'd do if I lost him, too."

"You won't. I'll keep your secret. Or I'll come there and hide out with you and find myself a local man with a big cock and balls."

"Wow, that's...pretty specific."

"What can I say, I have standards."

"Right."

Damien opens the door and steps in. He comes straight for me, biting my neck and making me squirm. He slides my sundress down off my shoulder and kisses behind my ear. Then his hand roams down my cleavage to capture my breast. I tip my head back and he kisses my forehead.

"Who is it?" he whispers.

"Carrie."

"Tell her I said hi."

"You smell like fish," I say, making a face.

"Don't pretend you don't like it."

I push him away and he goes to the bathroom, taking his shirt off on the way. I lean over, watching him through the open door as he drops his drawers. Shower sex would be awesome right now.

"Are you even paying attention to me right now?" Carrie asks.

"I'm sorry. Did you say something?"

"Exactly," she says with sass. "Ugh, can you hang on, someone is at the front door." I hear her scuff her feet across the floor and I imagine her in her fuzzy slippers. She never picks up her feet.

"Fuck," she says.

"Who is it?"

"Cruella Deville."

"Jocelyn?"

"Why won't she just leave me alone? I swear I'm going to tell her you went to some remote island in Asia. That ought to keep her occupied for a while."

"Carrie—"

"Talk to you in a few days."

Click.

Shit. Biting the very last bit of my nails off, I march to the bathroom, sit on the toilet seat and worry. Damien quietly sings while he showers and I see him moving behind the transparent curtain. I must be upset because it doesn't get me excited to see the outline of his cock. Usually, the sight of it has me begging to be bent over.

When he's finished, he yanks the curtain open and jumps when he sees me: sitting, thinking, stressing.

"What are you doing?" he asks as he wipes the beads of water off his perfect chest. When I don't answer immediately, he adds, "Is everything okay?"

"I don't know. Jocelyn's been hassling Carrie."

He rolls his eyes and wraps the towel around his middle. "She won't hurt her. And I doubt she's showed anyone the envelope yet, because if she did, it would be the Dantes on Carrie's doorstep, not Jocelyn. And that's if they even care. Mickey is dead. You're one girl. And a small one at that. I can't see them feeling all that threatened."

"If you felt this way, why did we leave home?"

He retracts his head like I've slapped him. "In case I was wrong. And running away with you was an adventure I was pretty excited about."

"Really?"

He grins at me. "Do you have to ask?"

I sigh. "I guess not."

"I'd follow you anywhere," he says.

He kisses my head before he makes his way to our bedroom.

"Do you think I'm worrying about nothing?"

"Carrie isn't Jocelyn's family. So yeah, she might be a bitch to her, but she knows Carrie is important to me. And even though she's fucked up and twisted, she does care for me—in her way."

"You sound like I did when I talked about Mickey."

"I think maternal bonding is a little tougher to break than a sociopathic uncle."

I clear my throat. "May I remind you that your mother is also a sociopath?"

"You're probably right."

"So Carrie's safe?"

He nods. "I'd be on a plane now if I thought she wasn't."

SATURDAY IS Damien's day off. He has a friend who let us borrow his boat for the day. Damien seems to have a lot of friends. This doesn't surprise me. Mona didn't like anyone, but she bought this guy a forged passport to take off with me, so if he can charm her, he can charm anyone.

Ladies love him too. I hate the way they look at him.

We anchor a little distance from a coral reef and snorkel for an hour or two. The ocean floor is full of fish in all different colors. Every time I see a new one, I jab Damien and point, all excited like a kid. I can see him laughing at me through his facemask.

When we're done, we lounge on the deck of the boat.

"I wouldn't mind having one of these," I say, checking it out. It's a speed boat with a small cabin below, just large enough for a bed and some storage. "We could spend some nights out here, on the ocean, under the stars."

"Did you think it could be this good when we left?" he asks as he wraps his arms around me. I lean back against his chest and sigh. "Not just when we left. I never dreamed life could be like this... happy. No bullshit. No drama. Just happiness."

He kisses my cheek. "This is all I ever wanted. Just this. A quiet, peaceful life with a girl who creates just enough drama to keep me on my toes."

I smile at him as I elbow him in the ribs.

"And the swearing. I'm not sure I could ever find another girl who swears so much she makes me blush."

"Fuck you," I say.

"There she is," he says, rolling over on top of me and pressing his erection in tight between my legs. I reach between our bodies to wrap my fingers around his length and circle my thumb along the tip.

He crushes his lips to mine and pumps his hips in a rhythm that matches my hand's. His eyes close and his back arches as he moans. It's easy to please him and sometimes I want that and nothing more. I push him off me and remove my top. I straddle him and he palms my breasts before lightly squeezing my nipples. I lower my mouth to his neck and place delicate kisses along his chest, stopping to lick his nipples. His hands move to softly rest on the sides of my head and he strokes my hair.

When I reach his navel, I look up at him from under my lashes and he smiles as I trail my tongue even lower before freeing his cock. While my hand pumps the base, I mouth the tip, swirling my tongue around him and licking his pre-cum. I swallow as he moans and I go deeper until I feel him at the back of my throat. His cock twitches and his hands tangle in my head as he gently urges my head to glide up and down his shaft. I giggle a little and the vibrations make him gasp. His back arches as he lets out a low, "fuck."

"Go slow or I won't last."

I remove my mouth and smile. "I don't want you to last," I say, my voice husky. I spread my lips again and glide them over his shaft and I don't stop until he tickles my vocal cords.

"I love you," he says with a sigh.

WE LAY NAKED on some towels on the deck after our bodies are exhausted from sex. It wasn't enough for me to make him come; the second he found his sweet release he flipped me over and spread my legs wide so he could return the favor. My hand rests on his cock now and absentmindedly I stroke my thumb along the line of one of his veins.

"If you keep doing that, we might not ever make it back to shore."

"Fine by me," I say.

He kisses my forehead and pulls me close and we stare up at the stars and the moon overhead as violet clouds wave across it. "Come on, babe." He squeezes my shoulders, "I promised I'd have the boat back," he glances at his watch, "over an hour ago."

I feel like a petulant child right now as I groan, wanting to pout and chant, "but I don't want to." Of course, I don't. I just roll my eyes at him instead. I could have stayed out here all night. But then, I can't ever get enough of just being near him.

We tie the boat up at the marina and hand the keys off to Damien's friend who lives nearby. Although they invite us in, we don't stay. I'm ready to have Damien all to myself on the hammock. Maybe even sleep there again. When we turn to leave, Guillaume— or Guy, as he likes to be called—hollers the name Lucas. Damien doesn't respond at first; it still takes us both a moment to realize that's his name here, the same name that's on his passport.

"I almost forgot! Lana met one of your friends at Port Zante."

"Friends?" Damien asks. I link my elbow with his for comfort. I don't like the way he says "friend," like it's someone visiting the island, someone who doesn't belong here.

"Yes," he says, before calling out to his wife inside.

"Lana, what was the name of that man you met today who asked you about Lucas?"

Lana sighs and taps a finger to her lips. "You know, I don't remember his name. He showed me a picture, said not to tell you he asked because he wanted to surprise you. But he seemed odd to me, and a little tense, otherwise I would have let him have his surprise."

"What did he look like?" I say, jumping in quickly.

Guy and Lana glance at each other and she frowns before she responds. "Well, tall and thick"—she pronounces it tick—"maybe forty? But an old forty."

"Tattoos?"

"Oui," she says, her French accent coming through. "Many. I didn't notice what they were, except for a sun, a big one, on his arm." She runs her hand down over her long braid that falls over her chest. "Mon dieu," she whispers. "Is there a problem?"

"No," Damien lies, hiding his apprehension well, as if he rehearsed all day.

I can't hide my fear like he can, because I feel like I'm about to collapse. "I knew this couldn't last," I whisper as we walk away. "I knew it."

"Shh," he says, caressing my shoulder. "We'll get through this."

"Damien, you said you didn't think they'd feel threatened by me. You said you didn't think they'd care enough to come looking."

"Well, it seems I was wrong."

I stop and spin around to face him. "What now? If we react and get rid of them, Frankie will only send more."

"We need to find out how they found us."

"How?"

"Leave it to me," he says.

Our cabin is on the hillside, tucked in between tall, green, lush trees. You can see a glimpse of it from the ocean, but it's only because it's painted such a bright color. We know the area well now; we've explored it a fair bit in our spare time. There's a path through the mountain that we can take to get to our cabin from above. We take this route, figuring Frankie's men would take the most obvious way, on the dirt road that meanders off the main one.

We crouch in the trees, watching, waiting. We don't have long to wait. An hour or two. I fidget, almost breaking my fingers and Damien reaches out to grip my hand to stop me. "We're fine," he says. "We just need to maintain the upper hand."

"I don't feel fine, Damien. I feel like we're about to lose everything and I want to pull the gun out of my purse and start shooting."

"I promise you, reacting without thinking will get us both killed. Just trust me." He reaches out to touch my face and his thumb strokes my cheek. "You trust me?"

"With my life," I whisper.

There are two of them—but that doesn't mean there aren't more on the island somewhere, holding our photos up and raising suspicion about us. If they disappear, people will ask questions. Cops will come looking for us, the two people those assholes were searching for. Guaranteed. Damien wants to think we can get out of this and continue on like it didn't happen. He's delusional. I'd love to believe that, but I've always been a realist. Don't react, he says? Does he know me at all?

Damien pushes the tall, dark green weeds apart and crawls on his hands and knees closer to the edge of the ledge we hide on. Some mosquitoes buzz around me, and I swat them away, killing one mid-bite on my hand.

I follow after him, watching intently. I half-expect Damien to start putting lines of mud on his face and go all soldier on me, but his expression is calm, thoughtful, intent. The wheels are spinning in his beautiful head and I want to know exactly what he's planning.

One of the men walks around the back of the cabin while Sunny —the one with the sun tattoo—goes around front. I remember Sunny well. At one point, he and Mickey worked together. I'm not sure if he helped him kill people, but I assume that's why they spent so much time together before Mickey took an interest in other pursuits.

The other guy is Simon Trent. I hate that fucker to death. He came on hard to Carrie one night, and usually Carrie's up for whatever, but this guy had some kinky shit in mind. If Damien knew... well...not sure how he'd take that. Might want to tuck that information in my pocket for later.

There's a crash of glass and Trent sticks his hand through the door to unlock it. As he goes through the back, Sunny waits on the front porch, sitting in my fucking chair.

Trent comes out the front door and they enter together, waiting for us.

"Do you think there are more of them?" Damien asks.

"I don't know. Maybe. Maybe not. Frankie's numbers are down since Mona took down a bunch of them. They wouldn't be able to leave the country while on trial. But...who knows? If they have our address, I would think they would all have it and they'd all be here waiting."

"Look around, what do you see? What do you hear?"

"The ocean, trees. I hear the wind, some music in the distance. Fucking flies buzzing around my head driving me crazy."

He frowns at me.

"We're looking for their friends. Look for movements in the trees, in the distance. People who look suspicious. Rustling leaves, moving branches. Anything that suggests they're not alone." He points straight ahead. "Watch our left flank, and I'll take the right."

"Flank? What the hell is a flank?"

"Just watch left of the cabin. If the coast looks clear, I'll go in and you can stay here and keep watch."

"Not a chance."

"Beth, I let you have your way all the time. This is familiar to me and I'm good at it. I'm not going to fight with you. You'll stay here and you'll do what I say or I'll tie you to the fucking tree over there."

"Did you just swear at me?"

He lets out a frustrated sigh. "Beth..."

"All right, fine."

He glares at me.

"Fine," I say again, because he seems to need additional confirmation. But we both know I'm lying.

"I swear to God..."

"I'm staying," I say, full of sass.

He snatches my purse and pulls out my gun. "Just in case." He tucks it into the back of his pants. His gun is snugly situated in one of his work boots that he insists on wearing all the damn time. He crawls forward, but I yank him back, and slap him across the face. He stares at me blankly.

"In case you don't come back. I won't forgive you." I know I shouldn't respond this way, but I want to tell him I love him and this just isn't the time for that. I can't let myself be vulnerable when our lives are at stake.

He opens his mouth and I swear I'm about to get an earful but instead he says, "I love you, too," and presses a kiss to my lips.

"I'm sorry," I whisper.

"You can make it up to me later."

He crawls off, and the trees and weeds are thick enough that I am unable to see him. But he's there. The weeds sway just a little more than they should with the light breeze and I hear his hands and feet scuffing along the foliage with tiny snaps and cracks of stray twigs and branches.

I bite my lip and draw blood but swallow it down.

Damien, you better come back.

Please come back.

He moves to his knees and I can only see the back of his dark shirt. The moon is full and bright now and as it hits the ocean there is more than enough light for me to make out shapes and movements.

As he reaches the edge of the weeds and bushes, he rises to a crouching position. He pulls his gun from his boots, and still crouching, he jogs to the western wall of the house. I cover my open mouth and my whole body clenches with worry as he cocks his weapon and opens the door.

CHAPTER SEVENTEEN

"Fuck this," I say, moving forward. I don't have my gun anymore, but I'll be damned if I stay here and let him try to take them out on his own. That is what he's doing, right? How would I know? Because he never let me in on his plan. I want to scream in frustration.

It's not okay for me to kill people but it's okay for him?

I crawl forward, through the weeds, wincing as I pass over some small rocks and some thorns. The mosquitoes follow me, nipping at my neck. I try to focus on Damien, and try to be quiet so I can hear what's going on.

I hear nothing.

How can that be, unless he's taking them out quietly? But he had no knife. No silencer. Nothing. When I reach the edge of the overgrown grass and weeds, I stand and do as Damien did—duck down and run for the house. With my back to the wall, I sidestep to the back door.

Wait.

Listen.

I hear voices. Then I hear crashing. I can't go in the back door; I'll be a sitting duck. The window to our bedroom is open slightly and inside I can see that Damien is aiming a gun at Sunny and Trent. They have their hands up. How the hell did he manage that? Impressed and completely relieved, I let out a breath and the tension in my muscles relaxes.

I stride to the back door and open it, stepping inside. "Damien?" I say so he knows it's me. I don't want him to think he's got more company than the two assholes in front of him.

I snatch a knife from the counter and it scrapes along the stone. The noise barely registers in my ears. I'm too focused on Sunny and Trent, who are sitting on the couch.

"What now?" I say.

"Get some rope."

Rope? Where the hell am I going to get rope? There's a shed out behind the cabins that the yard workers use. I dash into the darkness to the building. With a big, sharp rock, I smash the combination lock that hangs from the latch connecting the doors. It takes me a few tries and I'm sweating when I finally hear the clank of metal as the lock drops to the concrete skirt around the base of the structure.

I open the doors and fight to see through the darkness. Then I have a bright idea and pull out my phone, pushing the flashlight button. Shovels, lawnmowers, gas tanks, paint, brushes, broken chairs...and aha! Rope. I snatch the cord and run back to the cabin, worrying I've been gone too long. It only takes a minute for a situation to change completely. But I can relax. When I get back, everyone is right where I left them. I'm not sure if they even blinked.

Damien nods to the men and I tie them up, so tightly that Sunny winces. So I pull it a little harder just for good measure. That's for ruining my new life, asshole.

Damien yanks Sunny up and drops him in one of the chairs at the kitchen table. He is in the middle of the room as Damien circles him like a predator. *He would have been good at this.* He would have been an asset to Jimmy and his crew. Jocelyn saw this easily, but not me. I couldn't see through his soft nature. Not even in those moments where I drove him crazy. This realization hits me hard.

"You took them easy," I say softly.

"They weren't a challenge," he says.

Hmm. When I'd trekked down the hill to help him, I worried he'd be in here bleeding and I'd have to find some way to save him. But he didn't need my help.

He kneels down so he's eye to eye with Sunny. "I need information. And you're going to give it to me."

Sunny scoffs at him. Then he snaps his head back and spits in Damien's face. My hand flies to Sunny's face and I slap him hard. Damien frowns and looks at me with a raised eyebrow. "I can handle this."

That much is very clear. "So handle it."

"How did you find us?" he asks.

"I didn't," Sunny says. "I was told where to go."

"And how did Frankie know?"

"Frankie?" he scoffs. "Frankie didn't send me."

"What did you say?" I ask, grabbing his shirt to make him face me.

"You know, Beth, I always thought you were a sweet kid. I didn't realize you were a raging bitch like your aunt."

Damien stands and holds me back while I kick and flail, trying to get close to Sunny.

"Enough, Beth. Enough."

When I agree to be calm, he lets me go. But as I walk by Sunny, I punch him in the junk.

"Beth!" Damien yells.

Sunny tries to bend over, coughing and sputtering and retching. I'd say I'm sorry but I'm really not and I promised I would never lie to him, so...what does he want from me?

When Sunny collects himself, Damien tries again. I sit in the kitchen, a few feet away because Damien won't let me get closer.

"Who sent you?" he asks.

Sunny keeps his mouth shut, and Damien hauls off and punches him in the face. Damien's knuckles are bloodied and I'm not sure if it's his own blood or from the open cut on Sunny's nose. Damien looks at his hands and I see a shift in him, though he recovers quickly. Our eyes meet and I mouth, "I love you." He returns from wherever he retreated to and focuses once again on the man in front of him. It warms me to know I could do that for him. And it also makes me feel better to think he might need me as much as I need him. We make each other stronger. Even if it's not in the same way for him as it is for me.

Sunny laughs at Damien and I know this is going nowhere quick. Damien doesn't have the stomach to push Sunny in a way that'll make him sing, and I'm happy for it. I love him for it, but that doesn't help us today. Because right now we need to be warriors and fuck the costs.

"Was it Jocelyn?" I ask.

Sunny's lips remain sealed.

"Fine." I stand up and start rooting through the drawer underneath the microwave. I find a pair of pliers and, satisfied, I go to Damien's side.

"What are you going to do with those?" he asks.

"I'm going to rip off his dick."

"Beth?"

"Damien, if you don't want to watch, you can go outside. But he's threatening our lives right now and I won't let anyone take anything else from me. He talks or I make him. That's just the way it is."

Damien licks his lips, pretends to debate it, though we both know he's not letting me rip anyone's dick off. Guys are weird about that, anyway.

Sunny opens his mouth. "All right, all right."

"Well, that was easy," I say, swinging the pliers around my finger.

"Fuck," Sunny says. "You're fucking crazy!"

Trent screams at Sunny, "I'll kill you myself if you talk!"

"It was Jocelyn," he says. "She beat it out of the Knowles kid."

I gasp. "Carrie?"

"Yeah, that's her."

"Is Frankie looking for us?" I ask.

"How the fuck should I know? I worked for Jimmy, not Frankie, and Frankie's pretty fucking selective about who works for him these days."

"We can't let them leave, Damien," I whisper.

He shakes his head and props his hands on his hips. "She'll send someone else and then where does it end?"

"It ends when we kill them and move somewhere else. We don't tell a soul where we've gone. And we take Carrie with us. Jocelyn won't find us again."

"This is what you want? To kill them?"

"It's them or us, Damien. Don't you see that?"

He hands me the gun and steps aside. "Then do it."

I hold the gun in my hand, take my stance, and grip it the way he showed me, with two hands. I point at Sunny, see the sweat building on his brow. Trent sneers at us, spitting on the ground as his friend did.

I cock it and point, line up my sights, aiming for his head. Sunny's eyes widen, and his body tenses. He closes his eyes and under his breath, I hear him whispering something that sounds like a prayer.

"Just fucking do it," Trent yells. "Fucking pussy!" he screams.

I bite my lip; my hands start to shake. I can do this. I know I can. I just have to pull the trigger. *Just pull the trigger.* That's it. But my arms get weak and my eyeballs are wet and it's only now I see what Damien knew all along. No matter how hard I try to pull this damn trigger, I just can't do it. Tears spring to my lids and they fall and I hear Trent taunting me in the background but it just enters my ears as noise. Damien's warm hands cover mine as he takes the gun from my hands and wraps his arms around me.

"You're not that person. You never have been, no matter how tough you try to be," he whispers in my ear. "But you needed to see for yourself to really believe it."

"I'm sorry," I cry. "I thought I could. I really did."

"I know, Beth."

"Now what do we do?" I ask, as I wrap my arms around myself.

"I have an idea," says a female voice, drawing my eyes to the front door as Jocelyn saunters inside, in her alligator skin heels. *Bet the bitch skinned one herself*, I think as I sneer at her.

She's in a red dress and it's the color of blood. It perfectly matches her freshly applied makeup. I don't even know how she manages to keep her makeup on in this heat. Or why she'd put lipstick on right before our reunion. She has her priorities straight, I guess. Her image and appearance being number one.

Damien grabs my arm and steps in front of me to shield me. But I don't need his protection. I still have the pliers in my hand and I can use it to gouge out her cold, black eyes. I couldn't kill Sunny or Trent, but her? I don't know. I might just find the strength for that.

Evil bitch.

"Put the gun down, Damien," she says. "I'm not going to hurt you."

He lowers his weapon. Jocelyn isn't holding anything but a purse, though that doesn't make her harmless. I'm not sure if Damien recognizes this or not.

"What the hell are you doing, Mother? Just when I thought you couldn't get any worse."

"Oh, please. I won't apologize for wanting my son home and safe." She glances between her goons. "You can let them go. They won't hurt you. I've paid them handsomely to bring you back without a scratch."

"He's not going anywhere with you," I say, but Damien nudges me to be silent.

"This isn't going to end the way you want," Damien says to his mother.

"It's going to end exactly the way I want it to."

"Or?"

She smiles. "Damien, I *will* kill her. Slowly. She's no match for me. Trust me, I've already had it out with her. She's weak. Not just physically, but her mind."

"I'll show you weak," I say, attempting to step around Damien but he grips my arm and blocks me. No matter how much I fight, he won't let me go.

"I won't let you touch her," he says. "And you're wrong, there's nothing weak about her mind."

Jocelyn scoffs at that. "What are you going to do to stop me? Kill me? Your own mother?"

"If I have to," Damien says.

"No. You wouldn't." She takes a seat on the couch, by Trent. "I have that envelope. I've kept it to myself and I will continue to do so, but only if you come back with me. Her—on the other hand," she points to me, "she needs to leave Sterling permanently. I don't care where she goes, but she stays away from you. Forever. You will never be who you were meant to be with her by your side. She's not strong enough."

"Fuck you!" I say.

Jocelyn rolls her eyes and it's all I can do not to lunge for her. She pulls a gun out of her purse and Damien raises his. "Don't worry. It's not for you." She twists on a silencer and like a silent dart, a bullet shoots from the end to hit Trent on the side of his head. Brains and blood and bone particles splat on the wall and I cover my mouth to stop myself from screaming. She turns the gun to Sunny and a bullet darts out to land between his eyes. His head rolls back and blood drips to the floor.

"Why?" Damien asks. He sighs and his shoulders slump. It seems as if she's draining the life from him and I want to hurt her for it.

"No one knows I'm here," she says. "I had to kill them to protect you. I don't want them talking when we get back to Sterling."

"I love her, Mom."

She laughs. "What's love got to do with it?"

"Everything."

"Come home with me and she'll be safe. I'll give you the envelope. And we'll move on. Like we've done all our lives. You and me. It was always that way until you joined the army! Don't you see?"

Damien sighs and looks out the window. "So you're telling me that you never told Frankie about the names?"

She nods, pulling out the envelope from her bag and tossing it onto the coffee table. Damien takes a few steps forward, still keeping me close at his back. He opens the envelope and pulls the sheet out. Satisfied, he nods and puts it back down. "Beth's safe?"

"Yes. And she'll stay that way."

What is he doing? He can't be serious. He can't actually be considering this? She'll turn on him! Ruin him! I grip his shoulder and force him to look at me. "No, Damien. You can't. She's poison and I can't handle the thought of her influence on you. I won't give you up."

He tips his head down until his forehead meets mine. "I won't give you up either," he whispers. "You mean everything to me."

I touch my lips to his and feel them tremble. It tears me up to see him so torn. I want to do something to make his hurt go away, but I have no idea what that something is. "I love you," I say, hoping my words give him comfort. "More than I've ever loved anyone or anything."

"I know. I love you, too. And I'll do anything to keep you safe. *Anything*." He lets out a sigh before pulling away.

Then, without warning, he raises his gun and fires.

WE'RE on the ocean in Guy's boat, three bodies wrapped in tarp on the deck. I stare at them, glad they're all dead, but sad for Damien because I know what killing his mother is doing to him.

It will haunt him for the rest of his life, and he did it for me. The weight of that decision affects us both. For him, for obvious reasons and for me, because I also feel responsible. And I know one day he may come to resent me for it.

It's inevitable.

He ties bricks to Sunny's feet and rolls him off the edge of the deck. The body enters with a splash, water shooting up to wash over the edge of the deck and the tips of my toes. I take a step back and fold my hands over my chest. Damien does the same to Trent now, pushing him into the water with his foot. He saves his mother for last, staring down at her through the clear plastic.

"I'm so sorry," I say, touching his shoulder.

He bends down and closes his eyes, says a prayer, and then

pushes her off. He keeps his eyes on the blue-green water as she sinks, her image first clear and then suddenly cloudy. He keeps staring in the same spot long after she's disappeared. I have no idea what to say or to do, except to reach out and intertwine his hand with mine.

"She never would have stopped," he says. "She said she'd leave you alone, but I could tell from the way she wouldn't look me in the eyes, she wouldn't have been true to her word. She's killed people for less—a lot less. She would always have seen you as the girl who took me away from her and she would have made you suffer for it."

"I wish I'd done it, so you don't have to feel this guilt."

He scoffs. "Guilt? I'm not sure that's what I feel." He sighs. "She killed my dad, you know?"

"What?"

"I was five and she thinks I don't remember, but I do. He was cheating on her. I know because he introduced his girlfriend to me one time. He told me he was leaving my mother for her and taking me with him. When I told her, she just snapped. She told me to go to my room and I heard yelling, first in the house and then outside. When I went to my window, I saw him walking away and her running after him. She spun him around and started hitting him over and over. Then he slapped her. I was about to run for her but I couldn't move. It's like my feet were glued to the carpet and I couldn't even call out to her. He said he would make sure I never saw her again. When he turned his back again, she grabbed a rock and smashed it over his head."

"Why didn't you ever confront her about it?"

He smiles. "One of the reasons I fell so hard and so quick for you was because I felt like we were the same. Like you could under-stand me and I could understand you because like you, I've always felt alone. Loved, but not really. Not the way you're supposed to be."

I wrap my arms around his chest and rest my head on his shoulder.

"I knew from the moment I laid eyes on you in high school."

"Really?"

"Really," he says.

"So what do we do now?" I ask.

"I don't know. I love it here, but I hate pretending to be someone else."

"So we leave."

"Yeah. And go where?" he asks.

"I don't care. As long as I have you, I'm home."

He places a tender kiss on my forehead. "I would have forgiven her if she was sorry for all that she's done. I would have let her be a part of my life still."

"Yeah, I know what you mean. But people like her and my Uncle Mickey don't change. You either accept it and love them as they are or decide life is better off without them."

"I don't like either option," he says.

"Neither did I."

CHAPTER EIGHTEEN

Damien smokes a cigar outside the pub. I can see him through the window. He's with Henry. Henry is probably pushing sixty, so at first it seemed weird that they became such good friends, but the more I see them, I think they're kind of perfect together. Damien is a bit of an old soul.

I sit down on a stool and kick off my shoes. The pub just closed and I can finally relax after a grueling ten-hour shift. Carrie is behind the bar. She works here now. Partly because Jocelyn got her fired and also because I trust her and enjoy having her around. She's a hard worker so that whole business-and-friends-don't-mix bullshit is moot. And I don't treat her like a boss.

I have Carla for that.

Carla. What can I say about Carla? I don't love her. But when I found out she has a business degree and she ran her grandparent's restaurant until it burned down a few years ago, I decided to give her a chance.

She makes my life easy. And it turns out I like easy. Who knew?

The pub door opens, the bell above it jingling.

Henry and Damien make for the bar and Carrie has drinks in hand, ready to pass one off. For me, it's a virgin Bloody Mary. Damien bends at the waist and kisses my swollen belly. Five months and I swear I look ready to burst. We didn't even find out until two months ago, after we decided to come home.

At first I thought coming back here was a mistake, but now? As my friends surround me and laugh and carry on? I know I made the right decision. Jimmy is in jail for good now and so are the other assholes who had a hand in my aunt's death. And Frankie forgave me for running away on his debt, because I paid him what I owed plus interest. A businessman at heart, he couldn't deny the fact that keeping me alive is more profitable than killing me.

Mickey is still missing.

One day his body might turn up, but for now, I play dumb when the cops come by to bother me and Damien.

Life isn't perfect in Sterling. But I have everything I want and more on the way.

And as Damien kisses my forehead and showers my face with kisses I know that I'd repeat the last seven months of my life again and again if it meant I would end up just like this.

Crazy in love with the one guy who proved me wrong.

FLAWED

EXCERPT FROM FLAWED, ALSO SET IN AN INCAPABLE WORLD.

NIKO: A buzzing noise echoes through the cellblock; this noise has taunted me all day. Every time I hear it, I spring from my paper-thin mattress and wait for a guard to call my name, and each time I'm met with disappointment.

Six years is a long time to wait for freedom.

I stay where I'm seated, my back against the cold cement wall and my gaze on the small window I've looked up at every single day since they threw me in here. Through the bars, I can still see the cloudy sky. My bunkmates sit across from me, playing cards, yelling at each other over the rules of some stupid game I've never heard of before.

"Nikolai Kosh!" The CO's low voice booms through the block.

My bunkmates stop, cards in tight against their chest, and grin at me. A stupid smile claims my face. I'm a fucking sixteen-year old girl invited to prom. Not having someone dictate every detail of my life will be a welcome adjustment. I can sleep when I want, keep my light on as late as I want—if I want it on at all—wear whatever I want or nothing at all, and I can finally taste alcohol that's not brewed in a dirty bucket. And I can see the few people in my life that mean the most to me—if they're willing to see me too.

I stand and lean my elbows onto either side of the door frame of my cell. MacDonald, a burly correctional officer with a thick mustache, saunters into the open common area, his control evident from the ring of keys hanging from his fat finger. He sets his eyes on me. "Bed and baggage."

Bed and baggage, the call sign for 'pack up your shit, you're sprung.' I toss my things in a laundry bag. Each of my roommates stands and slaps the palm of my hand before gripping it and bumping their shoulder to mine. As far as roommates go, I could have done worse. At least I didn't have to keep one eye open at night with them. Both of them are light-fingered but neither of them is violent.

I hike my bag over my shoulder and wave to the few things I leave behind: some chips, a brush, candy, and toiletries. "Take what you want."

They forget about me while they fight over a box of mints. I shake my head and say good-bye, touching my hand to the wall by my bed with the lines carved into the wall for each year I spent in here.

I wave good-bye to the other guys in the common area and MacDonald and I walk to the doors. He looks up at the camera and within seconds the door opens and he escorts me out. This time I'm not in cuffs and it feels good. I wrap one hand around the opposite wrist and can almost feel the cool steel still biting into my flesh. Once we're through, I look back through the glass at what's been my dysfunctional home and quietly say, "Never again." I don't mean for the CO to hear. Honestly, I didn't even mean to say it aloud.

"You know how many times I hear that?" he says.

"You've never heard it from me." I bite the inside of my cheek and resist the urge to say something smart. I don't need him reminding me how many people fall through on those plans. The guys leaving before me weren't me. And I mean what I say. Always.

"I give you a month," he says with a sneer. "Maybe six weeks if you're smart enough not to get caught."

The CO dumps me in a holding cell, like the one I sat in on admission, but now, instead of changing out of my street clothes, I'm changing back into them. I pick my old clothes up and shake my head at them: jeans frayed at the bottom, and a black, long-sleeved shirt. I can tell they don't fit just by looking at them. It's an effort to push the button on the waist through the hole and the legs are sitting pretty high above my ankles. The sleeves of my shirt strain from the added muscle in my arms. A rip starts near the shoulder. I just shake my head.

I was still a kid when they put me in here. Long and lean. I'm harder now, with sharp angles and muscles. And I'm pretty sure I've grown half a foot. Other than working in the kitchen, I've spent a lot of my time working out: lifting weights, pushups, sit-ups, running in place, running around the yard. I tried my hardest to keep myself busy so I didn't rack up more time. It's hard to be on the straight and narrow behind bars when there are so many rules to be broken. And the drugs? They're everywhere. I can't tell you how many times I wanted to shoot up or snort something in the beginning. The promise of an escape from this cold, hard place and the monotony of it all is hard to resist. Riding a hallucinatory wave where I can feel, touch, and see the things that matter the most is awfully tempting.

It was so tempting I almost broke.

The CO walks me to the main doors. While we wait, his eyes scan the length of me and a small smile covers his lips. He's laughing at my clothes. Fucker. I can't even be irritated right now when I'm practically bouncing on my feet. How many more doors are there?

"Cute," he says.

I roll my eyes and sigh. "I must remind you of your boyfriend." I only have so much willpower.

He glowers at me.

A buzzing noise rings out and the door slides open. We walk through two more doors and two fences topped with barbed wire. And then I'm on the outside, turning my back to the final door as it closes behind me. I take a deep breath. The air smells different out here. Fresher. The cells smelled of dirty socks and sweaty men or mold or backed up toilets. Out here, I smell pine and smoke from nearby burning wood stoves. The trees are full of leaves in every color. It's the beginning of November and the wind is a little chilly, but not enough to make me shiver.

This is it. It's over. It's what I've been waiting for, and yet, now I'm on the outside, my grin starts to fade. Why aren't I happier? I should be. This is what I wanted up until thirty seconds ago. Now my excitement is replaced with a needling in my chest. Don't get me wrong, I'm glad to be rid of this place and the people in it, it's just that while I stayed here, stagnant, the world moved on without me and I don't know if I'm going to like the life I'm going back to. I've made a mess of things. Royally. My mistakes cost me my mother and the only girl I ever gave a shit about. And they also cost me a chance to say good-bye to my sister. Ain't no way to get right about that, that's for damn sure.

My brother Vik pulls out from the parking spot near the end of the lot and pulls up to the curb where I stand. He drives an old white muscle car with a black racing stripe down it. It's as perfect as I remember it. When I was sixteen, I built this beauty from a rusty frame, and she still runs like a dream. The roar of her engine is like music to my ears. I gave her to my brother for safekeeping when I got locked up. He's totaled three cars in his life, so I'm impressed he's taken such good care of her.

He climbs out, rounding the car and heading straight for me. Looking at Vik used to be like looking in a mirror. Though we were always different on the inside—Vik is a borderline sociopath—we always looked similar on the outside, even though he's a few years older than me. Vik is still neat and clean with a short haircut and a clean-shaven face, and I'm looking a bit rough with hair long on top and an impressive beard that I might be able to braid in a month. My face and neck is scarred, the biggest mark by my Adam's apple from where a man tried to slit my throat a few years back. Vik is as pretty as ever. A wolf in sheep's clothing. Yet I love him all the same.

He opens his arms wide and I wrap my arms around his middle and squeeze, picking him up off his feet. We were never affectionate as kids, unless you count fist bumps and brotherly punches. Dad was cold and mean and showing affection was discouraged. The only people I ever got affection from were Ivy and my sweet sister, Claire, before she died. I never thought I would miss something as simple as touch. Turns out I did. I squeeze him a little tighter and he starts to wheeze. I chuckle and set the pussy down.

"Shit man, you're like the fucking Terminator," he says. He wraps his hands around my bicep, and I swat his hand away. "You spend all your time lifting, or what?"

"It's good to see you too, brother."

"Man, you don't even know," he shakes his head smiling, as he looks me up and down. "Nothing's been the same since you left."

"For me, either." It's funny. I was trapped in small spaces and surrounded by people and yet I never felt so alone in my whole life. Without anyone I could really talk to or trust, I might as well have served my time in solitary. At least with Vik, I know he has my back. We'd die for each other.

He scratches his face. "I bet." He eyes my clothes and lets out a low whistle. "Wow. If I'd known you were into tight, I would have brought spandex." He strolls to the trunk and opens it, tossing me a backpack.

"Laugh it up, fucknuts." I catch the backpack and unzip it, letting out a relieved sigh at the clothes inside. I never asked for them, but he still thought to bring them.

He slams the trunk shut and I put the bag on top of it, pulling out a shirt. I remove mine and put on the new one, grateful for sleeves that actually reach my wrists.

"I couldn't remember what you went in with, but I figured you might want something new."

"Perfect fit, brother. Thank you."

He shrugs. "I'll send you a bill."

"I bet you will, you little shit."

Without an ounce of modesty, I drop my pants and slip the jeans on over my boxers. The length is right, but the waist could be smaller. Thankfully, they're not loose enough to fall down over my hips.

I shove the old clothes in the bag and shoulder it. Vik tosses me the keys and I catch them easily. Driving a car—something I missed but didn't realize until this very minute.

Inside the car, I take her all in while I breathe in the musky scent of the leather upholstery, tempered by the sweet vanilla air freshener. I slide my hand over the smooth leather covering the edge of the chrome steering wheel. I did something right when I built her. Betty—that's what I used to call her. I rev the engine and listen to her purr. I'm smiling wide as I peel away from the jail, squealing my tires as I wave good-bye to this shithole.

I want to speed, feel the wind on my face, and brace for the rush of adrenaline as I career down the highway. But when I reach the limit, I back off. Nerves, and the angel on my shoulder, win out.

"Give 'er," Vik says, tapping the dash. "Come on!"

I curse under my breath and relax my foot, settling in comfortably at five miles above the speed limit.

"You go soft in there or what?"

I shake my head and keep to the limit.

"What the hell is wrong with you?" he teases.

"Got no desire to go back. I get so much as a speeding ticket and I might be visiting some old friends."

"That's the way it's going to be?" he quirks an eyebrow. But he's smirking. He doesn't believe me.

"I don't know. Yes. No. *Maybe*. I haven't decided yet." But I have.

"Be a better criminal," he jokes. "Don't get caught this time."

I laugh without humor. "Don't get caught?" I wasn't exactly thinking about getting caught when I put Darren Black in a coma just after my eighteenth birthday. *Horrific*, that's what the judge said about my crime. No matter that the guy deserved it, as I'm sure everyone in that courtroom agreed. The only thing horrific about that whole situation was what my 'victim' did to my sister, Claire. He's lucky the cops came before I had a chance to end his life. And I *would have* killed him. Wouldn't have debated any other resolution for *his* crime. It rots me that the court didn't think I was justified. But then, in my experience, the law is pretty fucked up. My only regret is that it kept me from Claire in her last minutes. That bastard's fate could have waited.

"I think I'm done with all that," I say, keeping my eyes on the road ahead. I don't need to look at my brother to know he's looking at me right now with perhaps the sourest expression he can manage.

"You're serious, aren't you?" He runs his palms down his face and groans. "We'll see about that. An ex con can't bank the same money Yuri can offer," he says. "You know that."

"I can't do it, man."

"Yuri ain't going to be happy about that. He's got plans for you."

Yuri is the head of the family, and my uncle by relation. In our town, he has his fingers in everything. My family does construction as a front, but in the underground we deal in trafficking—mostly drugs. Every man in my family has a role in the business, both criminal and legal. I was only sixteen when I started contributing. That was back when all I wanted was to earn money and respect, back before Ivy Parker fell into my lap. Literally.

"I'm not the same person I was back then," I say.

"Because of Claire?"

Hearing her name out loud tears the scab off the empty hole she left in my chest. I try not to think about her much, and I don't like the reminder. Sweet Claire. She was the antithesis of my dad. A girl with a golden heart who happily gave more than she received. A girl who practically raised me and Vik because our dad was in jail and our mom worked more than any person should be allowed. She never deserved what she got—unlike the guy who hurt her. He cost me my sister, and after her death, he cost me my mother and my girl too. I blame him for all of that.

"Ivy, Claire, Mom, take your pick."

"I'm your brother, and I know you. Going straight won't take, no matter how hard you try. We're not cut from that cloth, brother. We were born for this life and we'll die living it."

I give him a half-hearted shrug. "I can't believe that, man. Otherwise, what's the point in trying?"

"People don't change," Vik says. "It's great in theory, but people always go back to their roots. Sorry, brother. That anger deep inside of you that screams to be let out when you want something you can't have...or when someone wrongs you or someone you care about...or breaks your trust...rats on you... You can't lock that up. It comes out. Trust me."

"You say that like you tried and failed."

He shrugs.

"The fuck? You tried to go straight? When?"

He lights up a cigarette and rolls his window down all the way to hang his hand out the window so I don't lose my mind. I smoke myself but I don't want my car smelling like it. Or my clothes or my hair. I love the taste and the release a smoke gives me, but I can't stand the stench. But fuck, if I'm going to sit here and watch him smoke without having one myself.

"Give me one of those," I say, reaching out for one.

He taps one out of the pack and hands it to me. After I put it between my dry lips, he lights it, his hand protectively covering the flame of his lighter so the wind blowing in doesn't put it out. I take a long drag and it burns all the way down my throat until it hits my lungs. The taste lingers on my tongue after I hang my arm out the window to keep the smoke outside.

"I tried a few years back," Vik says. "And not going straight, exactly. I tried to work a job separate from the family."

"Yeah, you mentioned you got another job. I thought you were fucking with me."

He sighs. "Yuri laughed at me when I told him I found another job. He said I'd be back and he'd welcome me. Of course, I wanted to prove him wrong. But I wasn't there a week before my boss tried to yell at me for taking a break during my shift when I wasn't supposed to. Did it in front of the whole factory." He smiles a wicked smile. "Fuck that. Disrespected me, the prick. My anger came out hard; if you'd seen me, you would have taken me for Dad. I was smart about it, though. I did him after hours when no one was around. Tied a rope around his neck and tied the other end to a rafter in this old barn out back of his house. Kicked his ass out the

hay bay door. They ruled it a suicide. Decided after that I'm probably not suited for honest work."

"Nope. Probably not." And the smile on his face confirms it. In
some ways, he's just like our dad—no shred of remorse for something as big as murder. It's hard to hear sometimes, but I can't judge
him, though. I'm no innocent, and I have the criminal record to
prove it. Then there's the other crimes I committed but haven't
been caught for—though I hadn't committed murder before jail.
Do I regret my crimes? I don't know. Before jail, I would have said
no. And now? Maybe. Some of them, at least. I have Ivy Parker to
thank for that. After falling for her, I questioned everything I did.
Before her, I had a temper like my father. He's in a super max jail in
Sterling City now, and he ain't ever getting out.

Dad killed a cop when I was eleven. Vik and I saw it all. He was
in a fight with some guy that owed him money and cops came to
break it up. They tried to get him to the ground but Dad pulled out
his knife and sliced the throat of one. The other tasered him then,
but he was on drugs and it only seemed to fuel his fire. He beat the
one with the taser until he laid bloody on the ground next to the
one holding his neck as he bled out. Vik and I watched from the
other side of the road. I remember reaching for Vik's hand, but he
wouldn't take it. He put his arm around me instead and led me away
from the fight. We were back at our house when more cops came
and questioned us.

"Out of curiosity, why'd you try going straight?" I ask. "I didn't
realize you were interested in a normal life."

He scoffs at me before blowing out a circular puff of smoke. "So
little faith in me. I found Jesus."

"Serious?" I say, flabbergasted at his response.

"Fuck no. It was a girl."

A girl. I laugh, shaking my head. Then my laughter fades and we both sit in silence. It's always a girl, isn't it? Like for me, the girl I never forgot.

I turn off the highway onto Cortland Street and Vik quirks an eyebrow "Where ya going?"

"Nowhere."

He eyes me, and I hate that he can see through me so easily.

"She don't live there anymore, man," Vik says.

I make a face. I want to deny I'm going to see Ivy, but Vik would see right through the lie and I don't want to argue with him about it. I don't need him to remind me that I broke it off with her and she's probably moved on. Because none of that matters. All I know is I thought about her every day in prison. Her face in my head was the only thing that made that place bearable. She's the reason why I want to be better, and she's the reason why I managed to rein myself in and stay out of trouble—mostly. If I have any chance at all at overcoming who I am, I need her help. The only problem is I'm pretty sure she hates my guts.

Purchase Flawed now to keep reading.

ABOUT THE AUTHOR

Sara Hubbard is a bestselling author of romantic fiction. Her debut novel BLOOD, SHE READ released fall 2012 and was a NEORWA Cleveland Rocks winner and a RCRW Duel on the Delta finalist. Her latest novels, Beautiful and Broken and The Last Shot, are Amazon Bestselling Novels.

Sara lives in Nova Scotia, Canada with her two children (four if you count her husband and her needy Labradoodle) and works as a registered nurse with the military.

Sign up for Sara's mailing list for notifications about new releases: http://eepurl.com/NDwi5

Connect with Sara:
www.sara-hubbard.com
author@sarahubbardauthor.com

ALSO BY SARA HUBBARD